"This year's best local debut novel."

—*METRO*

"*Baby* is a funny, taut, relentless fever-dream of a novel. Buy it and read it now, and you can brag about it one day the way people who bought and read Emily Perkins' *Not Her Real Name* in 1996 do today."

—LOUISE KASZA, *THE SPINOFF*

"An amazing, fresh voice in New Zealand fiction."

—JENNA TODD, *RNZ*

"In Cynthia, she has crafted a memorable monster. Creepy and subversive, *Baby* is a classy debut."

—LINDA HERRICK, *NZ LISTENER*

"Sparse and tantalising in its unfolding, it never quite allows you to get your sea legs."

—RUTH SPENCER, *NZ HERALD*

BABY

ANNALEESE JOCHEMS

SCRIBE

Melbourne • London

Scribe Publications
18–20 Edward St, Brunswick, Victoria 3056, Australia
2 John St, Clerkenwell, London, WC1N 2ES, United Kingdom
3754 Pleasant Ave, Suite 100, Minneapolis, Minnesota 55409, USA

First published in New Zealand by Victoria University Press 2017
Published by Scribe 2019

Printed and bound in the UK by CPI Group (UK) Ltd,
Croydon CR0 4YY

Scribe Publications is committed to the sustainable use of natural
resources and the use of paper products made responsibly from
those resources.

9781947534957 (US edition)
9781912854271 (UK edition)
9781925849349 (Australian edition)
9781925693799 (e-book)

Catalogue records for this book are available from the National
Library of Australia and the British Library.

scribepublications.com
scribepublications.co.uk
scribepublications.com.au

to Nicholas

1

Cynthia can understand how Anahera feels just by looking at her body. Today Anahera's wearing a pair of loose orange shorts. Their quality is obvious from the way they stretch at the crotch when she lunges. Her singlet is very tight, and Cynthia thinks it must be one of those sophisticated ones that button up between the legs. Anahera's quite tall, so if it is that sort it must be extra tight down below when she leans or bends.

That's just it, the leaning and bending – that's how Cynthia knows. Anahera yearns for strain, she courts it with her every movement, and Cynthia can see this, because she feels precisely the same way herself. She's squatting now, and she's been squatting for minutes. The agony in her thighs and ass is desperate and profound, but she continues to squat, as instructed by Anahera.

Classes are held on Anahera's lawn, surrounded by bushes; forceful, gloriously cultivated bushes that spill against each other and onto the lawn, pressing against the seven members of Anahera's class. It hurts, the squatting, but Anahera wants it to, so Cynthia holds the pose. Anahera herself is over by a lavender bush, kneeling and telling motivating things to a very puffed-out middle-aged woman. She can't always be motivating all of them, Cynthia understands. They've got to take turns because Anahera doesn't have a microphone and her throat gets sore. Now she yells that it's time for everyone to plank.

How to describe Cynthia's feelings? How to catch the

sensations so hot in her body, and hold them still enough to measure their edges? It's out of exhaustion, not disrespect, that she stops planking, and sinks down into the grass for a brief rest. Her whole body hurts in the most exquisite way. There are daisies, and she spots three of them by her nose in a near-perfect line, evenly spaced. She picks one and dabs the soft yellow at its centre, smears gold on her wrist. The lawn isn't wet, but it's got that good grassy taste and smell. Something big is happening inside Cynthia, and all around her. She feels herself on the cusp of some enormous event of infinite meaning. She licks some grass thoughtfully, then nibbles a bit and spits it gently back out. She loves the blades, furry and soft on her tongue, and pauses to wonder – how must it feel to be Anahera, to instruct? There's such luxury to Anahera's body, such glory in it. All of her is the same brown, flexing into shades under the sun. Just looking at her helps Cynthia feel the stirring and readiness for action held in her own belly.

Soon, she feels sure, Anahera won't be able to resist her in such repose among the other exercisers. She'll press a shoe into Cynthia's back, and Cynthia will get up, panting, and work out a bit more. For now, she watches the little bugs. They're very fit, clearly, jumping from blade to blade and scuttling along the edges. Bugs don't have feelings, and if there's one thing Cynthia's learned from Anahera's classes, it's that feelings are a hindrance in the game of physical excellence.

The shoe doesn't come. Cynthia looks up, and Anahera's marching past a big bush to stand on the deck beside her barbecue. 'Alright,' she shout-talks hoarsely, 'weights.'

Cynthia puts 1 kg on either side of her bar. Everyone else has at least 2.5 kgs, but that doesn't matter. Anahera's already told her not to compare herself to the other ladies, and to put her bar right down each time she needs to change her grip.

'Where are your muscles?' Anahera asks them all. 'I want to see them.' Cynthia feels like a child but also sexy, like always at this part, and she tenses obediently. This is the sixth lesson of Anahera's limited participant class, and Cynthia's attended all of them, although she's known Anahera for longer.

Whenever they do weights the same 50 Cent song plays, and the same lady, Evelyn, puts out a small snooty puff of air about it. This time she exhales only three seconds in, long before the lyrics have even started. She's wearing a blue tracksuit, and Cynthia puts a glare on her. She's got a kid doing puzzles inside, but that's no reason to be superior.

The singing starts. 'Damn, baby – '

'Oh my gosh! I am so embarrassed. I really will sort this out,' Anahera says – like always, in a rush – picking up her bar and not moving at all to change it. Cynthia nearly laughs. 'Lower,' Anahera says, calm again. 'Yes, and lower. Hold.'

After twenty-five minutes with the weights they all lie down in the grass, even Anahera, who shows them how to kick their feet in a very specific way to work their abs. Cynthia closes her eyes and tries to keep moving in the same pattern. It feels right, it feels good. But, 'No,' Anahera's head says, appearing above her. She takes a firm grip of Cynthia's right foot, and moves it so it's no longer comfortable. 'Alright,' Cynthia says, because her whole body's been repositioned. Anahera gives her ankle a little rub before moving on, and when Cynthia closes her eyes again there's sun caught and sparkling inside them.

A car parks at the roadside, Cynthia hears it and looks up. It's a red Toyota, not so flash, but obviously regularly washed. That sort of guy then, and he is: a puffy, pinkish man with floppy hair and a fake pocket sewn at the left nipple of his shirt. He gets out and leans over Anahera's fence, sighing and impatient, waiting for her to notice him and stand up. 'Kick, kick, kick,' she finishes saying to the assembled exercisers, then looks up at him.

He sighs again, seeing that she's not going to stand. 'Ana, where's my laptop? I'm supposed to be at work.'

'Kick, kick,' Anahera says, nodding at Cynthia. 'Then go to work?'

'But I need my laptop. I'm just asking if you've seen it around.' His hair's a dull, light brown, the same colour as his chinos. His mouth hangs limp at the end of his question.

'I don't know, Simon, I'm instructing a class.'

'You haven't seen it then?'

'I don't know, Simon.'

'Bloody alright then.' He marches past them all, up the garden path and into the house. Anahera says, 'Kick, kick,' again, but stands to watch him go in, scratching her eyebrow. Cynthia tries to kick, but she's lost it now, completely.

Minutes later he comes out with nothing under his arm, looks at them all, and drives off.

What a bland man! Just another part of the world which simply isn't adequate, not for Anahera, and not for Cynthia either; not with all its roads leading to more roads, its lines and lines of houses, its dogs on leashes, and all these ladies in Anahera's class, on her lawn, so heaving and entitled. The feeling is boredom and disappointment to the point of excruciation, and Cynthia understands it absolutely.

She first attended Anahera's muscle class at the gym nearly a year ago, and she went to those classes for months. One day, and it was a bad day – the third in a row of non-stop rain – she heard

Anahera speaking sternly to the gym manager in the hallway. 'I don't care,' Anahera said, then, 'No, I'm not going to.'

He spoke sternly back. 'If you care about your job, you might –'

'I don't care about my job,' Anahera said, Cynthia heard it clear as day. Then she was coming down the hallway, towards the corner, and Cynthia ducked into the bathrooms. A week after that, Anahera left his employ and offered Cynthia and six other select individuals places in her limited participant class.

Once they've stretched, Anahera comes over to see how Cynthia's feeling. She pats her own hot cheeks, and Cynthia does the same. They exhale together. The only male class member's petting his poodle at the gate, with one of the ladies. Cynthia can't think of much to say, but she smiles and shrugs. Anahera grins back, and everyone follows her inside.

Anahera's house is quite big, Cynthia supposes, and there are things around: half-read books and not-completely-drunk teas. A big dog roves in circles at the edges of rooms, pausing at the doors, shut inside because of the poodle. The snooty woman, Evelyn, gives her kid a mandarin from Anahera's table.

Cynthia's about to go after Anahera, to help make everyone's drinks, but Evelyn sits down at the table and says, '*Hmm*,' in a very pointed way.

'*Mmm*,' another lady says, her friend.

'It isn't just me then?' Evelyn says. 'The quality of these classes is definitely slipping.'

'Sorry, um – you just stole her mandarin?' Cynthia says. She looks around the table but there are no expressions of outrage on her classmates' faces. Several people are nodding, slowly.

Particularly a woman in a bright orange sweatband, Evelyn's main friend, her sidekick.

'Well,' the friend says, her eyes glimmering with excitement, 'at the facility her classes were incredible. I mean, really, she was the *best* –'

'Excuse me, just a second,' Cynthia starts up, surprised at the high noise of her own voice. 'Anahera's mum died, do you know?'

'That was well over a year ago,' Evelyn says quietly.

Cynthia's loud this time, 'So? Her mum fell off a horse, rolled down a cliff, banged her head on a rock, and *died.*'

Everyone is silent. The man coughs, and Evelyn puts on her cardigan. They've all noticed at once, a moment before Cynthia, Anahera standing in the doorway. They all look away, at the table or out the window, except Cynthia, who can't. Anahera blinks, with her hands on her hips, waiting for an explanation.

Cynthia starts choking, but Evelyn interrupts and says in an aggrieved, solemn voice, 'Some of us have been feeling less than satisfied with your class.'

'Who?' Anahera says. 'Who else?'

Evelyn's friend tilts her head sideways, as if shy, and puts her hand up. Anahera taps the carpet with her bare foot. 'Anyone else?'

Two more ladies raise their hands.

Anahera nods. 'Okay.'

'I'm so happy with the class,' Cynthia says, breathing now. 'I actually think it's improved since we started at your house. You have a lovely garden, that's how I feel.'

'I don't garden. Those are overgrown bushes.'

'Oh.'

'Don't wait around,' Anahera tells everyone at the table. 'The tea and biscuits aren't part of your fee, they were complimentary.'

Then she says, 'Anyway,' and walks off down the hall.

'Well,' Cynthia says, 'that serves everyone right, I'd say.'

The man gives her a nod, or at least she can see him thinking about it, then goes out to his poodle. They all sit and watch him untie it through the window.

'It's another structural issue with this style of class,' Evelyn says. 'There's no way to place feedback anonymously.'

Her friend nods, and yanks off her sweatband.

'Does that thing even catch sweat?' Cynthia asks her. 'How much sweat do you have.'

'It's a sweatband,' the friend says, and she and Evelyn get up and leave.

The three remaining ladies look sadly at Cynthia, then they tidy themselves and go too. Just because they can afford Anahera's $75 class fee, doesn't mean any of them deserve even to speak to her, let alone learn her fitness skills, obviously. Cynthia picks up a *National Geographic* and moves through it quickly, looking only at the pictures: a series of frogs of varying colours, one of a couple of elephants trying to communicate, and then two of sand. She goes right through, then back to the frogs, and she's looking at an orange one when Anahera sits down beside her, sipping coffee.

'I'm pleased it's just you here now,' she says.

Cynthia nods and waits.

'I've noticed a definite improvement in you, you know,' Anahera says. 'You really are getting stronger.'

'Gosh,' Cynthia says, and feels herself rocking back and forwards in her seat. Her face is hot. She cradles her cheeks and they're lifted into smiling, warm and soft. 'That's an achievement you can feel amazing about, too,' she tells Anahera. 'I could never have improved without you. As for some of those other ladies.

Well. They'll just be fat forever, it's in their nature.'

Anahera nods and asks, 'Tea?' Then she goes to make it.

Cynthia sits, thinking. When Anahera comes back she's prepared. 'Okay, so,' she says, 'imagine for a second that you start another, even more private class? A one-on-one sort of thing. I could pay. My dad –'

Anahera interrupts. 'It's not sustainable, Cynthia.'

'I don't care about sustainable,' Cynthia mutters, and she squeezes Anahera's arm. It's astonishing, the solidity of it. Anahera lifts a long finger to her mouth, and bites the knuckle before turning to Cynthia. She blinks, as if coming out of a daze, and with a new, peculiar concentration, puts her hand on Cynthia's arm. Cynthia's skinny-fat, and Anahera's grip pushes through her like custard, and holds her bone.

'I have $30,000,' Cynthia says, 'and I've been thinking about leaving this dump-hole city. What do you say?'

Anahera shakes her head, and stands up. 'Class is on next week, as usual.'

Cynthia nods and moves to sip her tea, but it's too hot.

Anahera's trying to get her to go, she wants to be alone – it's obvious. But Cynthia stays sitting. She drinks a bit of the tea and it's definitely far too hot. While Anahera stands, still waiting, she prints her phone number out clearly on a scrap of paper, then double-checks it.

Cynthia misses her bus, she doesn't see it till it's already driving away, but she doesn't mind. She misses one more and walks home. Cars pass her but she doesn't notice a single one of them. She passes houses but doesn't see them either. At the traffic lights someone swears at her, but she doesn't hear properly. She should've waited, they were probably saying, but it doesn't matter. There's afternoon light all over everything, hitting the leaves from the sides and making patterns of glow and shadow. She picks several leaves and crumbles them up in her fingers to smell them, then drops some on the footpath, and more in her pocket.

For months or even for her whole life, Cynthia's felt a furious desperation to go somewhere, to feel things, and be a real person. Well, Anahera is the over-heated centre of the world, the point of rupturing where it becomes too big and too strong to hold itself, and Cynthia feels close to her now. At last, she's content.

2

When Cynthia got home she did things on Facebook, got in bed, did more things on Facebook, slept, and now it's the next day, afternoon, and she's still in bed. Nothing has happened at all. Anahera didn't call. Cynthia's struggling for hope, and looking at a picture of her own pool on Instagram. The underwater lights are turned on, so the water glows blue and purple. A very attractive, very tedious boy called Randy took the photo just a few days ago. Then they had sex, and afterwards she made him watch a documentary which he found boring. Actually, it was lurid. It was about a young soldier who met a girl on the internet, but really he was lying – he was middle-aged and dull. He'd never even shot a man. Also, she wasn't the girl – she was the girl's mother. But he didn't know that, and he killed another man in jealous rage. What Randy failed to understand was the doom bespoke by the middle-aged guy's smugness. After killing the younger man the older one was trapped in his own naïve satisfaction, and he will be forever; to think again will destroy him. Randy will never see that, and that's just typical. Cynthia has a lot of options in regards to boys, but none of them are able to comprehend depth.

When it finished she told Randy she's not interested in men who don't like educational television, and he went home. Earlier this morning he sent her a picture of a Labrador, but that's just more of the problem – that's the only way boys of his sort ever like to have sex.

Cynthia flops on her face, bends her knees to lift her crotch up, and throws it hard back down onto the bed. Her dog, Snot-head, was sleeping between her knees, and now he's flung off. He moves quickly, panting, in a hurry to readjust and settle back into sleep. Cynthia can't breathe so much in this position, with her face shoved into the pillow, but it hardly matters. Anahera hasn't called. Cynthia should probably text some boy. Her dad's away on business, in Australia, and if all her dreams aren't going to come true today, she should at least make some use of the house tonight. Snot-head lets out a big wheeze, and she breathes heavily too, out her nose against the pillow.

Snot-head snores, and she dozes. The bell rings downstairs. It twangs and hurts. Cynthia hasn't bought anything online lately, it won't be for her. It'll be one of her dad's employees, or some other ridiculous person. Still, it keeps ringing. She moves carefully, turning onto her back, this time trying not to wake Snot-head. He wakes anyway. He's a French bulldog, fat and de-testicled. He snorts and she adores him, even though she's not in the mood to. He wriggles under one of her knees, between her legs and up, onto her belly, lifting the blanket in a hump, then settles down to sleep again. Whoever's downstairs is rude. They knock now. Loud and then louder.

Cynthia topples Snot-head off, and heads for the stairs. He trots after her, hoping to be fed. The knocking continues, louder again. 'Yup!' she yells. Down the stairs, through a big pointless area, to the door. Her dad got a peephole put in, and she leans forward to look through it. Snot-head's butting her ankle, hungry, but she forgets him.

Standing right there, at the door, with her hair wind-licked and curling loose, is Anahera. There's no pause, the door is open. Cynthia deep-breathes twice. Anahera's car door's swung wide and her lips separate. Her eyes are raw, red. She's about to ask a big question. But then she only says, 'Is this your flat?'

'My dad's house. I, um, live here.'

Anahera steps back, towards her car and her own open door. 'Oh, ah – shit.' Snot-head runs out and licks her toes. She's wearing jandals. Cynthia wouldn't have thought she'd own jandals, but there they are.

'He's away,' Cynthia says.

'I'm getting a divorce,' Anahera tells her, then notices her car door and jogs back to shut it. When she returns she says, 'I just decided.'

Cynthia didn't know Anahera had a husband. It doesn't matter, she decides immediately. She looks up at Anahera, and all she wants is to put her in bed, then make her tea and carry it carefully up the stairs. She imagines Anahera not waiting for it to cool, just talking about being alone and how it feels. Cynthia's ready to see it burn her lips, and to understand burning. 'What do you need?' she asks.

Anahera glances up at the house, right at Cynthia's window, although she can't know that. 'Money,' she says, 'to leave.'

'Okay, me too,' Cynthia says. It's warm in the hall where she's standing.

Anahera pauses, then nods. 'Don't ask about him,' she says.

'I never will.' But what Cynthia means is, not until she's earned the right to.

3

Cynthia grabs Anahera's arm, and Anahera comes through the door. It clangs and the cold's shut out behind them. They look at each other. Anahera's lashes are long, and her head seems to be at a more accessible height now they're standing so close. She relaxes, she's indoors, and she leans against the wall with a hand holding up her head. 'Did I wake you?'

'No,' Cynthia starts, 'I was just –'

Anahera laughs, so Cynthia sees her tongue. There are some stray hairs at her eyebrows, and some tiny, soft, nearly invisible ones above her lip. Her eyes are bold and black in a way that makes Cynthia peer down and feel serious. She adjusts her pyjama pants, and looks back up. There are lines under Anahera's eyes. She's exhausted.

'We'll get a boat,' Cynthia says.

Anahera pauses, then replies, 'I need to go somewhere,' and that's agreement.

Cynthia makes sure to under-react. She waits, then, 'Okay!'

The fingers of one of Anahera's hands pinch the leg of her pants, and those of the other pull at the collar of her shirt.

'Okay,' Cynthia says again. 'I'm not sure how much I have, but we should be good.'

Anahera lets some air out in a surprised way, but that's all.

'We'll take care of each other, for a while?' Cynthia asks.

Anahera nods, and Cynthia sees she's waiting to be invited in further. In the living room, Anahera looks around briefly, then curls up on the couch to sleep. Cynthia doesn't touch her at all; she sits down in a chair opposite to think.

Once, late at night when Cynthia was twelve, she looked out her bedroom window and saw a woman in a navy blue jumpsuit and bangles standing on the driveway, buttoning up her coat. Her dad wasn't visible, but she heard him say, 'Yeah, alright. Good. Suits me.' Then a taxi arrived, and the woman was gone.

Before school the next day she asked him if the woman had been a prostitute. He said, *Well, yeah, yeah she was, sorry*. She didn't mind, she wasn't surprised. Her dad had always stood for long moments in the hallway on Saturday mornings before entering his home office; he'd always been a lonely man. She was proud of him for taking ownership of his needs and feelings, and she's even prouder now, remembering. Now she knows for herself how hard it can be, and how necessary. He said she couldn't meet the lady, and she understood.

You have to ask for love, and do anything for it. When Anahera's eyes blink open Cynthia tells her, 'I'm ready to do my best, and earn some respect.' Anahera nods and sleeps more, and Cynthia watches her till she feels herself less frightened, and then completely brave. She goes to sit down at the computer in her dad's office.

He doesn't leave it locked, and he's got an auto-login on his computer and a password saved online for ASB. She winces. There's only $16,650 in his cheque account, and nothing in the others. She transfers herself $16,400, and wipes her eyes.

Anahera comes in then, and stands tilting her head side-to-side, as if to tip the sleep out of it.

'$16,400,' Cynthia tells her. 'It's less than I thought, but I think it's enough. I took a bit from my dad.' She's trying very hard not to cry. She never planned to leave him with nothing. He probably has another account, she thinks, with another bank. She doesn't know him very well in some respects, she has to remember. After she finished uni, when she was looking for a job, he said he didn't have any contacts in the media industry. She's at least forty per cent sure he was lying. He'll have more money somewhere else, of course he will.

Anahera's looking at the hedges and the lawn, and close behind them, Auckland city. She doesn't ask another question, she says instead, 'We'll get jobs. We can pay him back if you want.'

Cynthia's not really interested in jobs anymore, so she waits.

'My husband caught me fucking a guy I used to know,' Anahera says. 'Everything's ruined for me now.'

Cynthia fries bacon so the fat crackles and drips, loud. Anahera can probably hear it from where she's sitting in the lounge, thinking, most likely about her marriage. Cynthia's always been what you'd consider a lonely person, but also, she's someone with a limitless sense of meaning. It wells up hot in her, and ebbs away cold, and she often does have to be careful not to get sad, but mostly she's able to make sure she feels inspired instead. Now, with Anahera in the next room waiting for her, the feeling comes easy.

She's made pancakes too, beautifully puffed, and she's pleased to bring them through to the lounge, balanced on her wrist, to present them to Anahera. Anahera doesn't want bacon, but Cynthia doesn't mind, she just gets some maple syrup.

'We'll leave tonight,' Anahera says.

Cynthia nods.

'Or tomorrow?'

Cynthia thinks. 'Tomorrow.'

'Okay.'

There's a pleasing dab of syrup on Anahera's lips, and a smile there too, maybe. Cynthia's not so hungry, she's just looking, and waiting for some nice new thing to do for Anahera, who pauses, then licks the syrup and says, 'Good.'

Cooking is not one of Cynthia's things, so this is an incredibly good sign. She watches the food admiringly on Anahera's fork, then at the entry to her mouth. 'Oh!' She jumps up. 'You need clothes?'

Anahera starts to say no, but Cynthia jogs off and up the stairs, into her father's room. She takes some navy blue pyjamas, a pin-striped shirt, an All Blacks one, and a cowboy hat one of his business friends gave him in Australia.

She dumps it all in front of Anahera, looks up at her face, and straightens it into a neat pile, with the hat on the top.

'Won't he notice?'

'Nope.' But Cynthia hopes he does, and knows that she left with someone.

Anahera puts the last of her pancake in her mouth and grins, rubbing the silk of the pyjama pants with her thumb. 'He definitely won't notice?'

Cynthia shakes her head vigorously.

'I feel better now,' Anahera says. 'Thank you.' She puts the hat on, and Cynthia begins to nod again, encouragingly. *This is who I'll love*, she thinks, then knows. Anahera stands up and does two very good lunges, tips her hat, and grins.

'I got into the postgrad thing I applied for,' Cynthia says, lying and surprising herself. She didn't apply. 'But I'd much rather come with you.'

Anahera does one more lunge, which isn't perfect because she's confused. 'Okay, good,' she says. 'Will we take some food?' She gestures to the pantry, which Cynthia's left open.

'All of it.'

'Okay, most of the things.' Anahera gets up and does the dishes – all of them Cynthia's, from when her dad left two days ago.

'You don't have to do that, you just put them in the machine,' Cynthia says.

Anahera keeps washing them, then puts them in the machine. 'What do we need to pack?' she asks.

'I have a solar phone charger, unopened,' Cynthia answers proudly, 'from when my dad nearly went camping. And I've got data-unlimited on my phone.'

'Cool,' Anahera says.

'Other than that, we'll be wild! We'll abandon everything, and everyone!'

'Canned food,' Anahera says.

Anahera finds a gas thing in the garage, and wants to pack food, but after she's packed her clothes Cynthia says, 'Will you lie with me a while, I'm scared.'

Anahera looks almost relieved – she must be a little nervous too – and follows Cynthia up the stairs to her bed, even reaching up for her hand. Snot-head hears their feet and comes too.

They all get in Cynthia's big bed together, warm like a family. Cynthia and Anahera don't touch directly, but Snot-head wriggles against Cynthia's belly, and he must be touching some part of Anahera too. Just in their togetherness, and their shared heat, it seems to Cynthia that they become a new place. A small home they'll take with them wherever it is they go.

4

They move forward in tired but certain silence. Snot-head sleeps and they let him. Cynthia picks up her duvet and sheets in a muddle, and at the car, whispering, Anahera tells her to fold them. 'It's easier if everything's compact, so we know where things are.' Cynthia finds this silly, but insignificant, so she puts everything down and picks it all up again, piece by piece, packing it neatly into the boot. They take all the food in the house except a bottle of wine Anahera says looks *very decent*, some bread, butter and coffee. Anahera says they should leave some canned tomatoes, but Cynthia's father doesn't cook. 'Then why does he have canned tomatoes?' Anahera asks, but it doesn't matter, they take them.

'The shop's just down the road,' Cynthia tells her. 'He can get apples.' She packs dog food, Snot-head's little spiky collar, and his lead with the hearts. They're quickly in the car and Anahera hands Cynthia some camembert from the fridge. Cynthia's got some cranberry juice.

A bit of cheese doesn't stay in Anahera's mouth and Cynthia picks it delicately off her shirt, careful not to push it in, then tongues it from her finger. Anahera's got a beautiful chewing smile, although it doesn't make sense to chew that sort of cheese.

They drive north. Cynthia checks her phone and there are five texts from Randy, the last three extremely sulky. How exciting for him not to matter anymore! She smiles brightly and they go down an avenue, between a line of trees. 'Both of us will become entirely new to ourselves! Just you wait!' she tells Anahera. 'We'll save each other from this ugly place.' The leaves shine in the new morning light, hanging like gems alongside the road ahead of them. It's when they reach the end of them that Cynthia remembers: Snot-head!

'We've got to go back,' she says. 'My dog.'

They've not driven far, only a few minutes, but Anahera pulls over instead of turning around. 'What?'

'My dog.' Cynthia enunciates very clearly.

'Your dog?'

'Yes.'

Anahera sits, licking her gums.

'There's no way I can go without him,' Cynthia explains. 'There've been times in my life with him as my only friend. He's always stood by me. I can't leave him there.'

'Cynthia, I thought we were getting a boat?' Anahera's using a patient, adult voice, tilting her head. 'That might not actually be so good for him.'

'All he does is sleep!' Cynthia holds her voice down, carefully. 'Sleep and love me, and he can do those things anywhere!'

Anahera sighs.

'I can't leave without him, simply.' Cynthia won't say more.

Anahera sighs again and gets back on the motorway, in the direction of Cynthia's house.

'Thank you.' Cynthia squeezes Anahera's fingers on the wheel. 'I can't say how much I appreciate this. Really, I can't.'

Anahera watches the road. But they're going back down the avenue, and when they're on a quiet street near Cynthia's house she turns and smiles.

'He's a great dog,' Cynthia says.

At Cynthia's, Anahera doesn't get out of the car. Cynthia feeds Snot-head, and waits impatiently for him to eat. He does so dutifully, staring forward for long moments after each swallow.

The car honks.

'Yup!' Cynthia yells back, pushing Snot-head's bum gently with her foot. He turns and looks at her solemnly, then continues eating at the same pace. When Cynthia loses patience and picks him up, jellymeat falls from his surprised mouth onto her white pants.

They're all together in the car, and Cynthia expects Anahera to say something. She doesn't, she looks at the dog and turns the key. Snot-head licks at the meat stuck to Cynthia's pants, and it falls onto the seat between her legs. He shuffles on the bone of her thigh and leans down to lick it from where it's fallen on the upholstery. Anahera pretends not to notice, which is good.

They drive for a while. Anahera's phone rings and she answers it. For a while she just makes annoyed noises, then she says, 'Paihia.' A sigh. 'Yes, with someone. Someone I know.' She turns and grimaces at Cynthia. 'Do whatever you like,' she says, and hangs up.

It must be her husband, Cynthia thinks. 'Paihia,' she repeats, and likes the sound of it. She's heard of Paihia. Part of *The Bachelor NZ* was filmed there. Beautiful scenery, and quite a historical focal point, actually.

They drive longer. Cynthia touches Anahera's arm, then thinks she's been touching it too long and stops. 'I've had this boy since I was fourteen,' she says proudly of her dog. Anahera doesn't seem that interested, but Cynthia continues anyway. 'I definitely noticed a big change in his personality when they lobbed off his testes. *Definitely.*' Anahera doesn't ask about the change, but that's fine. They're together, and what that means is potential.

They pass three KFCs and Cynthia points each of them out, but Anahera says things about saving money. They'll stop at twelve and eat stuff from their cans, she says, but then she looks at Cynthia and Snot-head, and pulls over so Cynthia can get two bananas from the boot. They eat them leaning on the car, and Snot-head trots around it three times, then pees on a wheel.

'Watch this,' Cynthia says, but then Anahera is watching and she's nervous. She hasn't done this in a long time. The ground's gravel, but she gets on her hands and knees facing away from Anahera. 'Ride,' she says to Snot-head. It seems he hasn't heard, or he's forgotten. She hears a rock shift under Anahera's shoes, and she says it again. Then, suddenly, she feels his weight land with his four paws on her back. Anahera laughs, and she keeps laughing. She gets on her knees beside them and Cynthia can feel his paws pressing down while Anahera pats him. 'Excellent,' she says, 'that's just excellent.'

Encouraged, Cynthia crawls in a small circle around Anahera, careful to make slow, even movements so Snot-head doesn't fall. Then she stops, and explains, 'It's really hard for him, with his weight and all, he doesn't always make it.' Anahera laughs again and there's a sound of her kissing Snot-head between the eyes. The gravel hurts her knees, but Cynthia stays there till Anahera's done patting him.

5

Cynthia suggests mini-golf, and Anahera reminds her of the money issue. 'But haven't we gone insane?' Cynthia asks. 'I mean, aren't we just doing whatever we like?'

It doesn't matter. Cynthia's never had a sister, and she thinks – Anahera will be her sister, a whole new half of her. She's letting her money go, letting it run to Anahera like blood to a cut-off limb. She's venturing into a new wilderness with a friend at her side, and she won't turn back. All she wants is to be physical and real, beside Anahera's body and entirely in her own.

On a corner there's a big, sudden thudding noise. 'My weights,' Anahera says. Cynthia soothes Snot-head. They pass two more KFCs, but she doesn't mention them. She pats her dog. They're going away, to where no one will look at them and they'll look only at each other. It's such joy to see Anahera's eyes narrowed on the road, and her hand hard on the gearstick.

'Let me know when you want to drive,' Anahera says.

'Oh, I don't – drive,' Cynthia replies.

'That's fine,' Anahera says.

There's a word in Cynthia's mind, an enormous one: divorce. They stop at a bathroom, and while she pees she says it to herself. She says it quietly, but it's loud. The walls are unpainted wood, and she rubs them with her hands till the fat of her fingers catches a splinter, then she bites it out.

When she comes back out she's still walking through the awe of it, and she's awed even more to see Snot-head sitting cosy on Anahera's knee. Perfectly, Anahera looks a bit embarrassed, coughs and shoves him off.

Three more hours of driving, and Cynthia says, 'I think with the way my dad is – I think we'd better get cash.' They'll stop in Whangarei, Anahera says.

In Whangarei they wait in a queue at ASB. Cynthia keeps thinking Anahera's leaning down to whisper something, or about to, but she never quite does. They shuffle forward, like everyone else.

The lady says hello.

'Cynthia would like to withdraw everything from her account, in cash,' Anahera says.

'Would you?' the lady asks. She's got blond hair, but it's cheap, supermarket.

'I've decided to purchase a boat,' Cynthia says, and hands over her card. She's shorter than both the bank lady and Anahera.

'She and her father have been discussing it for a while now,' Anahera tells the woman, and pats Cynthia's shoulder.

She nods. 'Well, good on you!' she says. She puts a phone to her ear and dials. 'Pete, yes, Pete – I've got a youth here – '

Cynthia interrupts her: 'I'm twenty-one.'

Anahera's pat becomes a squeeze. A man walks through a door, past the tellers. He's blond too, and very combed. The blond woman shifts off her seat so he can stand in front of her. 'She'd like to empty it,' she tells him from behind.

Pete looks at the screen and he laughs. '16,800, eh?'

'For a boat,' Cynthia says.

'Hi, I'm Anahera.' Anahera puts her hand through the gap in the glass. Cynthia introduces herself too, and when Pete's laughed some more he says, 'Look, ladies, it's a bit humdrum, but I'm going to need you to sit down and sign some papers.'

They stand where they are and wait for him to walk along, back behind the tellers and through the door he came from. The blond woman smiles at them, then at the man behind them in the queue. Anahera pulls Cynthia aside to let him past, and Pete appears from a different door. 'Follow me,' he says, and gestures towards a third door. It's windowed, and opens to a little room where they both sit in cushioned chairs and wait while he prints forms. The printer makes a rasping noise, but he speaks louder, saying, 'Now, I'm going to need some proof of identification.' He laughs. 'If that's not too rude a demand.'

Cynthia hasn't got it on her. Anahera hands her the keys.

When she comes back Anahera's touching her face, laughing, and he's laughing too, with his crotch forward, his shoulders back, and his two hands gently caressing his belly.

'She's just finished uni,' Anahera says, nodding at Cynthia.

'Yeah,' Cynthia says, handing over her 18+ card. 'I have a degree.'

Pete nods, and Cynthia signs the papers he slides her. He checks them, turning each one over although some aren't double-sided. 'Righto,' he says, 'and next time – you can trust us – but next time, remember to read the small print on any documents you sign.'

Anahera nods and pats Cynthia's hands, which are held together in her lap.

'Righto,' he says again, and goes off to put their forms somewhere, and presumably get their cash.

He comes back with a surprisingly large padded envelope. Cynthia squeezes it. There are five wads in there, rubber-banded. 'Why not just a cheque?' he says. 'What sort of boat is this?'

The envelope's clutched tight in her fist, and Cynthia wants it back in her account, or her father's; intangible again, put back into nothing. She wants to eat it. There's no wind on the street, and people are looking at her. Should she dig a hole and bury it, like a dog? Put it down on the street and piss on it? Anahera is waiting quietly. Should she run?

'I'm sorry about in there,' Anahera says.

'What for?'

'I don't know.'

Cynthia sees her properly then, and understands her own terror as a ripping, a new place being made in herself for love. Anahera must be feeling the same way. A car goes past them quickly, loudly, but Anahera doesn't seem to notice it, or the people all around them pausing to gawk. She's not looking down at the envelope either, but at Cynthia's face. Anahera's eyes are brown in this light, on the street. She's doing nothing but waiting, with the sun on her face, for Cynthia. Neither of them can run, or will.

'It doesn't matter,' Cynthia says.

'Do you still want KFC?'

'Nah.'

They get back in the car. The passenger window is fogged with dog breath, and imprinted by his nose. Cynthia hands over the envelope, and Anahera puts it in the compartment between them.

'What kind of boat do you want?' Cynthia asks.

'Probably the cheapest one.'

'Yeah.' Cynthia nods. 'A little one then. Good.'

Anahera laughs. The dog's quite heavy after all the sitting he's already done on Cynthia, but he's warm.

6

Cynthia's been trying to explain for a while precisely what it is that's so tragic about *Talhotblond*, the documentary Randy so pathetically failed to understand. Snot-head's wheezing gently, and Anahera's been mostly listening for twenty minutes now. Cynthia jolts Snot-head awake, remembering something that could be crucial. 'The spelling of *tall* in the title is actually incorrect, they miss one of the "l"s, because the lady herself misspelled it in her username! And then – in real life she was actually quite short, so.'

'Okay,' Anahera says.

Knowing Anahera gets it makes Cynthia get it even more. 'But they're in an impossible love!' she says. 'They can never actually meet each other, because she's too old and he's a loser! It had to end in death.'

'Don't you think people just need to make things work?' Anahera asks.

'What I know,' Cynthia says, 'is that there was no possible ending without Brian's death, and everyone else's heartbreak.' She looks at Anahera and sees she disagrees. She disagrees, but she understands. She's a force to be reckoned with.

'You know,' Cynthia says, 'I think we three are going to save each other.'

'From what?'

Cynthia doesn't answer, they won't know exactly till they're saved.

Cynthia gets out first at the boatyard, then Snot-head, then Anahera, then Cynthia catches Snot-head and puts him back in the car. She's got to hold his small body back after she's put him down, inch her hands out the door and slam the last gap quickly. Anahera puts the envelope in her hands. They walk together up to a brown box-shaped office.

A guy sticks his head out the door. 'Hi!' he says.

'Where's your cheapest?' Anahera asks him, coolly.

'Oh yeah, I got a little pretty one for $18,000? Come in and I'll show you a picture.' He shifts aside and lets them in first.

It's tight and tiny in his wooden office. He sits behind a desk and Anahera takes a plastic chair, gesturing for Cynthia to sit on a padded one. He pulls out a worn photo album with yellow and blue flowers on the cover, opens it and shows them a photo at the very back. 'Comes with plates, anchors, some buckets, bedding, spoons,' he says, and he keeps listing other things, but Cynthia is in love.

It's got *Baby* written in wispy orange lettering on the side. It's bluish-white, with dirty bits at the water line, and the sea clinging at its little hips like low-waisted pants. There are bigger boats around it, but *Baby* catches the sun better.

'That looks alright,' Anahera says.

'Belonged to an old couple,' he says.

'You'll have to reduce your price,' Anahera tells him.

'How much have you got?' He nods at the envelope in Cynthia's hands.

Cynthia's about to answer, but Anahera says, 'Doesn't matter how much we've got.'

He pauses, thinking.

'Cash,' Anahera says, and Cynthia's thrilled and proud to be with her, to be her girl. She shuffles in her seat and covers her mouth with a finger.

'$18,000,' he says.

Anahera shakes her head.

'We could sell your car?' Cynthia asks her, chuffed to have an idea and be involved.

The guy looks at Anahera.

'Do you have a wife?' Cynthia asks him, then. 'Kids?'

He laughs. 'My wife drives a better car than that.'

Anahera laughs too, but only for a moment.

'We won't do more than $15,500.' Anahera straightens her face. 'Looking at that picture.'

He stops laughing, and Cynthia can tell this is going to take a while. She goes out to find water for Snot-head. They sit and wait. 'Bureaucracy,' she tells him. 'It does go on and on.'

Eventually, the door opens and the guy emerges with Anahera. 'Ron!' he yells. 'Ron!' Then he looks down at Cynthia and grins. 'Not his real name, but you'll see why I call him that.'

A red-haired boy arrives from a back corner of the yard, he's excessively freckled, and eating Twisties.

'See?' the guy says, taking the packet.

'Yeah,' Anahera tells him. 'That's good, alright.'

'Look, Ron, buddy, you take these ladies in that car' – he points at Anahera's car – 'and show them where' – he's leafing through his notebook – 'thirty-three is. You know the one? *Baby*.'

Ron's watching his Twisties swing in the guy's hand. He looks up, squinting – he doesn't know *Baby*.

The guy says, 'Anyway, thirty-three,' and eats a Twistie.

'Can I keep the picture?' Cynthia asks the guy, nodding at the album hanging in a hand at his side.

'Yeah, that's ten extra. Nah, just kidding.' He slips the photo out, clumsily, then nods at her envelope. '16,000,' he says. 'Plus the car.'

That sounds good, so Cynthia opens the envelope and lays the notes out on the step, counting them. There's no wind, and Ron steps forward to shift Snot-head out of the way. Cynthia can feel Anahera standing above her, but she tries not to rush. It does take a while. She turns back, and hands the money to Anahera, who passes it on to the guy. 'Good,' he says, without seeming to look at the notes or the numbers on them. Then he yells, 'Ron,' again, jokingly, because Ron's already there.

Just before they get in the car to go, he trots back up to them. 'You people want a dinghy?' he asks, blowing air out his nose.

Cynthia shrugs and Anahera says yes.

'Yeah,' he says. 'You'll need one. I forgot. Nothing extra. You want a motor in it?'

Cynthia's about to say yes, but Anahera speaks first. 'A paddle is good.'

Ron puts an old dinghy on the roof of the car, and Cynthia stands holding Anahera's arm and looking down at Snot-head. When Anahera's moved stuff around in the back seat to make room for him, Ron says, 'Or should I drive?'

'Nah,' Anahera says, waves at the guy, and they go.

Snot-head snorts, snuffles, sniffles and finally settles on Ron's knee. He's quiet in the back. Cynthia turns and asks him, 'How old are you?'

'Sixteen and a half,' he says.

'You look nineteen,' she tells him suggestively, and turns back around to flash a smile at Anahera. Anahera looks very ambiguous, and flicks the indicator.

Ron and Anahera carry the dinghy down a metal causeway, to the jetty. It's narrow, so Cynthia walks behind them. They tie it up in the water, and when they turn around she's embarrassed to be standing there with nothing, so she marches back to the car. She opens a door, and as soon as she does Snot-head runs out and begins pooping. Anahera and Ron both nod to show they understand, he's got to do it. He starts and stops, first under the tree, then a rubbish bin, then back under the tree again. Anahera and Ron take a second load, then a third. Before he takes the rest of the stuff, Cynthia stops Ron. 'Give me your number,' she says. 'We're probably gonna throw some parties on there.' He does. Anahera pauses and goes off again.

'That's the thirties,' he says, gesturing off at some boats anchored a little way from the wharf.

'Right.' Cynthia points at exactly where she thinks he means.

Anahera comes back, and stands beside Cynthia. 'Maybe you'll show us how it works?'

'Um,' Ron says. 'I'm not too good with those older ones.'

7

Baby appears gradually from behind all the bigger, more robust boats, dancing like something imaginary. The water lifts her sometimes, then drops back under, exhibiting her dirty underneath.

Snot-head runs around fast, sniffing everything, and Cynthia watches on. Big houses with a lot of glass windows look down on them from the hills. That must be where the boat salesman lives, she decides.

Anahera goes back in the dinghy for the rest of their stuff. There are windows, curtains and lots of little cupboards for Cynthia to open. There's a trap-door in the ceiling, so they can keep things up there. A little cabin, with a short, narrow bunk bed. It's all wooden, which Cynthia likes. She finds that the tops come off the built-in seats on either side of the table, and that inside them are long panels of cushioning, presumably to make up another, third bed. Opposite the table is a kitchen sink, a small counter and some cupboards they'll keep food in. She opens a little door and finds a toilet, and a sink. The boat has everything a house would – a toilet, beds, sinks, only smaller and more fragile, like a tiny set of organs. It's all perfect for Snot-head; he's little too. At the back of the boat there's a steering wheel, and an unsteady seat that flips out under it. There's a ladder which can be pulled up or dropped into the water. Along the boat are bars to hold while you walk its perimeter, and a thin panel for your feet, one after the other. At the front there's a washing-line, and a flattish area underneath where they can lie down, although of course it won't be safe there for the dog.

This is what Cynthia has now: her boat, Anahera and Snot-head. Her money was like water, in its big nothingness and the way it slipped away before she really had it. She doesn't mind. Money runs downwards, and people are always trying to position themselves under it like drains, but she'll never involve herself in any of that ever again.

When Snot-head's sniffed everything twice, he goes to sleep in the cabin. Cynthia crawls in after him, to touch the lift and fall of his little ribs. He's a very soft dog, with a nose he only occasionally lets her touch and ears he can stick up but never does. He's golden, and wrinkly, with a diva walk; he's got a big little swingingly seductive bottom. Sometimes he likes to stretch his legs apart and press his crotch into the ground, that's one of his cutest things. She lifts his ears and looks in them. They need to be cleaned, she'll remember that. She shuts the cabin door quietly, and sits at the table to wait for Anahera.

They're together, newly, looking at each other newly. Cynthia doesn't know how to work the gas, so Anahera puts the kettle on, then she says, 'We might not have any parties.'

Cynthia shrugs, that doesn't matter. It was only something she said, not her dream. Anahera pours boiling water carefully over her coffee, and Cynthia's herbal bag. The boat shifts gently right and left, and Anahera doesn't adjust her body in any perceptible way.

'Do you know my dog?' Cynthia asks.

'Yup,' Anahera says. She's lying down on the wooden bench,

half obscured by the table.

'Well,' Cynthia says, and begins: 'When I was fourteen I cried every single day. Sometimes three times. I wasn't my best self then, and I was bad-looking. I had no friends. I looked at myself in the mirror every day, crying. Sometimes I'd watch myself cry for whole half hours, in my pocket mirror, in my bed. I caught my tears in a jar, but they always dried up.' She peers over the edge of the table to check Anahera's listening, and Anahera sees her and nods.

Cynthia's pleased. She continues: 'And one day, my dad asked me what I wanted, you know. It was our best moment of love together. He didn't hug me, but if he'd been that sort of guy I know he would have. He told me he'd heard my crying all that time. I felt better then, when I knew he'd been listening. He said, "What do you want? I'll give it to you."'

'And?' Anahera asks, although she must already know.

'So I got Snot-head.' He's on her knee, looking up at her and listening. He looks like he's been hit in the face with a plate, a bit. But that's how he always looked. He's just got a head that's squarer than other dogs, with their pointy noses.

Anahera sits up, and nods again.

'Yeah, and I still cried. But it was better. I always had Snot-head in bed with me, and he knew.'

'That's actually really nice,' Anahera says.

'Yeah. He's my true love.'

'Okay,' Anahera says. 'We'll keep him.'

Cynthia hadn't considered it up for question, but she nods.

'Where will he shit then?' Anahera asks, looking around their new boat.

Cynthia hadn't thought of this.

'In kitty litter,' Anahera suggests.

'We can get it tomorrow, he only needs to once a day.'

'Okay,' Anahera says.

The sea is gentle with their boat, and very blue. They find romantic novels in a little cupboard above the door, and read them together sunbathing on the deck, under the washing-line. The sun's going down – so Cynthia goes around the side of the boat for blankets. There's a loud thud, which Anahera says is just her weights. When it's too dark to see they go back inside and Anahera makes some miso soup with broccoli and other stuff in it. The thudding happens again while they eat, but Cynthia isn't frightened, she's expecting it.

While Anahera's cooking, Cynthia finds a small fresh circle of spew on one of the cushions in the cabin. Snot-head looks up at her, and she pats him three times slowly on his head. His eyes close and he nuzzles into her hand. Tomorrow she'll sneak the whole cushion into the water. He only needs to adjust.

She kisses him and leaves to ask if Anahera needs help with anything. She says no, but Cynthia sits and watches her cook. She cuts the broccoli quickly, then slides it into the pot. Everything's simple, when she moves.

They sit and eat. Anahera says not to worry about the dishes, and Cynthia stands back to watch her puzzle the table into a bed. There's a steel pipe holding it up, and Anahera loosens a screw so it can contract. Then, it's level with the seats. They lay the cushioning from inside the seats over it, and it's a bed. Cynthia gets their sheets and pillows, and Anahera sets it all up. It isn't till they're settled in and warm that Cynthia remembers Snot-head. He hates sleeping without her, but she's caught in Anahera's warm and quiet, and she says nothing. At ten, when Anahera's asleep and she almost is, she hears him under them, scratching. He whines. Cynthia's on the wall-side, so she's got to clamber over Anahera to reach him. Anahera shifts her legs, but stays mostly sleeping.

Snot-head twitches and settles into Cynthia's spooning, and Anahera lies close and breathes gently.

In the morning Cynthia wakes early, excited, and it's like she's slipped into reality, but not out of her dream. She moves quietly, and dumps the spewed-on cushion into the water outside. Under the sunrise, she eats a packet of biscuits and watches the cushion float, sink a little, and float away.

Anahera comes out, yawns in the sun, and gives Cynthia a good-morning smile. Her shoulders are postured soft, and her hair's a sweet mess on her head. She ties shampoo and conditioner to the corner of the boat – they'll be washing their hair in the sea. While she's back inside putting her togs on, Snot-head retches twice more on Cynthia's knee. Nothing comes out either time, which is great.

Anahera's togs are an old-fashioned black one-piece, which exposes the solid bones of her hips and the smooth of her back. She stretches her arms and legs, and her smile while she does so is peaceful and controlled, almost religious. Then she dives into the sea, cutting a smooth, perfect hole, precisely the size and shape of her body. She emerges metres away, and Cynthia and Snot-head watch the sun wrench the last of itself from the horizon while she swims towards it. When she's vanished, Cynthia takes her dog in to feed him. He doesn't chew, he just takes hunks of jellymeat between his teeth, lifts his head backwards so his neck squashes into rolls at the back, and lets them fall down his throat.

There are ten texts on Cynthia's phone, all from her father. They're all one long continuous message, split by his cellphone into parts. They say, 'Hello, Cynthia. Now, I see that you have stolen $16,400 from me, and some of my clothes. Without even mentioning the intensely hurtful nature of your behaviour, I must emphasise that I consider this a serious issue. I expect to receive contact from you in the near future, wherein you will apologise, and describe a detailed series of steps through which you plan to make this up to me. Sincerely, your loving father, Thomas.'

She reads it twice, and composes two draft replies but doesn't send either of them.

8

Anahera's back and she's saying all at once, 'Are you ready? Put a lead on your dog. We're going to town. Pants, Cynthia!'

Cynthia is wearing shorts, they're just tight and small. She puts on a sweater. Snot-head sees his lead and gets so excited it takes seven minutes to catch him. Anahera changes, then stands waiting. She's in the dinghy first, and when Cynthia passes the dog over there's a moment before she takes him. He trembles, and his legs wriggle in the air. 'We should definitely bring him along,' Cynthia says. Anahera takes him then, and he shakes in her hands. When Cynthia leans forward and pats his head his eyes stay wide open. Anahera paddles, and Cynthia holds him tight, tight enough to still him. 'I know how we'll make money,' she says. A gull swoops near their heads, the wharf's getting closer.

Anahera looks up abruptly from Snot-head. 'Oh, how?'

'Well,' Cynthia leans forward, over her dog. 'We'll sell undies online.' She pauses. 'Used ones.'

Anahera stops paddling.

'Horny men,' Cynthia says knowingly. 'We just have to photograph each other's bums in them.'

Anahera's paddles thoughtfully, slower. 'You've done this before?'

'Course I have,' Cynthia lies. Snot-head's a bit calmer. 'Our bums are quite different, but I've looked at yours and I think we'd do well.'

Anahera looks at Snot-head, but it's okay, he's not trembling so visibly now.

There are so many children, too many children. The footpaths are laden, and not a single person is walking down them with the same verve or purpose with which Cynthia follows Anahera, pulling Snot-head behind her. They all get out of the way. First thing, Cynthia shouts ahead to Anahera, they should stop at a café.

Some backpackers are at the table behind them. One says, 'You've just gotta breathe, man. That's all I do, breathe. And think, when has the universe not provided?'

Anahera lifts her eyebrows, and Cynthia suppresses a giggle.

'I was down to my last pair of shoes,' he says, 'you know, I was gonna have to cough up and buy some. But then – my buddy was like, he goes, "Hey, I found some shoes? I think you were saying you needed some shoes?" And, like, I'm not saying they fit me perfectly, but – '

Anahera's eyebrows are still up.

'Yeah, I can see,' the other guy pipes up. 'They've got Velcro *and* laces.'

'Mmm.'

A lady comes with Cynthia's coffee – Anahera isn't having one – and a bowl of water for the dog. 'So,' Cynthia says. 'We get G-strings, and cotton ones. Cotton ones are less sexy, but more absorbent. We make a $200 investment, and we start photographing tomorrow.'

A man comes out of a pub across the street while Cynthia's talking, and nods at Anahera, but together they ignore him.

'$200?' Anahera says.

The backpacker's pulling off the Velcro on his shoes, and putting it back down again.

'Yup,' Cynthia says. 'Gotta do it properly. Spend to make.'

'$200?'

'Alright,' Cynthia sighs. '$80.'

Anahera looks uncomfortable even with that.

It's a very small town, Paihia. Everything's either on one street, or in the little mall tucked in behind it. There's a shop with jeans, togs and two bras in the window. Cynthia walks straight in, with Anahera following. Then she has to go back out to tie Snot-head to a rubbish bin. '*Retirement knickers*,' she says under her breath to Anahera when they meet again in the lingerie section. The bras are mostly huge, and the undies too. A lady comes up to them so quickly Cynthia worries maybe she heard her joke.

'Can I help you?'

'G-strings,' Cynthia says, but she can't see any.

'Hmm,' the lady replies. She gestures to the rack they're standing beside, then wanders off a bit. They're all enormous. Cynthia wants to say *big old curtains*, but the lady doesn't quite leave. She nods at them, and adjusts some shapewear on the hangers. Because Cynthia's concentrating hard on not glaring at the woman, she's surprised when Anahera says, 'You'll look good in this,' and holds up a little red lace thing. Cynthia's head gets suddenly hot, and her shorts feel too tight. Still, she moves closer to Anahera, being careful not to look sideways at the woman who must still be there. 'So would you,' she says. Anahera holds up some blue cotton ones, jiggles them, and puts them back.

'Should we try them on?' Cynthia asks, but panics at the rasp in her voice.

'Go,' Anahera says, and hands her the red ones. Then, after thinking, the blue ones too. 'I'll find more.'

A sign says you're supposed to leave on your undies while you try on the shop's, but that's ridiculous if you're buying a G-string. Those rules are for people who aren't serious about making a purchase, not for Cynthia. They look good, both of them. Cynthia turns to see the red one from the back, and catches her own eyes in the mirror. The blue of them looks dark, she blinks. Should she call Anahera to come see? She's probably been in there a while.

There's a knock at the door. 'Are they good?' Anahera.

'Yup.' A pause. 'Do you want to – '

'Yeah, there's only one changing room.'

'So I'll get out?'

'Okay. Yeah, cool.'

Cynthia rushes with the undies, and they make a stretching noise like ripping. 'I've got the same ones,' Anahera's saying from outside. 'Just bigger and different colours.'

'Alright,' Cynthia says, sorting out her little shorts. They make brief eye contact on her exit, and she passes the undies under the door, then goes out to see Snot-head sleeping happily by the bin he's tied to outside. She's pleased to see where he's peed on it. He looks like he's melted into the concrete, he's so soft and wrinkly. His ribs are warm and she gets on her knees to pat him, and nudge his stomach with her head. Anahera laughs from above her, and touches Cynthia's bum with her shoe.

They cross the street, and Cynthia and Snot-head wait at a

picnic table while Anahera's in the supermarket. She puts him on the table so she can look at him. He's shy of the height and lowers himself to a grovel against the wood. As a youth he was very energetic, then he started humping Cynthia's legs while she slept and, although she told him a thousand times not to worry, her dad got the dog's testicles removed. Now he's very submissive and lethargic. His eyes are brown, and choc-chip flecked. She puts his head through the leg hole of the pink knickers, then the big one for hips, then the other leg hole. Anahera's taking a while.

The guy from before, who passed them while they had coffee, comes out from Countdown. Cynthia can't properly see his face, but from the way he holds his limbs he looks like all he does is walk around hoping someone will try and thump him; he's a smug, huge body with a big head settled on top. Snot-head feels the lack of her attention and panics at the tightness of the underwear. The man's pretending to watch a tree behind their table, but he's looking at Cynthia.

Anahera helps pull the last of the dog hair from the lace, then they have a biscuit each, with Snot-head looking from one mouth chewing to the other.

Either Snot-head trembles less on the way back or Cynthia's got used to it. Anahera watches, frowning and thoughtful. When they're back on the boat he won't sit down. He runs from one end to the other, snuffling and sometimes making little barks. Anahera leans back, closes her eyes, and scratches her neck. Then she opens them back up, black and bright, smiles at Cynthia, frowns, and shuts them again. 'Want to play cards?' she asks a little later.

Sure Cynthia does. 'Snap?'

'Nah,' Anahera says. 'It's always the same.'

'Aw, then nah.' Cynthia goes to the toilet, and when she comes out Snot-head's sitting on Anahera's knee, retching.

Anahera looks up. 'This doesn't seem normal.'

'Oh, it is,' Cynthia says. 'It's absolutely normal for a French bulldog to do that. They started with a very small gene pool you know, so there are those things.'

He quiets, and Anahera holds his head in the soft of her hands. 'I'm not entirely sure,' she starts saying.

'Well I am, and he's my dog,' Cynthia tells her. Anahera keeps patting him like he's nearly died, and Cynthia looks out the window, at its small cut of sky.

9

Cynthia thought they'd get right into the underwear and photographing, but they don't. Anahera joins her outside and says, 'You can have that boy Ron over, if you want?'

'Why would I?'

'I'll sleep in there,' Anahera gestures through the window, to the cabin. 'I don't mind.'

'But why would I?'

Anahera shrugs. Cynthia thinks she looks guilty, almost, but whatever she's feeling she doesn't hold it like guilt. Anahera has excellent posture, and a chin almost like a man's.

They read their books for a while under the washing-line, but Cynthia feels bad about leaving Snot-head alone and goes in to see him. She tells him to sit and he doesn't, so she squashes his bum down while telling him again. Dogs are like children's toys were in the nineties. They can only do about five things, but they still make you immensely happy. When he's stayed this way for one hundred seconds she kisses and lifts him above her head. He's got a pasty, pink bald belly and quite short legs. She loves him, and she says so a lot of times. His head crooks down and thrusts towards her face, trying to lick. He's heavy, and eventually she lowers him. He lands with his uncut nails digging into her chest, and tongues her face fast and wetly. Cynthia tries not to shut her eyes – this is intimacy – and to look steadily back at him. When he's done she wipes his spit off on her shirt.

She goes out to rejoin Anahera, but Anahera's coming back in.

'Business,' Cynthia says, sitting down at the table.

Anahera nods with a flirty smirk, and moves to sit, but Cynthia asks if she'd like coffee. So Anahera stays up and turns the kettle on, and Cynthia says she'll make them drinks when it boils. The slice of Anahera's mouth deepens, but her eyes don't lose their kindness.

'Alright,' Cynthia says. 'How many pairs of undies do you have, and do any of them look a bit new?'

'Five.'

'New-looking ones?'

'All together.'

That doesn't sound plausible, but Cynthia stays neutral. 'You should keep those for your own domestic use,' she says. 'I brought about, twenty?'

'Cynthia, if you brought twenty pairs, why did we spend $87 today?'

The jug boils. 'Okay. Okay, listen.' She'd thought it would be cool if they had matching ones.

Anahera does a listening face.

'Oh my god, I don't even know if I want tea now.'

Anahera switches the lean of her head from one shoulder to the other, and says, 'No, I'm sure you know what you're doing. You've done this before.'

'Well, yeah, I have,' Cynthia says, forgetting that she hasn't. She gets up to make the tea.

They sit, and Cynthia talks, making big gestures. 'Just think about it, I mean. It's money – what I'm seeing. Wads. I'm seeing our bums pressed together, you know, in one photograph. Two-packs could be a big seller. I don't think anyone's doing that. My undies and your undies. Two scents in one envelope. You know men. They're just' – Cynthia laughs – 'men are just, really.'

'How many of your own do you think we could sell?' Anahera asks.

Cynthia counts on her hands. 'Nine pairs, that's my surplus.'

Anahera spends minutes texting someone on her phone, then swims, and Cynthia sits down at the table with Snot-head to write ideas and do research. She looks at pictures on different sites: Perfect Panty Premium, Panty Deal and Stumptown Sniffs. She notes the names down to consult Anahera on later. In an article she reads, 'The inclination to smell is as natural as the urge to urinate. When you take raw meat from the refrigerator, you may smell it to determine if it's still fresh. Men approach woman in much the same way, and it's natural for them to find the scent of a woman arousing.' Snot-head's retching in the cabin, so she doesn't bother with the rest, which is about how to post things and use PayPal.

He spews only a little bit, and it's on an old blanket they got with the boat. She uses a jagged knife from the kitchen to cut the section off, and throws it into the sea.

He trembles and licks her hand while she holds him. 'Thank you' – she leans down – 'for everything you're sacrificing.'

When Anahera comes back she sits immediately, muttering, and writes down some numbers. 'Do you understand, Cynthia, that we're totally broke?' Two of her fingers rub into the fat of her cheek, but otherwise she holds her face still. She slides the paper over so Cynthia can see the figures, but Cynthia won't look away from her face. Her eyes are pierced, like a rabbit's. She's waiting for an answer.

Cynthia sighs gently and leans in. 'Don't worry, we can just float away. We'll end up somewhere.' They're not *totally* broke, she knows.

Anahera shakes her head, wriggling her hands inside each other.

'No. Hey,' Cynthia says, seriously. She needs to remember that Anahera was an adult, with a job and a husband, so she says the next part gently. 'I've been researching. We can make it extra big in the panty trade if we pee in them a bit.'

'A bit.'

'Yeah, you know, just a bit.'

'We own our own home,' Cynthia whispers to herself, twice, while Anahera sleeps. Soon, she knows, they'll talk about her father and about Anahera's divorce. She'll know who Anahera's been texting, and she'll know Anahera knows her. She's waiting patiently. Snot-head snuffles against her belly, and Cynthia's sure he's learning to hold his guts still.

There are little hills and islands all around them, and the water underneath lolls and loves them. In the bed, under all the blankets, in the warm with Anahera and Snot-head, it's like being in a tummy, under soft, mute fat and skin. During the day the sun comes through the windows and the way it yellows the old paint seems hygienic and purifying; simply healthy. Their togetherness is love or indistinguishable from love, and it's getting warmer, expanding like porridge and filling their little home.

10

Anahera goes swimming every morning and night, but that's fine. The waiting is exquisite. Cynthia's still not quite sure how to work the gas, but Anahera boils the kettle each time before she goes, and Cynthia drinks tea and watches *The Bachelor* on her phone. Snot-head spews daily, but Anahera stays out of the cabin, so it's easily handled. Her absences are also good times for Cynthia to use her face washes and pluck her eyebrows. Anahera's never gone longer than an hour, and they smell of the same soap and shampoo, so for a whiff of Anahera Cynthia only needs to sniff herself. Twice daily Anahera washes their dishes in sea water, so they dry salty, and while she's gone Cynthia licks the sides of cups like Snot-head, who, after she bathes, likes to drag his tongue down her now-spiky legs.

Each time Anahera comes back from swimming she's wet and shiny with new thinkings: 'We have to ration our food, Cynthia,' and, 'Do you want me to call your father? No, you're right, that would be inappropriate.' Mostly Cynthia isn't worried.

'You still look real good,' Anahera says one night while Cynthia's in bed watching her cook. 'Like when we left.' She flexes a leg, in Cynthia's dad's navy blue pyjamas.

'You too,' Cynthia says, and it's true. Anahera gets in with her, and hands her a bowl of something orange. 'You're good with cans.' Cynthia gestures with her spoon. Anahera's weights shift in the ceiling, gently but with noise. They must be dangerous, Cynthia thinks. This is how it must have felt for Anahera's husband, being married to her; risky and exhilarating. Cynthia doesn't mention it, instead she asks, 'How do you think a shark's stomach must feel, on the inside?' She imagines her own legs contained with Anahera's in the pyjama pants, and their breasts and arms buttoned in together under the shirt.

'I think they must stretch,' Anahera says, which is certainly right.

11

Cynthia leans in, with her mouth slightly open and her eyes a little popped, as if the tail of a fish were poking through her lips, and the fish itself were behind them pummelling her cheeks. She pushes forward, in need, with her face passive and open, held in quiet. She touches her own face, blinking for clear eyes. Her lips feel like they're plumpening, warm and tingling against the air.

It must make her even prettier, this leaning, this swaying in her body and blood. Pride swells her further. She thinks, *Here, I feel myself*, holds herself, and wishes to hold herself out for someone else. *I'm so warm*, she thinks, *who could not want this warmth of me; to take me home, and make a home for me, a home of me.* They're already there, in their new shared home, so it must have started – the looking, and leaning – the growing towards each other's light.

She touches her own warmth and softness, and doesn't see a need for it to be a secret. Still, she waits till Anahera's asleep.

Cynthia loves herself – it might be that. It's not so easy to tell the difference between self-love and a firm expectation of love from someone else.

12

It's the middle of the night. 'Cynthia,' Anahera says. 'Your dog spewed on me.'

'What? Sorry!' Cynthia says. She wriggles her hands around, trying to find her phone for light, but keeps hitting parts of Anahera's body.

'Cynthia,' Anahera says.

'Yes, Anahera, I know.'

'Yes, well, I have your dog's spew all over my stomach.'

Cynthia scrambles her hands faster, and scratches the back of Anahera's arm. She starts to apologise, but stops. 'Poor Snot-head, Anahera, I have to think of him too.' She wriggles her feet, trying to touch him, and kicks his skull. 'He spewed,' she says.

'Yeah, he spewed on me.' Anahera gets up.

'I know! That's how I know he spewed!' Cynthia moves down the bed to find him, and feels suddenly like he's running away. Anahera doesn't say anything, but goes outside. Cynthia hears the splash and slap of her wetting her shirt and leaving it on the side of the boat. She lies completely still, and after a while Snot-head snores lightly. Anahera comes back in to stand above the bed, in a different shirt, looking down. Cynthia can't see her eyes, but she sees her teeth, wet and white, in flashes as she speaks.

'This is probably not ideal for your dog.'

'No.'

Anahera waits, and so does Cynthia.

'So, just let him go, then?' Cynthia asks.

Anahera says nothing, and Cynthia's heart wrenches. She pulls at the skin of her neck and looks up. New, dim light falls through the window, on Anahera. She looks back. 'You don't like him,' Cynthia says, pulling in breath. 'You never did, and now he's puked on you.'

Anahera looks at the duvet, and the sheet, and pulls them back one at a time. Cynthia presses hard against the wall to give her space.

13

She wakes in light, to Anahera's humming. Right as she moves, Snot-head's on her face. His eyes come very close, and when she blinks he does too. She pushes him off, and sits up. Anahera turns with a warm bowl of porridge.

'I'm sorry,' Cynthia says.

'Me too.' Anahera puts some food in Snot-head's bowl and gets back in bed. 'Has he done that before, since we came?'

Cynthia shrugs, but Anahera's waiting. 'One other time, I guess.'

'Okay,' Anahera says, and her fingers are in Cynthia's hair.

Cynthia hasn't washed it, she pulls away. 'Dogs are really tough animals, and they love their owners.'

'He's real cute,' Anahera says. 'Nearly as cute as you.'

Cynthia puts some porridge in her mouth and quietly swallows it. Then she says, 'Are you even committed to this relationship?'

'What?' Anahera pauses with her spoon mid-air.

'With me and Snot-head. You haven't once suggested we photograph each other in the undies. You never pat him. Then he spews on you a little bit one time and – '

Anahera makes an interrupting noise, but then doesn't say anything. A moment, and she starts speaking but stops again. Then, 'Keep him,' she says. Immediately her mouth puckers in, surprised and regretful at what it's said. But she doesn't take it back, she adds, 'I thought we were waiting for you to join a site on your phone.'

'Well, I can't keep him if you're going to blame me and think I'm inhumane every time he spews for any reason at all.' Cynthia presses her head back against the wall, and spills a little of her porridge. Snot-head snuffles at her hip.

'We'll do it today, this morning. The photos,' Anahera says. She touches Cynthia's leg and her hand's warm.

'Only if you feel like it.' Anahera's overfed Snot-head, so Cynthia gets up and scoops meat back into the can.

Anahera goes off swimming, and Cynthia looks dumbly down at her dog. Would he prefer to die than spend another night with them, ill, on *Baby*? She's got no idea at all. They touch noses. Anahera's right; he wouldn't be alone, or even unloved for long. He'd only need to trot up to the right person. It'd take half a day. His eyes and nose are dewy, and he's excruciatingly soft. He's not obese, but certainly luxurious in figure.

Cynthia checks the cabin for more spew, and there's none. When Anahera comes back Cynthia holds her face blank, and says nothing about the dog. Anahera changes clothes and changes the table, then says, 'Right,' and smiles. 'Where do you want me to strip?'

Cynthia shrugs. 'Over there?' There's not much space, but she gestures towards the area in front of the toilet door, adjacent to the kitchen sink. It's near a window, so there's good natural light.

Anahera sticks her head in the cabin, looking for the underwear.

'I don't know if I'm in the right mood, sorry,' Cynthia says.

Anahera shakes her bum. 'Nonsense.'

Cynthia pulls Snot-head closer, and looks out the window. Anahera changes in the bathroom, and emerges in a T-shirt and the lace thong – sickly pink. She's embarrassed. 'Um,' she says, 'do I just turn around?'

It'll be fun after all. 'Yup,' Cynthia says, suddenly moving and disturbing Snot-head. He trots to the cabin. Anahera turns and takes awkward hold of the bathroom doorknob. Cynthia's not sure what the right, encouraging thing to say is, but it looks real good. She takes a picture. Anahera takes her shirt off then, so she's in just a bra, and shifts onto the toes of one of her feet so one butt cheek's higher than the other. 'Oh, yup!' Cynthia says, and takes another shot, then wishes she'd stayed quiet. But it feels weird to be quiet. Anahera turns and Cynthia says, 'Gosh!' then feels worse. She shades her eyes like the sun's in them, and squints.

'Alright?' Anahera asks.

'Oh, oh yeah!' Cynthia says. 'We'll roll in it. Money!' She takes one last photo, from the front, clipping out Anahera's face. Anahera laughs, relieved, and goes for her shorts and shirt. Photos in just one pair aren't enough, but Cynthia says nothing. They're only starting.

'Sorry if I made you uncomfortable.'

Anahera snorts gently, dressed now, and sits down to ruffle Cynthia's hair. 'You're doing it too.'

'I'll get rid of him,' Cynthia says.

Anahera's quiet, but they're sitting side by side, and Cynthia can feel through her arm that she's pleased. Neither of them looks to the cabin, where he's asleep. Cynthia shifts her eyes from her knees, suddenly, and stands up. 'Right then!' She gets the red underwear from the cabin, and changes in the bathroom. She adjusts the lace so there's no hair poking through, and pushes the tap-pump three times to wash her face in salty water. Then, she strides out.

Anahera's sitting on the bed in the still of the boat, waiting. She looks away from the window, at Cynthia, and Cynthia bursts into tears.

'Come here,' Anahera says, patting the seat beside her.

'It doesn't matter,' Cynthia says. 'My face won't be in the shots anyway.'

Anahera's face scrunches deeper with concern, but Cynthia ignores her and gets her phone. She explains how to work the camera. Anahera must already know, but she says nothing, nods, and takes a test shot of the kettle.

Cynthia makes a big smile, and gives two thumbs up. Then she stands and turns around, sticking her bum out. She waits, and Anahera doesn't take the photo. Snot-head's in the cabin with his ears flicked up; he's heard her sobbing. His eyes are wet and his wrinkles look particularly saggy. Cynthia only glances at him, then faces the wall again.

'Look, we can do this another time,' Anahera says.

'But we haven't done it another time ever!' Cynthia splutters. She doesn't move, gets herself quiet, and at last hears the camera go. That done, she turns and looks dully through the window behind Anahera's head, while she gets a photo from the front.

'There are other ways for us to make money,' Anahera says.

'What's wrong with this way?' Cynthia asks, holding her body still and barely moving even her mouth.

'Keep your dog,' Anahera says.

'Take the photo, Anahera.'

The clicking noise.

'Take another one.'

Anahera does.

'I'm not going to wear any other pairs today,' Cynthia says. 'I actually can't be bothered.' Anahera says nothing, which enrages Cynthia, but she holds in her rage, saying nothing either. Snot-head makes a little dry-heave in the cabin.

They both agree the milk smells fine and Anahera makes Cynthia a hot chocolate with it. She doesn't say anything more about the photos, the dog or money, she just watches Cynthia slurp up the drink. Snot-head watches too, from the floor.

'We'll do it tomorrow,' Cynthia says toughly, through her milky mouth, and nudges his ribs with her foot so Anahera can see what she means. 'And we'll get more groceries.'

Anahera nods, and rubs her back. The photos are good, but Cynthia doesn't get around to uploading them.

In bed that afternoon Cynthia runs her fingers through the crevices between Snot-head's wrinkles, and pauses every now and again to feel Anahera's own fingers wriggling through her hair. They are three spoons, but Anahera coughs and walks outside. Still, when she lies down again Snot-head makes a short lovely snuffle and she and Cynthia laugh against each other, his body a warm perfect nugget at their centre.

For dinner Cynthia asks if she can give him corned beef, even though there's jellymeat left, and Anahera says yes. After eating it, he walks in three little circles, slowly, then waits under the bed to be lifted up into it.

Anahera doesn't swim that night, and makes Cynthia a really nice soup. They wrap Snot-head in a blanket and eat it with him outside, under the stars, then a whole packet of Tim Tams.

14

The next morning Snot-head hasn't spewed anywhere at all. When Cynthia goes to the toilet, she lets him in after her and Anahera pretends not to notice. She sits with him on her knee after peeing, in privacy. After she's not sure how long, she stops patting him and forgets where she is.

When she comes back out, the bed's the table and they sit at it, side by side on the seat. Anahera stays out of the way. Cynthia writes a letter saying all the predictable things: How loved he is, and how lovely. That his name is Snot-head, and can it please not be changed? Also, you've always got to feed him less food than he wants.

The water under them is slow but rolling, so the note's a bit woozy. When she's done, she puts the paper aside and copies it carefully, pressing the pen down hard with each letter. It still doesn't look good, but you can see how hard she's tried by the pen's indent in the paper.

'He's very handsome.' Anahera puts her face close to his.

Cynthia shrugs.

'You have me,' Anahera says.

Cynthia pats him and doesn't look at her. Anahera always knows how to speak without promising.

Anahera waits a very long moment, then asks, 'Should we go soon?'

Cynthia says nothing, just affixes her note to his collar with some lace cut from her blouse.

'I just think, the sooner we drop him off, the more of today he has left to find somebody.'

They feed him and eat as quickly as he does. In her best clothes, Cynthia uses spit and her finger to clean gunk from the corners of his eyes, then her own, and they go.

In the dinghy she holds him tight – he's breathing deeply too. The water's slow, but the waves are big and moving up and down as well as towards the wharf. They keep coming up in leaps, and splashing Snot-head's tender face, so Cynthia takes her sweater off to wrap him up. Anahera pretends not to watch them, and makes a wince-smile when Cynthia catches her.

'Is it a weekday?' Cynthia asks.

'Thursday.'

'Then we'll leave him at the school. He likes kids.'

'That's a really, really good idea.'

Cynthia squeezes him, and smiles. 'I'll show him around a bit, so he knows where he is.'

They go to the supermarket and Cynthia picks Snot-head up and carries him inside. Anahera says nothing, and when Cynthia talks to her dog aloud to see if he wants the most expensive salmon, she stays quiet. 'Yes, of course you do!' Cynthia says, and she licks him between his two big eyes. On the checkout guy's request, she and the dog wait outside while Anahera pays.

She comes back out, hands over the can, and stands waiting. 'The school's just over there,' she gestures across the street, and moves her body in that direction too, suggesting they head off.

'We'd prefer to do this without you,' Cynthia says.

Anahera furrows her brow.

Cynthia doesn't watch her face for long, and busily fondles her dog.

'I'll get more groceries then,' Anahera says, and pats the pocket with her phone and card.

'Great.' Cynthia walks off.

'See you back here at twelve,' Anahera yells after them. She doesn't yell a second time, although Cynthia makes sure not to acknowledge hearing. After she's clipped the lead to his collar and put him down she notices a car's waiting for them to move; they're standing in the middle of the road. She's got no money for a snack.

They walk together past some quite nice houses, and Cynthia points each out to Snot-head. 'You see, that one's got a big deck, but the grey is no good. It'll depress you. Yes, it will. Yes.' Sometimes he looks where she points, or up at her when she speaks, but mostly he just sniffs the ground. 'That one's wood. Bricks, that one. Bricks are warmer. Three cars at that one. Yup, yup. *Three* cars.' When they've walked around two and half sides of the school they reach a carpark, which they hurry through. Cynthia doesn't want him hanging around that part of town.

Soon they're back at the dairy. It must be mid-morning. Over the road there's a bank at the bottom of which is the back end of the school sports field. She'll climb down it, wait for the bell to ring, eat a bit of salmon, and leave him on the field with the rest. The children will emerge yelling, and he'll trot to them. She'll be gone up the bank before he turns back to her.

She picks him up and clambers down, much quicker than she'd like to. He quivers in her arms. When she sets him on the ground he's very pleased, and she sees how small he is. She opens the salmon, and hits it hard against the ground so half falls out. There's less than she thought, and he eats quicker than she imagined. His share is gone, and he waits. She gets on her knees to kiss him goodbye and tell him not to worry, she loves him, but he won't look at her face. He gets up on his back legs and rests his front paws on her arm. 'No,' she says, careful not to be harsh because she thinks the bell will go soon. 'In a moment,' she tells him, and pushes his front legs gently from her arm. She holds him down while she kisses him, and cries a little.

When he hears her, Snot-head pauses and – this is his love – stops trying to reach the salmon. He looks up at her, confused. She pats his head twice more, and murmurs her love again. Silence, and he doesn't know why they're still there, or why he remains unfed. He uses his best manners and waits. Finally, Cynthia pats the rest of the salmon from the can onto the ground. He sniffs it, but decides he's had enough fish anyway. 'Yes, I love you. I love you more than her,' she tells him, but she can't make it make sense. He sniffs a second time, half-heartedly, and Cynthia remembers she was about to leave. The bell hasn't rung, he doesn't want the salmon. She touches her forehead, and scrambles up the bank. It's steeper than it looked. He's not eating, but standing with his head up, watching her, still waiting. She turns away, and struggles up the last bit in a big movement. At the top, she turns again, and he's left the fish to stand with his two front paws up against the bank. He sees her looking and struggles to follow her. Not hard, he's fat and lazy, and he doesn't know what her going means, but he tries. The bell rings then, but he doesn't look away. He's shuffling all his feet, the two on the ground and the two on the bank, and not moving at all.

Cynthia walks away, to wait for Anahera.

She sticks her head through the door of a bakery and sees she's half an hour early. She could go back now, to watch him meet the kids, but she doesn't. He'd see her looking, and she'd distract the children from petting him. He might run in the wrong direction, and what could she do to help, call him? No, she waits. She walks up and down the street and looks through the windows of a series of ridiculous shops. There are so many scarves for sale these days. Anahera arrives three minutes late. Cynthia knows, because when she sees Anahera coming she ducks her head through the door of a tourist shop and checks the time on a big paua-encrusted clock. Counting the time it takes them both to get back to the designated spot, Anahera might even be late by seven minutes. When they do meet, she knows better than to ask how it went. She's carrying seven huge bags of groceries, but she doesn't gesture for Cynthia to take any of them. 'I'm sorry,' she says, seeing Cynthia's face. 'You can go back and get him?'

They walk in silence back to the dinghy, and on the way Cynthia takes two of the bags.

That afternoon there's another text from Cynthia's father, split into five parts. It's the same one he sent before ('Hello, Cynthia. Now, I see that you have stolen $16,400 from me, and some of my clothes . . .') but he's added the words *very*, and *humiliating* so that the message now says, 'Without even mentioning the very intensely hurtful and humiliating nature of your behaviour, I must emphasise that I consider this a serious issue,' before continuing on to inform her that he expects to receive contact in the near future. He's also included a postscript stating that he's 'sorry if she ever felt he didn't support her in whatever career ambitions she had'.

This time, he's sent the message as an email as well as a text. She's got to have courage, so reads it in each format only once and deletes his number. She doesn't say a thing for the rest of the day, and Anahera watches her cautiously, touches her gently, and doesn't ask any questions.

15

The next day, before Anahera goes for her swim, she says, 'I thought because I liked sunbathing with you so much, and reading those books' – and she hands Cynthia a stack of pink-edged paperbacks. Four of them. 'This guy's on a horse' – she shows the cover of one – 'and this one's a Wall-Street wolf.' She makes a little growling noise at Cynthia, leans down, and bites her gently on the ear. Cynthia shivers from the bite, and jumps a little in excitement. After a moment lifting up and down on the balls of her feet, she growls back. Being in the sun with Anahera, and under the sunsets, knowing they're both reading books the other has read, or will read – what could be more beautiful? The men on the covers are all shirtless.

'Thank you,' she says. 'Thank you so much.'

Anahera beams back, and retrieves a packet of Tim Tams. 'I don't need to swim this morning,' she says. 'I just want to be with you.'

They take blankets around the edge of the boat and lie on them. They have cups of cold tea and of rum, and even though it's a bit warm it's cooler than the air around them, and sweet. Anahera reads from the blurb of her book, 'His face is that of a millionaire magnate, yes – but heavy and low in his Armani trousers lurks the cock of a lumberjack.' Her voice is sharp and cool, like a knife in water, and she laughs. Cynthia's probably in love. She laughs too, and unsticks her sweaty legs. Anahera pats them and says they'll read a bit, then go in for lunch.

Cynthia gets stuck on one page for an hour, and what she's imagining is Anahera saving her from drowning.

Anahera's stirring whatever lunch is on the stove. Cynthia's lying on the bed, and she sticks her foot up in the air. 'What do you think of this?'

'What?'

'My foot.'

Anahera turns. 'It's alright.'

Cynthia raises her eyebrows and waggles it. She worms her body on the warm, sun-heated bed, into the blankets. With her eyebrows raised, she waggles it faster and faster till Anahera says, 'It's good.'

Cynthia stops then. 'Thanks. It is, yeah.'

Anahera turns the heat down on the stove and stands looking at Cynthia, at her body. 'I had bunions,' Cynthia tells her, provokingly. 'You wouldn't think it, but I did.'

Anahera leans back on the bench. 'Bunions,' she repeats.

'And I've got a sensitive tummy,' Cynthia adds quickly. 'Weird ankles, too. Sometimes I just fall right over.' She rests her foot down on the bed and pulls her shirt up to reveal her tummy. 'I can drink those big bottles of apple juice, but I'll tell you what – I shouldn't. If I drink a small bottle of apple juice I can't jog anywhere, or even walk quickly, or have sex with anyone for four hours afterwards, minimum.'

Anahera looks down tenderly, as if Cynthia's belly were a kitten, and nods.

'You can touch it,' Cynthia tells her. Anahera squats down, beside the bed, and puts her fingers lightly on Cynthia's stomach.

'My body's a real disaster, in some ways,' Cynthia tells her, not showing off, just stating a fact. Anahera nods, and shifts her fingers like a whirlpool around Cynthia's tummy button. 'Anyway,' Cynthia says, 'you can touch my armpits, through my shirt.'

Anahera looks at her and her fingers pause.

Cynthia feels her lips pull in, but she's making sure not to be embarrassed. 'I like it sometimes,' she says. 'I touch my own armpits sometimes.' It's hot, the blankets are so hot under her, and her face must be like a capsicum. She lifts her arm up above her head and smiles playfully. 'Come on, love,' she says in a fake man's voice. 'Get to it.'

Anahera pauses a moment, but doesn't laugh. She leans over Cynthia, and with the long fingers of both her hands touches Cynthia's armpit. It tickles splendidly, like Cynthia's a pet rabbit, but she makes sure not even to smile. She can feel her eyes and lips opening, and she touches the inside of her bottom lip with her tongue. Anahera pauses her fingers, and Cynthia nods for her to keep moving them. 'It's sexual,' she whispers bravely.

Anahera nods, puzzled and hopefully pleased.

'Okay,' Cynthia says. 'That's enough, they lose sensitivity after a while.'

They gaze at each other. Cynthia notices again four or five stray hairs at Anahera's eyebrows, and her long blinking eyelashes, and realises: she's in love, definitely. Anahera stays close for a moment longer, then goes to circle the spoon around in the pot. She shifts from foot to foot, like dancing.

16

They're having a fabulous conversation, where words mean more than they do, and everything is true. 'We don't always understand each other,' Anahera has said, very frankly, and Cynthia has nodded.

Now Cynthia adds, 'We don't, no, no, we don't,' and she laughs. 'We're very different, but I try, and you try, and that's what counts.'

Anahera sips her rum, and nods. They look at each other, and this is what Cynthia has always wanted to feel – that by making eye contact with a dear, special person, she might become eternal. She feels herself expanding, and the enormous water laps at their boat from below.

The sun returns to them stronger with each day, and Cynthia stops counting them. Quickly, they finish the first bottle of rum, and Anahera produces a second. They lie close, nearly on top of each other, and at every full stop, between the sentences in Cynthia's romance novels, she imagines rolling over against Anahera, and telling her the dirty, truthful facts of her desire. Sometimes, Anahera herself rolls over and she says nothing, but Cynthia thinks her eyes press forward, like fingers. She's sure they both know, and are both waiting.

Cynthia could list her needs, and all of them are love. She could list what she's paid, given and sacrificed to Anahera, and it's so much more than money now. It's everything.

Anahera's swims are longer, twice as long. But Cynthia's happy for her – she must be even fitter! – and the time between them seems to have expanded. When Anahera's gone, Cynthia remembers Snot-head and wonders where he might be. She plucks herself, looks in the mirror and feels sad, but each time Anahera returns she's always pleased, and beautiful again.

17

They're re-reading their books now, which is a bit boring, but in a lovely, predictable way. Anahera gets up, slowly and hardly using her arms to lift her weight, and goes around the side of the boat and into the toilet. Cynthia sits still and watches the door once she's shut it. It takes Anahera less than three minutes to re-emerge. When she does, instead of returning to the sun and to Cynthia, she sits down at the table and looks into her phone, then types something. A message, she's sent it. Then she looks up and sees Cynthia watching through the window. She looks back, and sets her shoulders.

This is the third time this has happened, but Cynthia knows that, if asked, Anahera will assert her right to text whoever she likes. So, Cynthia rearranges her book in her lap, and peers down into it.

When Anahera's settled back onto her belly and elbows to read, Cynthia gazes down into the parting of her hair, and sees it as a crevasse. She asks, 'Where do you swim to?'

'Oh,' Anahera shuffles up, and points in the direction of an island. 'There.'

'To that beach?' Cynthia asks.

'Sometimes just towards it.'

Cynthia settles down to read then. She will not be unreasonable, she takes a glug of rum. Anahera has every right to send text messages, and visit a beach. 'Do you want to watch *The Newlywed Game* with me tonight?' she asks.

'Yup, what's that?'

The Newlywed Game is Cynthia's current favourite. Some couples even got divorced because of it. They answer questions about each other, and have to predict each other's answers to win. It's good to watch on a phone, because the definition's bad.

For lunch, Anahera boils two-minute noodles and canned tomatoes together in a pot, and the result is good. While eating they drink more rum. Afterwards Cynthia does some dancing. 'Wiggle it!' Anahera shouts at her. Cynthia bends and shakes her bum harder. Laughing, nearly wheezing, Anahera takes her head, holds it still, and puts some raisins in her mouth.

Cynthia dances her plastic cup up to Anahera and it's filled right up. She drinks half, and she drinks more while undressing for her midday wash-swim. 'I'm too drunk,' she tells Anahera, laughing. 'Too drunk for swimming.'

'I'll watch you,' Anahera says, and Anahera is watching her.

Cynthia strips down to her underwear, like usual, to wash. But she can feel Anahera's eyes pulling her body, sucking at her, and she can feel her own desire prickling, trying to escape her skin. It's hot. She swallows more and watches Anahera gulp back twice as much, and even flinch a little after doing so. Then, she puts her glass aside and leans forward with her elbows on her knees. Cynthia turns around, in a circle, unthinking, looking for nothing. Then she stops. She's facing a little to the side of Anahera, looking at the island. 'What do you do there?' she asks.

Anahera shrugs. 'Sit, mostly.'

'And, are you watching me still?' Cynthia asks, but she can't turn the rest of the circle, she can't look at Anahera while she speaks. Instead she leans over the edge, to feel the water. Its coolness reminds her of her body, and how smooth it is. She wants to shift her hand and touch herself, her hip, her waist, her ass, but she can't, Anahera's looking. She touches her wet hand to her throat, waiting for an answer.

'Yes,' Anahera says, 'I'm still watching you.'

Cynthia will slip in, underneath the water. She's about to. She can see the ladder, and the shampoo tied to it where the water foams against the side of the boat. She will, but she can feel Anahera's eyes holding her, and all of her body tingles, ready to be filled up and loved.

'I'm still watching you,' Anahera says.

Cynthia puts two of her fingers under the elastic of her underwear and wriggles them, wriggles them down, then kicks her two feet out of the holes. Trembling, she unclasps her bra. She can't hear it, not quite, but Anahera is breathing behind her, sitting with her eyes open. It's good, standing there in the cool light wind, under the sun. That's all you have to do to find yourself; tear everything else away. The air shifts against her new wilderness hair and her hardening nipples. She won't be ashamed. She turns to look back at Anahera.

Anahera's eyes shift away first, and she says, 'You know,' then gestures to the other boats around them.

'So?' Cynthia stands for one moment. Then, in her usual slow way, she gets in the water, wetting herself in very small portions at a time. Anahera's still watching her, she must be, but when Cynthia turns back to see her she's drinking more, and staring down at her hands.

Cynthia's careful not to do anything faster than she normally would, to get the roots of her hair washed properly, and not to miss any sections in conditioning the tips. When she's clean and a little cold, she shifts to the ladder and hovers on it, halfway up.

Anahera's untangling her hair. 'I don't know,' she says. It's very tangled today, a huge poof on her head, and she pulls a strand through the larger mass thoughtfully.

'About what?' Cynthia says, touching her nipple and trying to adopt a similar, contemplative expression.

'I don't know if sex would really be good for us.' Anahera drops her hair and watches Cynthia's finger, moving in circles now. The sun caught in her hair is godly. She raises her eyebrows.

'But why are you thinking about it?' Cynthia asks. She shakes some water from her hair and climbs up into the cold, fresh air. 'I play fast and loose,' she says, 'and I have since forever.'

Anahera's laugh is like biting, but she says seriously, 'So you want – what?'

Cynthia feels like a dashboard dog, nodding. Then she hears the question. 'You,' she says.

'I'm not looking for anything.'

'Doesn't matter, I'm something anyway.'

Anahera touches her own neck, and Cynthia begins nodding again. When it doesn't seem right to nod anymore she goes to sit on the bed, hoping Anahera will follow her. Anahera stands in the doorway, looking all over Cynthia's body. She's wearing Cynthia's father's pin-striped shirt and her workout shorts. Her feet are bare, and the muscles of her legs look almost tensed. The shirt's not buttoned all the way to the bottom, and she's holding one side from underneath, scrunched up in a fist. Cynthia can see her tummy button, a rude-looking slight outie. She shifts one of her feet, but doesn't come forward or stop looking. Cynthia lies back and twists sideways.

'What do you like, Cynthia?' Anahera asks, with her voice quiet like she's trying to be careful.

Cynthia thought she knew this. They both wait for her to stop thinking, and say, 'Come touch me.' Just then something clangs outside, and Anahera looks up, but Cynthia says it again, and Anahera does. Cynthia fingers the collar of her father's shirt, and then the buttons. Her fingers slip between them, and she's touching Anahera's breasts. Anahera laughs, but doesn't move to remove the shirt. Blood rushes through Cynthia, and lands hard and thumping between her legs. She squirms against the pressure, then she's squirming against Anahera's hand, and her fingers. With her second hand, Anahera presses down on Cynthia's chest, pushing her into the bed. Cynthia pushes back, and then she doesn't.

Anahera leans down and kisses her mouth, then, smooth and sudden, her fingers are in Cynthia. Cynthia moans and thrusts up, but Anahera's hand is pressure on her chest, holding her down. Her eyes shut, and the feeling becomes bigger, and becomes everything she's ever felt, or could feel. There's nothing in her mind but Anahera's eyes, looking down, with her pupils big and seeming to grow, then more, more, and Cynthia's feels she's lost her whole body inside them.

She blinks, and feels she's falling upwards.

'You're cute,' Anahera says, and Cynthia wants to touch her nose. The air between them sparkles, or Cynthia has fallen into Anahera's eyes.

'Are you alright?' Anahera asks, which is peculiar.

'I am, I don't want to move,' Cynthia says. There's no blood in her head, only an enormous, expanding sense of meaning. She says, 'I keep dreaming of Snot-head.' She hasn't been, really. She didn't think of him at all yesterday, but now she hears his name the soft, wet memory of his face comes right back to her. His tongue licking her cheeks. She touches them, and they're wet with tears. 'I knew we were magic,' she tells Anahera, 'I knew everything would be worth it.' She dabs some wetness from below her eye, and puts it to Anahera's lips, hitting teeth. Anahera had looked fierce only a moment ago, while her hands worked on Cynthia and pushed her down, but now through Cynthia's tears her face looks pliant and dewy. Confused, even. She shakes her head a little, so Cynthia's finger is flung from between her lips, and she goes outside.

Cynthia lies a moment, still deep in feeling, then follows her. The weather's changed, the sun's behind a cloud and there's wind. The water's a voluptuous mess. 'You're like my hero,' she tells Anahera. She wipes her eyes with her wrists and looks up, but Anahera isn't looking down at her. 'I think it's around the time of Snot-head's birthday,' she says. 'Today might be his birthday.'

Water is flung against them, and Cynthia remembers she's naked. 'It's his birthday,' she says, insistent that Anahera understand. But he wasn't Anahera's dog. 'Let me do you,' Cynthia says, but the wind takes her words before Anahera's had a chance to hear them, and she can't seem to repeat herself. They stand together.

Anahera waits for two more waves to disappear before wiping her eyes and looking down as if puzzled. 'Another time. Let's watch your show.'

'You're cute,' Anahera had said, and it made Cynthia happy, but now she can't find her show because it keeps distracting her, playing back in her mind in a dull voice. The air's gone cold, but Cynthia feels if she gets up to dress something will be over, so she snuggles in towards Anahera's warmth, and eventually finds the link.

She points out the couples who've matched their clothes; they're the ones you have to watch. Another thing: 'They call sex "making whoopee"!' Cynthia repeats it a second time. 'Making whoopee!'

Anahera laughs then says, 'Okay.'

Cynthia's hungover, so maybe she's not thinking properly, but it feels like their bed's gone saggy. She waits for the feeling to pass, but it doesn't. She presses play.

Bob, the host, asks the husbands, 'What percentage of your wife's body is jawbreaker, and what percentage is jello?'

Anahera gets squinty at the little screen, at Bob. The men all answer, laughing, but Anahera doesn't seem to get the fun of it, so Cynthia turns it off.

'Aw,' says Anahera. 'Why?' But Cynthia feels the space in the bed between them, and Anahera's body already readying itself to stand up.

'Never mind,' Cynthia says, and goes for her clothes.

That night Cynthia sits out late, with more rum, under the washing-line and the stars, putting Burger Rings on her fingers and eating them off. She's thinking, if you stop waiting for something to happen it won't, and if you start wondering if it will happen, you'll stop waiting.

She goes back inside, and Anahera's lying with her eyes open. 'Excuse me?' Cynthia says.

'Yeah?' Anahera barely moves.

'I saw your husband in town, and I know you've been texting him.' Cynthia shifts her feet, but keeps her head up.

A noise comes from Anahera's mouth, but it's a time before she speaks. 'My husband will never talk to me again, because I took his car and sold it to buy this boat. And because – *Cynthia, as you know* – he caught me having sexual intercourse with another man. Now, I can tell you very definitively that I have not been texting my husband, and that you did not see him in Paihia.'

'Oh, sorry,' Cynthia says, shrinking.

But Anahera leans over and tugs Cynthia by her arm into bed. They don't touch, not properly, but Cynthia thinks of how their bodies are lying in parallel lines, and feels tremendous relief at knowing there's no one else, anywhere, equivalent to either of them.

18

The following day Anahera's swim takes longer than any other. The waiting drags. Even when she's back the hours feel limp. They lie on the deck, reading in the sun, but spend more time not reading, and not doing anything else. Cynthia joins Panty Utopia, uploads pictures and writes the listing. She can't tell Anahera, because Anahera thinks she's already done it. 'You think we need jobs,' she says instead.

Anahera's hands stay far away from Cynthia, and her body far away from Cynthia's hands. They go inside, then Anahera goes back out. Cynthia turns the table into the bed and gets in. It's shaky and wrong, she's never done it before, but she won't get out and fix it. She watches a *Catfish* episode about a guy who thinks he's dating Katy Perry. Anahera comes back through, looks at her, and goes to pee. Cynthia turns off her show – she doesn't need to see him click any more faulty links to know his Katy's false – and turns to face the wall.

Anahera opens the door. 'What do you want?'

Cynthia wets her lips then blows air through them. Anahera always acts as if things are simple.

'I'll watch the rest of your show with you? I thought it looked really interesting.'

Cynthia makes another noise with even more moisture, and her spit lands on the wall in front of her face.

'I'll make biscuits,' Anahera says.

Cynthia rolls over to look at her.

'Okay,' Anahera says, then disappears back into the bathroom, and releases the water from the sink. 'Alright.' She re-emerges and sets about the biscuits. Cynthia sits up on her elbows to watch.

'There's nothing wrong with you,' Anahera turns and says, 'at all.'

'I don't need you to say that,' Cynthia grumbles. But the biscuits already smell good. It doesn't take long, and they're in the oven. Anahera gets on her knees on the bed above Cynthia, and touches her forehead with a thumb.

'Sorry about yesterday,' she says.

'What part?'

'They shouldn't take long,' Anahera says, of the biscuits. 'I made little ones.' She moves back on her heels to watch Cynthia.

'You're right, I'm totally fine,' Cynthia mumbles. Anahera seems to be waiting for more, so she adds, 'I only know how to be myself.'

Anahera gets up then, to peer through the foggy window of their little oven. 'First time we've used this thing,' she says. While they wait she goes outside, and Cynthia watches her feet through the windows, walking around the edge of the boat in loops. On the fourth loop, Cynthia joins her, then they come back in together to check the biscuits. They're nearly done. They walk three more loops together, and the biscuits are cooked.

In bed beside Anahera, Cynthia pulls one apart in her two hands. It doesn't crumble, it divides. The chocolate's in big parts, and the biscuit's fudgy. Anahera puts her arm up, near Cynthia's head, so it's touching the fluff of her hair. Cynthia can feel her in the static. She shoves both parts of the biscuit in her mouth and holds them there.

'We do need to make a plan,' Anahera says. 'About what to do with ourselves.' She kicks the blankets to the ground, away from their feet. It's hot. The biscuit dissolves in Cynthia's mouth, moving towards her throat and between her teeth. 'I don't know what,' Anahera says, 'but something.'

Cynthia just feels tired. She runs her tongue between her top lip and gums, and she doesn't mention her father, or her dog.

Anahera can't lift her legs straight up, because the ceiling's low over the bed, but she stretches them with her knees bent.

Cynthia reaches for another biscuit.

'What do you think?' Anahera asks.

'I'll get mussels with you,' Cynthia says. This is something Anahera's talked about more than once, but it seems brutal and scratchy; unfun. Still, Cynthia will do it.

'Okay,' Anahera says, but Cynthia can feel her still waiting.

19

That night in bed, Anahera cries.

'What is it?' Cynthia asks, but Anahera pretends to sleep. 'Please,' Cynthia says, stroking her fingers down Anahera's back, but the muscles stiffen. She waits, maybe for an hour, and then Anahera really is sleeping.

She takes $20 from Anahera's wallet in the drawer under the cutlery. She's going to buy nice food things. Sweet buns, possibly. They'll eat happily in the morning.

With the money tucked in her bra, she gets in the dinghy and the darkness, then unties herself, holding tightly to the paddle. The moon is magical light on the water, every part of it glimmers and beckons. She's not far from the wharf, and it's lit. Still, it stays the same size for minutes and minutes despite her paddling. Sometimes the work is easier, and she forgets this means she's holding the paddle wrong. Suddenly, the prickle of the money's gone from her breast and she looks around — as if it will be the sole bright thing fluttering in the night, but it's nowhere. Also: she didn't pay any attention when she walked with Anahera, she doesn't know where the shops are. They won't even be open. She turns, thinking she'll go back, and finds she's moved farther from the boat than she thought.

She struggles forward, and arrives. When she's tied the dinghy up and retied it a second time, there's the sound of people talking. Comforted, she squeezes her bra and finds the money there, as crunchy as when she first shoved it in. She wipes her sweat proudly, and gets out. The wharf's still under her feet, a peculiar feeling, and the surety of it strengthens her.

At the top of the steel bridge she's right by the tree Snot-head pooped under when they first arrived. It was the last one she ever watched him do on land, so she stands a while. There's just enough wind to shift the leaves, silhouetted by the moon, and to touch Cynthia through her shirt, where she's wet with sweat at her armpits. It's cold, she's wearing only her pyjamas, and she must move on.

She thought she was leaving to buy nice food for Anahera, but then she's in a pub. There are two men at the bar. She sees them, and sees them shift towards each other and see her. They're not attractive, but Cynthia leans on something out of habit – a high table. One looks Samoan, about twenty-five, and his hat's on backwards. He's the better one. The other's thirty, white, and he's walking towards her.

She remembers the sweet buns. His eyes are brown and his cheeks pouchy. He's looking at her hard, through an odd soft face. There's stubble on his cheeks, which should be good but somehow isn't. Suddenly his hand's out between them, and he's still walking. She doesn't move towards it. He hurries the last step and finally arrives too close.

'Where have you run away from?' he asks her.

'I'm just looking for the supermarket.'

'What?' he says.

'They're probably all shut,' she tells him.

He nods, and moves to go back to his friend.

'I'm having trouble with my girlfriend,' she says.

He looks right back at her. 'What?'

'I gave up everything to be with her.'

He nods for her to follow him, and they go back to his friend. 'Having trouble with her missus,' he explains, and his friend adjusts his hat and nods. They wait for more information.

'I had to let my dog go.' She nods as she says it.

'Ah,' they say, as if they've lost pets to women too. It's a poorly lit establishment. They sit there together, leaning on the bar and thinking. Cynthia orders a beer and drinks it. She goes to the toilet, pees, and comes back to sit with them and think some more.

'Him and his girlfriend never have sex,' the white guy tells her of the Samoan one. He doesn't deny it, just looks glumly into his glass. Cynthia doesn't say anything, but she does feel better, and warm in a way she misses. 'He's single,' the Samoan guy tells her, gesturing at the white one. Then he says, 'Love is difficult.'

Cynthia nods. Eventually she says, 'Okay,' and leaves. On the way back she stops at a liquor store and buys two packets of biscuits.

In the dinghy the tide pulls her in the right direction, and she doesn't worry about finding the boat. That's a whole town Snot-head can poo on she thinks, forgetting the regulations. Anahera was right, he'll be happier on land. She paddles slowly and wriggles, mixing up the beer in her belly to keep warm. Then she sees it, in its splendid curling script. *Baby*.

20

Anahera's gone when Cynthia wakes. It's still dark, and she stares hard at the ceiling, thinking. Her feet have always fit perfectly in her shoes, and her socks were always white, all of them, perfectly. Her handwriting's as neat as her toes, and till less than two months ago her eyebrows were as elegantly articulated as the dots on her 'i's. Now everything's slackening, she can feel it. She's shed her father, her dog, and now she's shedding herself.

Things have been happening since before she was born, she understands, in places she's never been, and Anahera seems to know everything. Cynthia must step forward or lose her.

She's reached a time and a place; Anahera will be back soon, and Cynthia wants only to be obedient.

'I'm going to town today, to ask about jobs. You can come if you want.'

'I'll come,' Cynthia says. Anahera's breasts are visible through Cynthia's father's damp All Blacks shirt, and Cynthia wishes they were touching each other, and that she didn't have to speak. 'I know you want stuff,' she says.

Anahera nods, and says, 'Okay, that's great Cynthia!' but then she doesn't say anything else. She makes jam sandwiches, and Cynthia sits thinking of Snot-head. Her dog, walking up to door after door, sniffing and begging. You can't think about it sensibly.

You can't think of anything important that way. Someone will have taken him in, surely, and he'll be in a room sleeping with them now, while they knit or talk on the phone. You can't think about need.

Anahera hands her a sandwich, and then two more wrapped in a plastic bag. 'Lunch.' The bread's stale, but they'll get more today. While chewing, Anahera says, 'I think sometimes – why can't I belong only to myself?' She looks to Cynthia for confirmation, and Cynthia eats her sandwich. 'My husband looked so *aggrieved* when he caught me, and I just think, he didn't have the *right*.'

Cynthia would like to argue, actually, but she chews.

21

Cynthia watches Anahera paddle, trying to understand how she was getting it wrong the night before. How do you know where you're going without turning to check? Anahera looks at Cynthia, who has dressed up very tidily. 'Do you know how to ask for a job?'

Cynthia adjusts her blouse where it's tucked into her pants. 'Can I have a job?'

'No,' Anahera says. 'That's wrong.'

Cynthia stares up at the sun.

'You say, "Hi, my name's Cynthia."' Anahera puts out her hand and beams when Cynthia shakes it. 'Then you say, "I was wondering if you happen to have any jobs going?"'

Cynthia makes a joke. 'This isn't the kind of role-play I want to do with you.'

Anahera pauses, pursing her lips as if she doesn't get it, then says, 'Say it back to me.'

'Hi, my name's Cynthia. I was wondering if you happen to have any jobs going?'

'Sure,' Anahera says.

Cynthia squeezes her sandwiches in their plastic bag.

Cynthia crossed this very same bridge only last night. Now, she trudges over it mutely, bringing up the rear. They go right past Snot-head's tree, and she can't remember how she hoped things would go today. She looks down the street before they cross it, and remembers the glow of the streetlights and how they led her to the bar like they were taking her home. They're so high and dull now she'd miss them if she didn't look up.

They arrive in town, outside the tourist shops. 'Back at the wharf in an hour and a half,' Anahera says, 'and focus on restaurants and cafés, I think.' Then she goes off in a direction.

Cynthia stands outside a café, and looks in the window. There's a boy in there, grimacing and vigorously wiping a table. He looks up and smiles. She walks into a gift store next door and inspects a watch. A kindly grey-haired woman approaches, smiling.

'Can I help you?'

'Yeah, um.'

The lady waits.

'No.'

The lady smiles and tells her to have a good day.

Cynthia decides to go back to the school and have a lie down where she left Snot-head. Then she'll come back, and go into more places. It's a small town, and she doesn't want to ruin all her chances in a rush.

She settles on her back and eats her sandwich slowly. There's a boy squatting low under the slide at the playground. He's wearing very, very tight denim shorts, and a loose long shirt. She looks closely, and he's holding a spray can. He turns and pulls the fingers at her, then waits, struggling to maintain his balance, to see what she'll do. She pulls the fingers back. He's a cute kid. He nearly topples, but rights himself and keeps spraying.

This is where she let Snot-head go, and she wonders, where

might he be? What might he have eaten this morning? She makes sure not to think of the shops, the people in them, or of Anahera. She closes her eyes and breathes in, then out.

A breathing noise that isn't hers. She looks up and it's the boy, puffed from jogging over. She shuts her eyes into slits, and watches him.

'Don't call the police,' he says.

She opens her eyes completely. She'd never have thought to call anyone.

He's a bit tubby, and red from the short run. 'I'm quick, I'd just sprint off. It'd be embarrassing for you,' he says. His face is concerned, squinting.

'You're not quick.'

His mouth falls open. She half expects a glob of spit to land on her.

'What were you drawing?'

'Aw.' He's ashamed. 'Just a dick.'

'I'll come look at it,' she says, and gets up. He's much taller than her, but not yet properly formed. He doesn't know how to hold his elbows, and they jut out like they might injure somebody. His face looks like putty.

'Dicks are classic,' she says, to reassure him.

He covers his mouth with his hand, but smiles and lollops after her to the slide.

'Now listen,' she says while they walk, 'have you seen my dog? He's a French bulldog. Quite ugly, but you know – a sweetheart.'

He listens closely. 'Nah.'

The dick's black, and he's barely started filling it in. 'What does it mean?' she jokes, pointing at it.

He scrunches up his face, puzzled, and answers, 'It's a dick.'

She laughs to let him know she was kidding, and he smiles. Cynthia doesn't want to go and lie alone, guilty in the grass, and she certainly doesn't want to go into more shops asking for jobs. 'What hobbies do you have?' she asks him.

He starts spraying again. He's at a difficult age, and she can see him deciding whether to trust her. He finishes the left ball, and says, 'Creative destruction.' The huge shirt he's wearing has a picture of a dead duck on it. He taps the dick with his spray can to indicate it as an example of his activity. Then looks around, for witnesses.

'Seems good,' Cynthia says. 'I don't know too many people who're into that.'

He takes a big, proud breath and begins the second ball. 'Yeah, well, me and my friend were supposed to pee over the wharf onto the tourist boats last night, but he didn't show.'

'Aw.'

'It's okay,' he tells her. 'He's only thirteen, prob'ly wouldn't be able to reach anyway.'

'Did you go without him?'

He sprays a little over the line. 'Nah.' Then smudges it with his finger, making it worse, and pats the problem spot with the pad of his thumb. 'Keep an eye out for teachers.'

She nods and sits down in the bark, then asks him, 'Are you bored?'

He shrugs, but looks down at her, differently now. 'I'll give you forty bucks for a twelve-pack of Cody's.'

'Nah,' she says.

She hears him spray a little more, then stop. He coughs, and says, 'You want something, or . . . ?'

'No,' Cynthia tells him, adjusting herself in the bark. Anahera's probably found herself four jobs by now. He doesn't start spraying again, and she looks up at him for a moment. His hair's orange, a very bad attempt at blond. He almost definitely thinks it looks good. 'You don't have a job, do you?' she asks him.

His eyebrows scrunch down, and his mouth puckers for a moment, then he says, 'I wash the windows and sweep the floor at my house. And I go to school.'

'Okay.'

'Well,' he says, 'what do you even do?'

She should tell him off. Instead she says, 'I have a boat.'

'Whoa!' He lifts up and down at his knees. 'With Wi-Fi on it?'

Cynthia remembers she's wearing her best blouse, her best pants, and that her shoes are black leather with sensible but serious heels. 'Of course,' she says.

'Fuck!' He switches his can from one hand to the other, then back again.

'Yup!' Cynthia nods. 'It's quite big, I guess, too.'

'I'll bet,' he says, solemnly. He touches a finger to his mouth for a moment. Then asks her, 'Do you drive through the rock hole?'

Cynthia doesn't know what he means. 'I have a girlfriend,' she says. 'We live on it together.'

He nods, bored. 'Do you have a drinks cabinet?'

'Yes,' Cynthia tells him.

'Oh my fucking god!' he says. 'I'll give you my forty bucks if you take me through the rock hole.'

Something about the way his nose twitches reminds her of Snot-head. 'I'm not sure about the rock hole,' she says.

'Ah!' he laughs. 'Can't fit, eh?'

Cynthia scratches behind her ear, thinking. 'There's an island,' she says.

'Is it deserted?' he asks, and she nods.

'Alright,' he says, and takes two twenties from his pocket. 'I will give you my forty bucks if you let me come drink four beers on your boat, and take me to the deserted island.'

She looks up at him and his money. She doesn't want to be alone with Anahera. 'Two beers,' she says. It's probably time to get back to the bridge, so she gets up and walks that way. He follows, gesturing back at his dick. 'Can finish that another day.' He gives her the money, and she pockets it.

'You'll have to let me stay the night,' he says, trotting ahead, then pausing to wait for her. 'Can't go home to my mum *drunk*. I'll text and tell her I'm staying with my boy Roger.'

They're early, and wait at the metal bridge together, under Snot-head's tree. The boy lies down and sends his mum what must be a very carefully worded text message – it takes a while – then clicks a finger above his head. 'Done.'

Cynthia nods. He shifts his legs around, trying to get comfortable, but he never will – not in those tight shorts. Snot-head's tree droops down and shades one of his legs. She points at its trunk. 'My dog pooed there.'

'Aw,' he says, and that's all. He coughs then, and she thinks he's faking. 'Is she coming?' he asks, of Anahera.

'Yes, I said she was.'

'Yeah,' he says.

'Um,' she asks him, 'what's your favourite subject in school?'

He grunts, and as he does so, Anahera appears around the corner with bags of groceries.

'Look!' Cynthia says, pointing at the boy. 'Isn't he good?'

Anahera peers at him for only a moment. 'Sure.' She looks bored, so Cynthia doesn't say more. 'There's nothing going,' Anahera says, about jobs. 'Nothing I want.' She waggles the bags. 'We're broke, pretty much.'

The boy's watching a seagull balance on one foot, pretending not to listen to them.

Cynthia presents the forty bucks, proudly now. 'I told him we'd show him our boat and some stuff.'

Anahera looks down at Cynthia for a long time. The seagull flies away.

'We're *broke*,' Cynthia mouths up at her.

'What?' But she got it. She walks off down the bridge to the dinghy.

'Don't worry about her,' Cynthia tells the boy, 'she's often quite obscure.'

He looks back at her, away from where the gull was. 'It's alright,' he says, 'my sister's a complicated person too, she says so herself.'

Cynthia can't help smiling. She tugs his shirt, and he follows her down the bridge.

In the dinghy he says, 'I can't see your boat.' He's big and he leans to the right, so the dinghy leans that way too. Anahera laughs and paddles.

Cynthia tells her, 'I thought we could go to your island, today or tomorrow.'

'Tomorrow,' the boy says. 'That's what I texted my mum.'

'He already texted his mum,' Cynthia explains.

Anahera nods. 'My island?' she asks.

'The one you swim to.'

The water's gentle around them, and the air's a little heavy and wet on Cynthia's shoulders; it'll rain soon. Anahera keeps paddling, and sucks her top lip. The boy looks at each boat they pass, craning his neck for the big ones, then back at Cynthia. She smiles.

'What sort of beer will it be?' he asks, and it starts raining.

Anahera swings her head around at Cynthia, glaring. Then back to the boy. She says, nicely, 'You won't be drinking any beer on our boat, sweetie.'

'That's fine, I guess,' he says. He frowns, and settles his elbows against his thighs.

'Do you want us to take you back?' she asks him. 'We'll give you your money.'

He looks at the water, and the rain falling into it in plonks, then lifts his shoulders and holds his hands together in front of him. 'No thanks,' he says. 'I want to go to the deserted island.'

Cynthia smiles at him, thankfully, and he grins back. Under his breath he's muttering the chorus from that one Kendrick song, 'Sit down, and drank. Stand up, and drank. Pour up, and drank.'

He's got the lyrics a bit wrong. Cynthia interrupts him. 'With most things, I'm allowed some part in the decision-making process.' The wind changes, and a lot of rain hits her face in a slap.

He waits till she's wiped her eyes and reassembled her face before nodding. Then he skips forward in his muttering to a later part of the song, 'I wave my bottles, and watch girls all flock. They all wanna – ' Mid-sentence, he looks up and sees her still looking at him. She smiles reassuringly, and he settles, quiet.

'Cynthia,' Anahera says, now he's stopped.

Cynthia waits.

Anahera turns to the boy. 'How old are you?'

'Sixteen.'

She keeps looking at him.

'Fifteen, and uh' – he calculates with his fingers – 'four months.' Anahera looks back at Cynthia.

Cynthia shrugs. He leans forward and takes an apple from their bags. His knees are high up, lifted at least level with his tummy button. She notices his yellow hair again, and touches her nose. It's got a spot. The water's a little rough, and the dinghy rocks now they're out in it. He stretches his legs out, and they're scabby. Rain runs down them in drops. He's got broad shoulders, strong thighs, and a wider than average mouth. He shrugs for no reason.

Baby's much smaller with him on board. They sit around the table, and he kicks the steel pipe holding it up. Anahera and Cynthia watch him quietly while he crunches through a second apple. When he's done Anahera asks him, 'What things do you like?'

'Uh,' he says, 'sports.'

'Oh!' Anahera jumps up a little in her seat. 'I'm a gym instructor, and I'm always saying to Cynthia, there's so much exercise to be had here.' She gestures to the little window above the sink, which is now being pummelled with rain. Cynthia nods, pleased to see her all perked up.

He breathes in and touches his ugly hair. She gets up to show him his bunk, in the cabin. 'It's a lot more comfortable than it looks,' she smiles and tells him, although she's never slept in it. As they're standing there, looking through the little door at the bed, the boat shifts suddenly sideways. She slips onto him, and he holds her up. His mouth smells thickly of lollies and Coke. Anahera's weights are heavy and moving above them, and Cynthia puts herself firmly on her feet.

'Cool,' he says, and laughs, then stands up on the table and knocks the panel in the ceiling. 'What's this?' Neither Anahera nor Cynthia answers, but he jumps up onto his seat, slides the panel back, and sticks his head through. 'You should renovate,' he tells them, echoing. 'Make up here a second floor for lying down in. Hot-box it. Shit-tons of cushions, I reckon. Psyche-fucking-delic.'

'No,' Anahera says, 'get down.'

'*Psychedelic*,' he repeats, as if he's not heard her. He thrusts himself up onto his elbows, so his feet dangle at Cynthia's eye level.

'That's dangerous,' Anahera says sternly. 'Get down.' Cynthia remembers her weights up there. He sighs, and his feet thump back onto the table.

Once he's sat laboriously back down beside Cynthia and taken a full minute to look around at everything in their one room, he asks, 'Where do you shit?' He's not looking at them, but up at the ceiling. Cynthia notices paint flaking there where she didn't before, at the edges.

Anahera gets up to show him the toilet and the bucket you dip into the sea for water to flush it with. 'It's on a string, so you don't lose it.'

Cynthia can't see his face, but almost hears his mouth pucker. Why did she invite him into their home? They come back and he sits again, beside her. She inhales and says, 'We're out of money,' dramatically, still trying to show him a good time.

'I know,' he says, 'I heard before.'

She forces a smile. 'Yes, well. We're unemployed.'

22

His name's Toby. There's a near continuous patter, louder than the rain, of gulls shitting on the roof. Periodically he gets up and swings around the side of the boat, trying to swat them with a rolled-up newspaper. The way Anahera looks at him when he returns from these expeditions is either indulging, or exasperated, Cynthia can't say for sure.

The weather gets nastier. Anahera bakes more biscuits, and he eats most of them. Cynthia eats most of the rest. They're delicious but he says so first. He goes to the toilet and doesn't flush properly. Anahera says nothing, and lugs in a bucket of water to do it for him. He doesn't seem guilty, or even to particularly notice.

They play cards. Toby only likes Go Fish, which Anahera seems to find endearing. Cynthia says, 'Maybe something a bit more grown-up?'

'You kept asking to play Snap before Toby arrived?' Anahera says. 'Snap is more grown-up.'

They play Go Fish. Anahera keeps smiling at Toby, then Cynthia. She seems to think Cynthia likes him, and that she's doing her a huge favour just by having him there. Cynthia goes for a lie-down in the cabin, in Toby's bed, thinking about her dog and almost pretending to be him. After a while she trudges past them, out to look at the water. It's filled with shit from the estuary.

At dinner, Toby's busy glancing around again, rudely, at the wood their home is made of – chipped in places, and blistering in others. Cynthia makes sure not to look at anything while he is. His eyes could pull her dream to pieces. She peers down, under the table, at his very clean high-top shoes. 'Are they leather?' she asks.

'What? Aw, yeah.' He rubs them against the steel pipe that supports their table.

'You definitely, actually want to come to the island?' Anahera asks him.

'Yeah, well . . .' He looks around some more. Cynthia actually wants to slam his head against the wall, a bit. 'I'm already here, and I already gave you my money, so yeah, I do.' Cynthia gives Anahera a look. He's not getting his money back.

'When I'm older I'll own an island,' he says.

After dinner they play more cards. Cynthia doesn't even nearly win, not a single round. She watches the rain fall against the window and the light fading behind the wet glass. Anahera shifts some hair from her eyes, and Cynthia waits for it to fall back. When it does she shifts it again. The boy tires quickly, and Anahera pays less attention to the game, watching him slump. The light falls lower, and soon they're not playing anymore, just all sitting there.

He sleeps in the cabin, and Cynthia and Anahera sit facing each other at the table.

'I went to places,' Cynthia tells her, 'but there were no jobs.'

'Yeah, well, we'll have to go back with lower standards,' Anahera says, not seeming to care if Cynthia's lying or what.

'You miss your husband,' Cynthia says.

'No.' Anahera doesn't ask about Cynthia's dog, or her father.

The next day Anahera wakes Cynthia, gently, with a hand on her arm. 'Let him sleep,' she says. Then, 'Why do you want to go to the island? Why does he?'

'Because we want to do something!'

Anahera looks for a moment like she's going to ask again, but Cynthia says, 'Please?'

'Okay, okay, sure.' Anahera shrug-wriggles, and gets quickly out of bed. 'We'll leave soonish, when he gets up. Make eight jam sandwiches, and cut one in half. You and I get two and a half, and he gets three.'

Cynthia lifts up on her elbows to see Anahera. She's being told off, almost. 'Please,' she says again. 'I really want to see your island. I wanted to anyway, before I met him.'

'Yeah,' Anahera says, 'well I said we would, so.'

Cynthia dozes for fifteen minutes, and while dozing she tells Anahera, 'I think about you a lot, and your needs.'

'Thanks,' Anahera says. 'We need jobs.'

They fix the table. There's noise from the cabin, Toby shifting into wakefulness. Cynthia makes the sandwiches, and Anahera sits out on the deck. While she's buttering, he walks in and opens a can of spaghetti, quickly, before she can comment. 'I'll only want one of those, thanks,' he says, nodding at the sandwiches. Cynthia shrugs and continues making as many as Anahera told her to.

When they're done she sits opposite him at the table. He's eating from the can with a spoon, and long strands dangle over the side. He tilts it so she can see how much he has left; roughly a third. 'They're so saucy,' he says disparagingly. It's on his face. He puts two more spoonfuls in his mouth, then tilts it again, grimacing; there's still roughly a third left. 'Can I have some bread?' he asks.

Cynthia hears herself breathe in. 'No, because you won't be hungry at lunch time, for the sandwiches.'

'I hate spag.' He stirs the spaghetti around, glaring at it.

'You have to finish it,' she says. 'We can't afford to waste food.'

He takes another spoonful, and fake gags. He's got spots on his forehead, and some on his chin. He gets up and walks outside, past Anahera, and throws the can into the sea. He comes back in and says, 'Now can we go? I want to see this island, but I've got shit to do today.'

'Actually,' Cynthia says. 'Do you know what? You told me you were into creative destruction, blah blah blah. I thought you were adventurous. Really, you're a little runt.'

He looks down at her quizzically.

'Psychologically – not in terms of size – you are a runt.'

He preserves the same expression. Anahera's looking in at them now.

'Okay,' Cynthia says, 'sure, we'll go. Whatever, but first you need to understand about our toilet, because it's very simple.' She makes him follow her to the deck, where Anahera's still watching them. She gives him the bucket and fixes the end of the string in his hand, then watches him drop it into the water. For a second she thinks he'll drop the string too, and she'll really have to ruin the whole day by making him swim for it, but he doesn't. The string's tied at three places, at opposing sides of the bucket, so he should be able to pull it up against the edge of the boat without losing too much water. However, as she knows he will, Toby yanks and three quarters of the liquid slops out. She looks him in the face, and holds the bucket between them. 'Now, is this enough to flush the toilet?'

'Should be,' he says. 'Or you'd have a bigger bucket.'

He's a typical teenager, a real little fuckhead. 'No,' she tells him firmly, and explains the string while he looks off into the distance, at the island.

'Cynthia,' Anahera says, 'what exactly is your problem?'

'Well,' Cynthia starts, 'I just don't like the way he's looking around our boat. He thinks it's crappy.'

'How am I supposed to look at it?' he says, far too loud. He's wriggling his arms, with his weird sticky-out elbows.

Cynthia doesn't want to answer. She loves *Baby*, it shouldn't be a problem if a teenager notices where the paint flakes, or complains that the toilet's laborious. But the ceiling seems lower with him under it, and the floor makes a noise beneath his heavy-stomping feet that she hasn't heard before.

'Okay,' Anahera says. 'Look, Cynthia – you can see he's sorry. He's embarrassed.'

His face is as red as blood, but that doesn't mean he's embarrassed or sorry for the right reason. Why doesn't Anahera understand how this matters? But Cynthia looks at her – standing there in her dad's Australian hat with the water moving behind her – and feels that if Anahera's not worried about it, she won't worry either.

'It's hot,' Cynthia says. 'It's so hot.'

Toby nods, relieved, and Cynthia sees Anahera watching her. She smiles back, and climbs up onto the edge of the boat, then jumps into the water. It's cool and fresh, and Cynthia doesn't generally jump off things. Toby jumps in after her. Then, after thinking about it, Anahera does too.

23

Even though he's in a man's body, Toby stands and watches Cynthia and Anahera drag the dinghy up the beach, twitching his foot, with the dark mass of trees waiting behind him. They put it down, and while Cynthia's puffing, he shoots Anahera a thumbs up and runs at a jog-trot into the trees. 'Go that way,' she yells at him, and he swerves to enter the bush where she's indicated.

Cynthia lets them go ahead together. Her feet are bare in the warming sand, and she hasn't been alone for so long. The water flickers. She'll have a new, fresh opportunity to understand Anahera soon, and she knows she can do better. Waves touch the beach and leave it wet, like licks over skin. She and Anahera will come back later, just the two of them, and the ocean won't have paused. She lies back to watch the clouds, just for a while.

Rested and warm, she follows their footprints along the beach, into the trees. In the clinging, striving mess of bush there's Anahera's bright orange workout singlet to follow, and then it disappears. When Cynthia sees it again it's stopped still. She can't see Toby. She concentrates on moving carefully, watching her toes and where she puts her feet, and holding the thicker trunks for support at the rocky parts. When she's closer she sees Anahera looking up, and she looks up too.

First she sees nothing but green, then – Toby's high in a tree. Anahera looks at her briefly when their shoulders touch, but turns quickly back to see him. This is the only way to admire people in his age group, Cynthia thinks: from a distance. He moves quickly and doesn't pause. He's done this before.

'Adults have forgotten the purpose of sports,' Anahera says. Cynthia looks at the side of her face and wishes she could be up there too; that she were a sportsperson. She can feel Anahera's arm against hers and, she thinks, a heightened pulse in it. The tree's high and tilting leftwards. He's near the top, at the surface of the canopy.

Down low, where Anahera and Cynthia are, there's no space for the air to move and they don't either. Anahera's breathing is steady. Cynthia knows what she wants, and she shouts up at him, 'Higher!' Her voice is a sudden break in the quiet, and she wishes she could suck it back in. It doesn't matter, he's too far to hear her, anyway.

He stops and waves, then looks down. He's ready to turn back, Cynthia can see it in his smallness, in how vague and unreal he looks. He lowers his left leg, and feels with that foot for a branch to stand on. 'To the right!' Anahera shouts, but Cynthia doesn't feel so patient. He's done now, he should just come down. He puts that foot back where he had it, and pauses, then lowers the other foot, and feels right. Anahera blows out air, and runs a hand through her hair. His hand slips as his weight shifts to the right, and she inhales again. He grasps again for the branch, but his left leg's shaking at the knee. He moves to pull his right foot back up, and the left slips. He's hanging from two branches, and one of them snaps. He falls, plonks.

The thud echoes, and the ground feels too solid under Cynthia's feet. Where is he? His tree, despite its height, has disappeared into all the others. There's no wind, and she forgets Anahera. For a moment nothing's alive, and all the trees might be made of plastic.

They're so still, and such pure green. Cynthia touches her eyes and they're dry. They blink. Her hands hang slack at her sides, like two wet towels. She sees his body then, a lump in the distance.

One of his elbows points skywards, she sees now, and his legs are tensed. A leaf shifts – and like that, there's wind again. The forest is alive once more with bugs, but when Cynthia touches her eyes a second time, they're still dry. Anahera's walking towards him. Cynthia follows, and when they arrive they see his eyelids. The right's shut, and the left's mostly open. Behind them, both his eyeballs stare up, and Cynthia and Anahera stand looking back down at him for a long time. His mouth is wide open and empty. Anahera squats for a moment, obscuring him with her back, then stands again.

Cynthia would like to know what to do. She moves away, and sits on a log to wait. She'd like to have a good thought, but she thinks only of how it wasn't her fault, or Anahera's. The sandwiches were squashed to mush in her fist while she stood looking at him, and she takes a bite of one now, chews, and spits it out. It sits in the dirt, as pink as guts. She pushes it aside with her shoe, and some gets caught on the toe. She won't feel guilty, she decides, and when Anahera sits down beside her, she pulls her sandwich apart and peers into it, to see the fleshiness, then takes a bite and swallows.

She can feel without looking how Anahera's lips are pulled in, and trembling like they'll be sucked down her throat. She tries to speak three times before she says, 'What can we do?' The edges of her eyes look sore, and her nose has swelled up red.

Only what they're doing, but Cynthia doesn't say it. She stands up and takes off her sweater, then walks to him. His mouth is slack at the corners, like it'll fall off his face. In his eyes, behind the wonky lids, there's a look she recognises from when he first arrived on their boat and looked about him. A slumped look, disappointed and aggrieved. She lowers herself to her knees on the rough, rock-studded earth. Her sweater is pink merino, thin and soft, and she puts it over his face. But his neck looks too exposed, pale, and his Adam's apple seems painfully sharp, like a stone pressed up through his body from the rough ground below. She piles leaves over him, so his thick limbs and neck are buried like roots. One of his hands sticks out, uncovered and limp, turned palm up, and she can see the veins running to it through his wrist. She's covering the hand when wind blows in a gust and exposes his knees and chest in patches. She piles the leaves back on, grazing his chest with her wrist. It's still warm.

She's finished, he's completely covered, and she sees the pink of her sweater and how wrong it is. It looks like the jam from her sandwich; it looks spat out. She can feel his face under it, can see the outline of his nose pushed through. There's still heat in him. In the dark under her sweater, behind his half-shut lids, he'll still have heat in his head. His brain, as pink as her sweater, is probably still twitching in the dark.

She takes it back. She doesn't want to look down but she does, and his face is exactly the same as before, except his mouth might have gone a little slacker. She goes back to sit with Anahera, and Anahera says, 'He's just lying there.'

Cynthia squeezes her sweater in her fists, it's still soft, and puts it back on. They sit for hours. She eats the rest of the sandwich she bit twice earlier, and it's too sweet. She used too much jam. She holds it between her teeth like a kitten in a cat's mouth, and leans backwards. She lands heavily with her head on the ground, and grabs Anahera's still, steady arm to pull herself back up. It doesn't work, she needs to be helped. Anahera doesn't move.

'Okay,' Cynthia says. The blood's all run to her head, and the jam's sickening in her stomach. She flops right down, and gets back up. Standing, she shakes her legs and stomps them into the ground to get the leaves off. She plucks every leaf from her sweater, and when she's done she drops it back onto the ground, back into the leaves. Anahera's sitting with her eyes closed, and her head lifted. Her mouth moves in little tremors. She's praying.

24

Cynthia pretends not to have noticed, and waits while Anahera mouths thousands of little words that can't mean anything. After hours, Anahera's eyes open slowly, but she looks down at her own hands, not at Cynthia.

Cynthia's lonely, so she gets up and walks. It's not a big island. She'll come back soon and they'll paddle home. She walks over lumps of roots and rocks, and through twiggy, sticky branches, falling and picking herself up twice without understanding that she's tripped.

He fell, and Cynthia thinks about the silent stillness of his body caught in the leaves. Now everything is moving again, there are sounds again, but that only means his quiet has turned into something else. She can't remember where he was. She looks up and feels she's being watched. She'd like to go back to Anahera now, but she turns and turns and every direction she picks feels the same as the one she came in. Then she sees something in the distance, blue, behind the vine-tangled trunks.

She walks closer. It's a tent. Beside it there's a dead campfire, dug into the ground, and a pile of wood. She approaches with her hands behind her back, and keeps them there, but bends to look closely. There's a pot, dirty with tomato sauce and dropped on its side. A stack of canned spaghetti and beans. Sloppy food, she thinks, and remembers Toby's fake gagging. The trees are loud around her.

She walks around the tent twice, then stops to touch its door flap with her fingers. It's unzipped and hanging open. She wants to hide, wrap up, and suck both her thumbs. Inside it's empty except for some blankets, a pillow and an exposed mattress. It would relieve her to crawl in, she thinks – maybe in there she'd cry.

But, Anahera. Cynthia didn't see her face when he fell, and not even for a time afterwards, but she saw the way it had swelled from crying when she left her alone on the stump.

Anahera doesn't look up, she hasn't moved.

'I found a tent, with a fire and a bed,' Cynthia says.

Anahera's twirling a leaf on a stalk, between her fingers. 'Did you.' She lets it go, and they sit longer.

Cynthia says, 'Do you think we should go back to the boat?'

She waits, but Anahera doesn't answer. It's getting dark, and quickly. Each tree has a shadow, long and distorted, mingling with the others, growing. She lifts Anahera by the arm, and leads her back through the dark mess of bush to the tent. They don't trip, fall or get lost, they simply trudge and arrive there, like they've been led. There's a can opener she didn't notice before, balanced perfectly on top of the spaghetti and beans stack. She opens some beans and they share them. Anahera weeps, and some fall from her mouth into the dirt. Cynthia wipes the sauce from her chin and asks, 'Do you want to sleep?'

The trees have disappeared into their own shadows. It's night. Cynthia leans closer, and asks again, quieter, 'Do you want to sleep?' but Anahera doesn't look at her, and shakes her head.

Cynthia crawls into the tent alone, and tidies the blankets as best she can in the dark. She'll give the pillow to Anahera.

'Anahera,' she says, and she says it again and again till she's not sure Anahera's still there anymore. She can't settle, and the blankets get messed up. She tidies them a second time, and leans out under the sag of the door flap. There's Anahera's hair, a dark mass looking so soft Cynthia thinks everything would feel okay if she could just touch it. She pulls at Anahera's shoulders, but they don't move.

When Anahera comes to bed she faces away from Cynthia, and Cynthia gives her as much privacy as possible, pushing herself against the side of the tent, so tight it makes a damp mask over her face.

Later she wakes and Anahera's holding her so close it hurts.

25

The next day Cynthia stirs slowly, and late, into the musk of the tent and her own sweaty heat. Anahera's gone. The nylon above her is illuminated in sections where light's struck through the trees. It's blue, and very bright in places. Lower down, it's mildewed, in some parts pure green. Her legs and arms are moist in the blankets, and she sniffs. The air's potent with the smell of mould, beans and something else. Anahera's left the door flap open, and through it Cynthia can see the pile of used cans. They're stacked, but most have fallen and rolled. A bird lands on top of them, and shoves its head inside so deep and quickly Cynthia worries it won't be able to retrieve it. A can shifts. The bird yanks its head out fast, and flies off. Everything is still again, but Cynthia thinks she can feel bugs on her. So many of them that they're like a new, thin layer of her skin. She looks at a plant so spindly it shouldn't be able to stand and remembers the boy, that he's dead. There are no insects to brush away, there's only Cynthia alone in the forest, and the time to wait before Anahera comes back, if she does.

The cans are still, and the trees shift only slightly behind them. Cynthia looks at the tent roof, then back at the thin tree. Anahera walks briskly into view then, and says, 'We're going. Get up.'

Cynthia does. There's nothing to bring with them. She follows as quickly as she can, not saying anything, but trying after each big tree they weave around to clutch Anahera's hand. Anahera's legs are her usual legs again, solid and abrupt, and when her hands swing back behind her they're fists. She doesn't look around, only straight ahead. They walk and walk, and the green brightens as they approach the edge of the bush, the beginning of the beach, and the sun. Cynthia thinks of asking about Anahera's feelings, but it doesn't seem appropriate. Anahera looks about suddenly, twice and twice again as if she's seen something. A pest, or a predatory animal. Cynthia looks too, at least three times in every direction, but only sees birds. The previous day she didn't notice them, but they're everywhere now. Some stop and peer at her, tilting their heads one way and the other. There are so many of them waiting along the path, and each flies off in its own direction. Then they all pause, even their necks with their shifting heads don't move, not at all. The leaves are bright, they're near the beach and it must be around midday. Cynthia's back is hot, and there's sweat on her top lip. She stops to suck it, and Anahera takes another step forward, and screams. There's a moment of her standing still, then she contorts and crumples.

The trees are huge above them. All of them loom. There's a steel trap clamped at Anahera's ankle. It's not bleeding, but the trap's made a horrifying dent in the muscle, and Cynthia's worried about the bone. Anahera moans, crying, and Cynthia squats down. She touches the metal and the skin, then sits back to look. Finally, with all her courage, she leans forward and pulls hard on the bars connected to the clamps. The trap comes out of her left hand, and her effort to open it slams it into the ground. Anahera screams again, for seconds and seconds, but there's nothing to help them. The trees grow more alive, closer. 'Shh,' Cynthia says. 'Hush, I'll take care of you.' Anahera looks at her, wild. The birds are moving again now, they're everywhere with their dark, darting eyes, watching. Anahera stares hard at Cynthia, and shakes her leg and the trap till she cries out again, and her elbows slip, so her head hits the ground with a thump.

Cynthia touches Anahera's hair, it's still soft, and she can still at least touch it softly, and says, 'I want to be good, I want to help.' But Anahera's moaning sharpens. Her whole body shakes, the foot most of all. The trap drags along the ground, lifting and thumping back down, and each time the sound Anahera makes is louder, and hurts worse.

'Please let me help you,' Cynthia says. Anahera's foot stops moving at a last thump after hearing this, but her screaming continues at the same aching volume. Her eyes dart everywhere around them. The birds are at a distance now, still looking and tilting their heads, but from behind leaves and branches. The noise is so much inside Cynthia's head. It goes on despite her.

Anahera stops suddenly and asks, 'How? How can you help me?'

Cynthia can't think. A hard, big reality has fallen on her. Might they die there? If they do they'll be alone, separated eternally by Anahera's noise. She moves forward gently, towards Anahera. It has to come off, so there must be a way to get it off.

'Don't,' Anahera says quietly.

Cynthia begins saying something about love, her love, and the anything and everything she's willing to do, but Anahera screams again, and her eyes bulge. She's looking behind Cynthia.

A person steps out of the trees. 'I am a German man,' he says, and comes forward. His moving is confident, his feet are big and in big floppy sandals but they fit perfectly between the rocks each time he puts them down. He touches the trees, but not for support; he touches them like loved and known furniture, like all of this place is his own bedroom. He's carrying a huge backpack with two pairs of shoes tied to it and holding a fishing line. He nods. 'A big one!' he says, gesturing to the trap. 'There.'

He's arrived and he's an answer, Cynthia understands. Anahera looks like she's about to pass out.

'Not legal,' he tells her sternly.

Anahera groans, glaring hard, but Cynthia sees she's looking at the man now. He's moving slowly. He gets on his knees beside Anahera's foot, without looking at her face. 'It's not serrated, you are alright,' he says. She yells and spits up at him, but it lands on her chest. He shifts back and waits for her to finish. 'Don't fight me.' He moves over her again, and Cynthia can't see the trap anymore. Anahera doesn't move, but she's breathing deeply, like something about to attack. His biceps flex, and Cynthia hears the metal pop open. 'This bad boy is not from this century,' he tells them, and he opens his pack and puts the trap inside.

'Have you already eaten?' he asks.

They don't answer.

'I have not,' he says, and takes a Tupperware container from his bag. It's white rice, drizzled with soy sauce. He brandishes a spoon from his pocket. 'I am a German man. Hello, I am Gordon. I'm only friendly. Don't fight me,' he says, then starts eating, ignoring Anahera as if she were an unnecessary table between himself and Cynthia.

Cynthia flicks her gaze from his spoon to Anahera's bulged eyes.

'Just sit quietly, you will be fine.' He nudges Anahera, and she moans again. Cynthia's very thankful he's arrived. He can carry Anahera back to the dinghy and paddle them home to their boat. She'll take it from there.

He talks through his food. 'I am on a nice-nice holiday with my girlfriend. But she left me on this island! For another girl! But I have all the money! You see, it is a twist. I am on a nice-nice holiday with myself!' He swallows and laughs, 'Ha ha ha. Ha. What am I to do with all this money which I have?'

Cynthia watches Anahera's face. She's not thinking, it's all scrunched up. Neither of them says anything.

'I am not even mad, you see? I am a friendly German man. But only a little stuck here, on this island.' He shrugs, and shoves another big spoonful in his mouth.

Cynthia laughs now, a hideous gulping noise she's been holding in since the boy fell. She laughs and she can't stop. Gordon watches her patiently. When she's done laughing she touches Anahera's arm, to show she's thinking of her. Then, 'You seem friendly,' she tells him. 'How much money do you have?' Anahera wrenches her body away from her hand.

'What are you girls?' he laughs, and looks down at Anahera, who's making a deep, hateful noise through her nose.

When he's finished his lunch and licked the edges, the corners and the lid of his Tupperware container, he moves towards Anahera, bashfully, with his hands.

'Under her knees, maybe? And her back?' Cynthia suggests.

But he picks her up instead so they're facing each other, and her legs are twisted around his stomach. 'Suck onto me like a mollusc,' he says, laughing. Cynthia can't see Anahera's face because it's pressed against his chest, but her nails are digging hard into his sides, and there's a rough, muffled noise coming from his torso, where her head is. 'You take my bag,' he tells Cynthia, and she does. It's big and heavy. She waits for him to start and walks behind.

They arrive on the beach directly in line with the dinghy, and stop next to it. He puts Anahera down on the ground, and she half falls, half sits in the sand. He turns to her kindly and asks, 'This is yours, yes?' pointing at the dinghy. She glares up at him, and Cynthia stands quietly alongside, out of sight.

'I am an abandoned man,' he says. 'I only want to help.'

Anahera spits again, in the sand, and tilts her head to one side. She makes a gurgling sound, and struggles to turn it into speech. In a dull voice she says, 'You only want to help.' Cynthia squats down next to Anahera and holds her face in her hands. Anahera looks right back at her, and says, 'I know this man. He only wants to help.'

Gordon laughs over them, good-naturedly. 'It's true!' he says.

Cynthia looks up at him, and sees he's begging like a dog. She's nearly waiting for him to get on his knees. He's lonely and lost, just like them. His face looks solid, as if beneath his skin are foundations of concrete, or carved wood. The skin under his eyes is baggy, but lifted by the hard muscle of his cheeks. There's a tough small line above his nose, and his forehead's another slab on top of it. His chin's divided into two parts. Above it his lips are fat, completely unlike the rest of his face, jutting out as if the wind would shake them; they protrude sweetly. His body's muscled, full, and strong. Cynthia estimates him to be about thirty-five. She stands up, and prods him in the sternum. 'What will you do for us?'

Anahera laughs cruelly, and bursts into tears on the ground beside her, but Cynthia thinks, *I am doing what's best*, and keeps looking at him.

He doesn't step back from her finger. 'Ah,' he says, 'I am a good company, yes, or you can tuck me away in a small place. I will give you a thousand dollars if you show me about to this beautiful environment.'

One thousand dollars! The man in sandals enjoys a moment of beauty in the sunlight, with the sea lavish and tumbling behind him. Then it's too long since Cynthia's spoken. 'Alright,' she says. Anahera will thank her later. She nods at him and says, 'Paddle us back. Our boat's over there.' She waves at it, pats him on the arm, and smiles comfortingly down at Anahera. He smiles too, then strides off and drags the dinghy down the beach.

Cynthia squats down to rub Anahera's back and listen while she says, 'He's a fuckhead.' The rubbing is light and smooth, but Anahera shrugs her hand off and says, 'Look at him.'

She looks, and he's just the back of a man, heaving their dinghy down the beach and to the sea. 'Try and be nice,' she says, and lays her hand back down, still, on Anahera's back. He's near the water now, and he turns and flashes a thumbs up. Anahera stands, and Cynthia holds her. It's a slow hobble, the leg is heavy and weak, and balance is difficult in the sand.

He jogs back to them, laughing. Cynthia steps aside so he can pick Anahera up. She doesn't fight, but he seems to anticipate it in the loose way he moves at her with his arms, then the tight way he holds her.

'Be gentle,' Cynthia tells him sternly, and he laughs and adjusts his hands. Anahera snorts. Cynthia wonders if she should carry her, or make Gordon put her down. But she doesn't, she runs ahead and pulls the dinghy into the water, then holds it still while he puts Anahera in.

26

Anahera shuts herself in the cabin, and Cynthia speaks with Gordon in hushed tones in the larger room. 'We're going through a difficult time,' she says. He nods sympathetically, and his kindness ruptures her. She's acting normal, she must be – he thinks she's normal, and that her problems are to the scale of a normal person's.

She pushes forward further, in relief. 'I was going to be on TV, announcing the news, probably. That was my dream, but I don't know if it will come true now,' she says. She's not as embarrassed saying this as another girl might be, she knows she's got a mostly stunning face and body, and that her elocution's good. The boy fell and hit the ground, but it makes her so happy to think of something else.

He nods. 'A worthy ambition.'

'I left everything for Anahera, we're in a real relationship. My father and I no longer speak,' she tells him, then realises Anahera can probably hear her through the cabin door, and rushes to change the subject. 'We could use some groceries.'

'Alright!' he says. 'That will be the first thing you show me of your beautiful land: the supermarket!' That isn't so funny, but they both laugh and laugh till there's no air left in either of them, and still laughter falls out of her. This is what she was waiting for in the forest, when she couldn't cry. She doubles over and bangs her head on her knees. He stops laughing first, and waits patiently while she continues to splutter.

She pats the cabin door, and whispers through to Anahera that they're off to the supermarket, and won't be long. There's no reply.

Gordon paddles Cynthia across the sea, grinning. His lips keep moving, as if he's silently practising to say something. She wonders if he's going to ask what they were doing on the island, but he doesn't. Instead he looks across at her suddenly, with his eyes clear, and asks, 'This water, do you look at it?'

The ocean is glimmering all around them, and how odd that Cynthia forgot all about it. She shuffles and peers over the edge of the dinghy, into the shifting murk. It must be in so many layers, like a pile of shadows, each with their own push. He nods when she looks back at him. He understands the water; he's an attentive sort of man, and his presence is comforting.

The beach is ugly, a lethargic expanse of grit speckled with bodies. Cynthia doesn't love everybody in the world, and certainly not in the way people at beaches expect to be loved. One of them gets up and strolls, then sits back down in a different place. She and Gordon share a look.

They arrive and the closest bodies are facing away from them: a middle-aged woman in a bikini with a bob haircut and man of the same age sagged onto his towel, asleep beside her. Gordon walks around so he's standing over her, but not too close. 'Hello,' he says.

She squeaks a little with fright – she was reading – but laughs.

'Will you be here for another hour? It is just, will you watch our dinghy?' He nods at it.

The woman looks at him oddly, and Cynthia almost explains:

He's German. But she smiles. 'Sure.'

Gordon shakes her hand and they move along, up the beach.

'I know this one, my girlfriend showed me the way.' His walk is big and confident. Cynthia hasn't been here before. She walks sometimes behind him and sometimes alongside, depending on his speed and the size of the footpath. 'You can take *anything* you like,' he tells her. 'Budget unlimited!' He's loud, but his snortle is cute. Before crossing the road they have to wait for a pair of police cars. 'Oh!' Gordon says. 'The justice system!' She makes sure not to turn to look at his face.

He takes a big family trolley, and Cynthia fills it right up. He drives it fast and zany, darting between people and around corners, and she jogs behind him, biffing things in. It makes her thankful to see his huge body jogging along in front of her, pushing the trolley and grinning, it makes her feel like she'll be alright. She punches him in the arm and he doesn't notice, he just keeps jogging. 'You have to try this! It's New Zealand's best stuff!' she tells him, dropping in a tub of hokey pokey ice cream, then two more.

'But,' he says, 'it will melt.'

'I don't care,' she tells him. 'We'll drink it.'

'You are a fun, adventurous girl!' he says. 'You are just getting *everything*!'

At the checkouts, they see four kids Toby's age smacking each other with Zombie Chews. One's been hit particularly hard, and he tries to make the others stop and look at the red on his leg. 'It's a welt,' he says, while the other three keep hitting each other. He's pulled his pant leg up around his hip, and he keeps saying, 'It's a welt. It's a welt, see,' but from where she's standing Cynthia can't see any discolouration in the private white of his thigh, and the other boys won't stop to look.

Their queue moves, and Gordon's hand grazes her shoulder. Remembering him, and herself, she looks away, and back at the old man grimly swiping groceries.

Gordon wheels the trolley right out of the parking lot, and down the footpath to the beach where he spoke to the woman. They take their bags in trips to the dinghy, and Cynthia walks behind, wondering if she's being too quiet; if she seems guilty. Before they leave he thanks the lady, and gives her a packet of Afghans. Cynthia waits with a foot in the dinghy, and thinks he might be flirting. The lady's beach partner is still asleep.

Anahera's on the big bed, with her foot raised high and a damp cloth over it. She doesn't watch the groceries as they unload them, or listen while they tell her what they bought. Instead she looks at Cynthia's hands, and at Gordon's big feet. Her eyes make it impossible for either of them to move properly in the small space between the bed and kitchen cupboards. Cynthia holds up the ice cream to tell Anahera how Gordon hasn't tried it, and Anahera says, 'Put some new water on this,' shaking her foot with the cloth on it. The foot, when it's revealed, is a blue-black mess with a mound at the front of her ankle, valleyed where the metal clamped down.

Cynthia comes back with the cloth, and Anahera's looking at the ice cream. 'Put it in the low cupboard,' she says. 'It'll be cooler there.'

Cynthia does so quietly, and Gordon moves apologetically to the cabin. He has to pull his shoulders forward and duck his head down to get through the door. Cynthia and Anahera sleep very early, at seven thirty. There's nothing left for either of them to say.

Cynthia wakes in the night, into musky hot air and Anahera's breathing. The blankets feel heavy, so she gets out and lies back down on top of them. Gordon shifts against the wooden walls in the cabin, and she's thinking about the boy. The weights move in the roof, and the water shifts below them. She never noticed Toby's eyes, but she remembers them now, blue, and in her memory peculiarly serious. She wishes, just for tonight, that she could lie alone, somewhere other than their boat.

27

It's afternoon, and Cynthia's talked to Gordon. They're taking him on an island boat tour. They're going to show him a lot of good things. First he gives her a lot of money, happily. He takes it in wads from different pockets on his pants and sections of his bag. It might be two, or eight hundred dollars. Certainly there are a lot of fives and tens. Cynthia takes it inside to Anahera, who makes a near-smile, and props herself up on her elbows to count it.

'The rest is, ah – digital,' he says, and having shed his cash, he gets down to just his underwear and into the sea to wash.

Cynthia sits on the edge of the boat, and looks down at him. 'You must have seen her before then?' she asks, gesturing back towards the bed, with Anahera on it.

'Nope.' He blows a lot of salt water out his mouth, then looks at her properly. 'Oh, who? No, nope – I was only on there for three days! How long do you think a man can survive!' His chest lifts and falls in the water, and she can see his legs green-tinted and kicking like he's running on the spot. They're like a frog's, thrusting out and bent. He's got long hairs on his chest, but not many of them. Cynthia makes sure not to stare. He's looking up, blinking from the sun behind her head. He chuckles at her imagining he'd been on the island for weeks; lived there. 'Also,' he says, still with laughter in his face, 'I would be so frightened at being alone with such a woman – I would shift my tent backwards, in terror, to the island's other side.'

He paddles with his hands and feet, and watches her face. After taking a big breath he says, 'I wandered in the forest all night, with my broken heart for my girlfriend. Then in the morning the light resumed with you two in it. I must now admit, I saw something beautiful, but oh, she was crying.' He shakes the water from his hair, and looks up at Cynthia shyly.

The tour's scheduled to begin tomorrow, when Anahera's better. They all sit at the table and pass around the last of the ice cream, which is a nice sugary slop. The gulls continue shitting and squawking, and Anahera's weights are gentle noise above them. 'These are things I will fix,' Gordon says quietly. He gets up and pours a little pile of peanuts in front of Cynthia, then Anahera, steps back with a flourish, and sits back down with the bag. 'Okay,' Anahera says. Then she turns to him. 'What do you know?'

He's caught, with a peanut only halfway between his lips, still supported by the finger he was using to put it in. It falls. 'Hey?' he says. 'Nothing.'

They're all of them reduced to their spit then; the almost-sound of it held in their mouths. Anahera and Cynthia share a secret look. Gordon's stomach makes a noise. He's clean after washing, and he's joined their pool of scent – he smells like peaches. Anahera separates her lips.

That night he goes to his little bunk again, and Cynthia sees briefly as he leaves the room that he's sad. He hasn't asked where he should sleep, just understood that the cabin's the only place available to him. Anahera's in bed, in the blue satin pyjamas, and Cynthia joins her.

'We can deal with him,' Anahera says. They're in sleepiness together. She touches Cynthia's hair, and throws an arm over her waist.

28

In the morning Gordon makes them porridge at the stove and they stay in bed. 'This boat is love music at night,' he says, sombrely. 'I couldn't sleep, I feel it all night.'

'No,' Anahera says.

'You do not think we are all in a big love?' He looks hurt.

Cynthia shuffles forward and touches his upper arm. 'It's just water, just lapping.'

'It's noise,' he insists. He's standing with a glass of milk and trying not to spill it. He puts it down and stirs the porridge. Cynthia's a bit miffed with Anahera. This is deep; this is a man sharing his feelings about the wide open sea and the silent noise of it. There is his heart and soul, displayed right there in front of them. That idea of music must have meant a lot to him; he must have been planning all night precisely how to phrase it, and Anahera's being very uninspired. Gordon inserts his thumb into his mouth and puckers his lips around it.

'What did it sound like – the music?' Cynthia asks.

He's confused by her English. 'Noise, I said.'

While they eat Gordon stands on their romance novels, and lifts the trap door in the ceiling up and aside. 'I will still those,' he says, gesturing up to where the weights are. Then, on his toes, he puts his head through the gap. Cynthia passes him her cellphone and he twists it back and forwards, trying to see them.

'It's probably very dangerous,' Cynthia murmurs to Anahera.

'One could just roll and knock him out.'

'Well, he doesn't *need* to be up there. I don't know what he thinks he's doing.'

'Ah, yes,' he says, muffled above them. 'I see, they have all rolled against that side, because of the tilt, and they are making the tilt.'

Cynthia looks at Anahera and shrugs, *What tilt?* Anahera grimaces back. It's like they're being accused of something. 'How's he going to get hold of them?' Cynthia asks, quietly.

Anahera answers loudly. 'He's going to catch them with his head, when they roll and hit his skull.'

Cynthia looks at her and she's unwavering. Has the boy's falling changed her? But it doesn't matter, if anything Cynthia loves her more. Gordon lowers himself back onto his heels. 'Pardon? What? Never mind,' he says. He steps carefully from the books to the floor, although they are only four and not high, and leans back against the kitchen cupboards, holding two by their small knobs.

'Cynthia! I know what you will do! You stand here, under the hole and wait for the weights to roll through it, then you catch them!'

Cynthia laughs, she won't do that.

He chuckles too. 'No, no, no. I am just funny. But you are very light, I will hold you up into the roof and you retrieve them.'

Cynthia's still laughing, she won't do that either, when Anahera interrupts. 'Gordon, how much money do you have?'

He shrugs, and laughs now at his own joke even though he didn't before. Anahera rolls her eyes and says she'll go swimming. She asks them to do the dishes. If they do remove the weights from the ceiling, she requests that Gordon put them back exactly as they were before she returns. They both nod, Gordon with his head right down, *Yes, of course they will.* She thanks them and sends them both outside so she can change into her togs. When she's done that she says it's cold, so could Cynthia find her wetsuit? It doesn't seem so cold to Cynthia, but she finds the wetsuit in a cupboard above the kitchen sink.

The foot is enormous, dark purple and blue, edged with green now. Anahera makes Cynthia hold the suit still, with the leg open, while she hoists the foot up and positions it in front of the hole. Gordon turns away to face the window, as he should. Cynthia stands with her legs wide apart for balance, and steadies herself, then nods for Anahera to shove it in. It doesn't go in, it might not have been lined up quite right, and Anahera howls and falls back against the table. 'I do not say it,' Gordon says, still facing away, 'but you should not be swimming.'

'Pah!' Anahera growls, and pulls herself up using the table. Cynthia's ready to get the hole positioned perfectly this time, but Anahera wrenches it from her hands. She shudders and breathes, and the suit stretches in stages as her foot moves through it, like a snake that's swallowed a rat. It's on, and she stands up suddenly, leaning hard on Cynthia's shoulder, then sits again to put her other foot through. Cynthia supports Anahera's balance while she gets it over her bum, then Anahera leans over with both hands on the kitchen bench so Cynthia can do the zip up at the back.

She doesn't say thank you. When it's on she limps to the deck and slips into the water with her bad foot first. Cynthia stands with Gordon to watch her go. She doesn't kick, so she's slow, and her damaged foot seems to drag her left side back, so she's crooked, but she's still got her powerful arms, and her determination. She absolutely remains an inspiration to Cynthia.

'I have been hit by a sudden love for that woman,' Gordon says. They watch several more waves fall in heaps over her body, and then she's out of sight.

29

It's quiet with just Cynthia and Gordon, even though Anahera wasn't talking very much. The weights have stilled, and Gordon's replaced the slat in the ceiling. Behind the window, in the distance, a flock of birds dive-bomb for little fish. They're the ones usually pattering about and shitting on their roof. Cynthia feels a new allegiance with Gordon; they both love a difficult woman. They wash the dishes together, as they were told to, and she asks him, 'What do you have in your bag?'

'Maybe a lot of shoes. I am a lot of men, sorry – man.' He laughs.

Cynthia's all hollowed out with her new knowledge of his love. She can see it's true. But he'll have to leave, he's too large – he's going to be hurt. She only wishes she could talk to him first, *really* talk, about everything.

Anahera returns, changes clothes, tells them she needs more time alone, and leaves again in the dinghy. The Island Boat Tour is postponed till the afternoon. 'Think up an itinerary,' she tells Cynthia before paddling off.

So, Cynthia watches a bit of *Bachelor Pad*. On season three there are three women whose heads and hearts boil with special love for Michael, a lovable goof from previous seasons. It's only a matter of time, and Cynthia observes carefully, looking for early signs of the downfall to come. Gordon boils the kettle so she can drink tea while watching. She sips, thinking – reality TV *is* society; it's about limited resources.

He grins charmingly and interrupts her programme, saying, 'You and I both know a thing in common?'

'What?' She pauses it. His arms are golden and she can tell from his face he's got no idea how bad his English is.

'Do you think it's about Anahera?' he asks her. It's the first time he's said her name. He pronounces it correctly.

'Well I do now!' Cynthia bursts out laughing. He looks at her, and she forces herself to be quiet.

'Oh,' he says, 'I can't say it, I'm very sorry.' He peers down at his knees.

Cynthia's giggling escapes her.

He laughs too. 'I am just funny,' he says. 'How would you know? You wouldn't want to know.'

Cynthia knows exactly. She laughs a bit more, and drinks her tea.

He retrieves some string from his bag and starts piercing holes in their used cans with a knife. Cynthia watches this during the boring bits of her show. Anahera will be annoyed about the knife. On *Bachelor Pad*, Erica's trying to convince Blake that they should spend the night together in the fantasy suite.

Gordon cuts his string into sections, and ties them to the cans. Then takes them around the side of the boat, clanging. Cynthia pauses her show and cranes her neck to see what he's doing. He sits them all upright, carefully, against the window at the front of the boat, then ties each to the washing-line. Two tip and roll away, and she's not sure if he notices. She could go and help him, but relaxes her neck and watches his feet.

When he returns, Cynthia's not sure why but she says, 'She and I made love, once.'

'Gosh,' Gordon says. One of his cans falls down from the line and clanks off the edge of the boat. 'For scaring birds, see. Yeah,' he says.

Cynthia changes the subject, to make it easier for him. 'I've thought of nothing for the itinerary,' she says, then waits for his reply. One of her friends got pregnant, and Cynthia went along to see it upside down in her belly, curled like a little moon. She touched her friend's stomach, and felt it hot with unfurling. Now, her boat's warm with Gordon. She watches, still waiting.

'Ah. Mmm,' he says. It's the beginning of his hatching, his clambering out. He says, 'Hmm,' and another of his cans falls and rolls into the water. He goes to tighten them.

Anahera comes back and says the tour can start whenever, it doesn't matter that they've got no itinerary. They'll just drive around a bit. She and Gordon fiddle with the motor out the back while Cynthia finishes her episode.

They have no petrol.

'That's okay,' Gordon says. 'I am very, very tired. Instead of having a good time today, could some of that money I paid be to sleep in the proper bed?' He gestures at the table, where Cynthia's sitting. Anahera's looking at him carefully.

'How long have you been up north?' she says.

'Less than a week in this area,' he tells her.

She says nothing, then shrugs – he's paid. When he's made the bed and settled in it they make tea and politely leave to drink it on the deck. They sit, and Cynthia waits for Anahera to say something about the boy, but his snoring starts, sudden and loud.

'Can I trust you, with the –' Anahera finally says.

'Yes.' Cynthia interrupts her.

'But later, when we're separate?'

'What do you mean?'

Anahera looks away, off to sea. Her hair's pulled back, tight and smooth, and she touches her lips. Cynthia pulls her own ponytail, and waits for her to turn back. She doesn't, she pulls her good leg up to hug it near her waist, and sips the last of her tea. Cynthia finishes hers, and runs a finger around and around the rim of her cup. Eventually Anahera gets up, and goes inside. Cynthia follows her.

They look down at Gordon's body, splayed out with his mouth open. Cynthia's about to ask what Anahera meant before, when she snickers and says quietly, 'Would you eat him with me?'

'Yeah!' Cynthia giggles. She might, but Anahera's only joking.

'I know how to tie them up – pigs,' Anahera says. 'I used to hunt with my dad.'

'He'd have to taste better than he looks,' Cynthia says, although from some angles she's thought him quite handsome. The cans on the washing-line tinkle. Cynthia listens attentively, and believes she can hear his naïvety in their strange, sad music. Anahera nudges him with her foot. He doesn't wake. Cynthia can see it in the rise and fall of his chest – loneliness. She's seen it in continuous flashes since he arrived; in the way he rubs his own hair and head with his hand, and cradles his hands held together between his legs. He wants to be touched.

30

The sea is a continual yes. They flush their shit into it and it closes its arms around them perfectly. It's like the boy's falling, their disaster, was a question it didn't hear. Cynthia marvels at the ease of the water. Their mess disappears into its holding, and maintains its same motions. A fly lands on Gordon's body, his arm. His sleeping mouth opens. He's been touched like a button.

31

They tire, and wake him. He goes to the cabin so they can sleep, and Cynthia pats his head before he ducks through the door. In bed they hold each other, and Cynthia knows the answer to Anahera's question, from before, about if they're apart – they won't be, can't be, not after what's happened. 'I know what you believe,' she tells Anahera. 'You believe in independence and strength. Well, I believe in those things too, and I believe in them through love.'

Anahera says, 'Is that contradictory?'

'Might be,' Cynthia says. 'That doesn't worry me.' In a few days, Cynthia thinks, when they're lying like this she'll touch Anahera's thigh, and that will be the beginning. Not even a question; an announcement. But it has to wait till Anahera's completely herself again.

The next day nothing seems to happen. Anahera swims twice and Cynthia watches some things online that she's already seen. There's a good bit on *Bachelor Pad*, where they have a pie-eating contest and Tamley spews pie back into her pie and keeps eating it. Gordon borrows Cynthia's nail-clippers and uses them sitting under the washing-line.

Sometime after lunch she's on the toilet, just relaxing. It's the boat's most private area. The water's shifting, and the seat's unsteady under her bum. She touches the doorknob, it's really cute – less than half the size of a normal doorknob. She doesn't have to flush, she's only peed and not much came out. She adjusts and imagines Gordon where she's sitting, with his knees to the side so he can fit in the bathroom with the door shut, and a huge dick hanging down, nearly into the water. She wonders if he has to hold it out, or rest it on top of his legs so it doesn't get wet.

32

Anahera sleeps and Cynthia closes her eyes and doesn't move them. She only listens. It must be eleven o'clock. Gordon moves loudly from his bed in the cabin and the little door squeaks as he opens it. Cynthia thinks again about her boat, warm and soft like a belly, or yes – a womb. She can be kind to him. She doesn't need to worry; those warm organs are engines of expulsion; he won't be with them for long, and so there's no need to be cruel.

When she wakes again, Anahera's gone and he's fishing. She asks if he wants porridge, and he says he's had some, there are leftovers on the stove if she wants them. The pot's still warm. Cynthia eats outside, and stands beside him. Together they watch the water ripple where his line slits into the sea. He's earnest, looking down quietly. It's sad, but he won't catch anything. One thing she remembers her father saying is that no fisherman catches anything in New Zealand anymore. He owned a boat for a while. Gordon mustn't know what's happened.

The weights are silent, but the cans tinkle. Anahera comes out in her swimwear and Cynthia wonders passively if she's annoyed by the noise. 'You and Cynthia get petrol today,' she tells him. 'While I'm on my swim, and we'll take you on your tour this afternoon.'

'Ah,' Gordon says. 'About that – but I would like more sleeping. In the proper bed.'

Cynthia waits.

'Well,' Anahera tells him, 'then that's $500, on top of what you've paid for the tour.'

He shifts on his feet, looking at them like a sulky boy. 'Well. I would perhaps not want to go on the tour.' Then he turns and looks at Anahera, suddenly glaring.

'Our contract is that you would like to go on the tour,' Anahera says.

'There's a hefty fee to change the contract,' Cynthia pipes up. Neither of them looks away from the other, or moves to acknowledge her speaking.

Anahera's mouth sets and her eyes harden. 'Tell us about your girlfriend, then?'

He hardly opens his mouth for the word, but it's loud. 'Blond.'

'Tell us more,' Anahera says.

'Blonder than her.' He gestures at Cynthia's head.

Anahera doesn't look away from him. Cynthia touches her roots.

Then, he changes. 'Oh. I am so sorry. I have been grumpy. I am hurt, hurtful. I am so sorry, tired.'

Anahera's tone doesn't change, but she says, 'We're not trying to pick on you. But we made an agreement, and Cynthia's been very excited – making plans. We'd love to show you our country.'

'You are such a good woman,' Gordon says. 'Your forgiveness is an unctuous balm.'

Anahera pats Cynthia's shoulder. 'What do you say we let him sleep, eh? And we'll get the petrol. I can skip my swim.'

Cynthia nods, and Anahera gets the fuel can.

'There's no way his girlfriend was blonder than you,' Anahera tells Cynthia in the dinghy, then laughs. It isn't funny. It's exhausting for Cynthia, sleeping in the bed when she knows he wants it. Anahera keeps paddling, and says, 'He'll be gone soon. I think.'

Cynthia moves her hand forward, to touch some part of Anahera's body, but Anahera doesn't pause paddling, so she retracts it. Are they both thinking about the boy? Is Cynthia only thinking about him herself to wonder if Anahera's thinking about him?

'I'll just get all his money first,' Anahera says.

Cynthia desperately wants to tell her of his announced love. It's unfair that Anahera never has to acknowledge these things. Instead she asks, 'How much do you think he has?'

Anahera doesn't pause. 'Twelve thousand, or something.'

The rest of their little trip is quiet with Anahera's seriousness and Cynthia's excitement. Twelve thousand dollars! At the fuel dock Cynthia spills a bit of petrol, but none gets on her, and Anahera doesn't see from the dinghy.

When they return Gordon's dressed very formally, in black long trousers and a collared shirt. 'I am very excited to view the beauty in person,' he says, as if he's been waiting since they left, and planning this sentence, rather than sleeping as he was supposed to.

Anahera chuckles from her throat. 'Where should we start, Cynthia?'

'Yeah,' Cynthia says. Then, 'Oh, at the rock? That seems like a natural place.'

'Great.' Anahera unscrews a little cap on the motor and pours in some petrol. Gordon leans back, watching, with the legs of his nice pants well away. He says, 'Okay, ladies! Alright, ladies!' and salutes. It's cute. He wriggles his knees in his trousers, which look freshly ironed. When Anahera's set the motor up she climbs around the side of the boat for the anchor.

'Sorry about this morning,' he says to Cynthia. 'My girlfriend wasn't blonder. I was only lying.'

She pats his knee. 'It's alright. We'll do this trip and set you on your way.' But she remembers: that isn't what they'll do. They want all his money; they'll have to keep him longer. He nods, sadly – so unaware. Anahera returns and smiles benevolently at both of them, then she moves back, past Gordon, and holds a button down on the motor. It makes a sudden, big noise, and Anahera jumps away and bangs her bruised foot on the side of the boat. Cynthia jolts a little.

'Oh,' Gordon says. 'Do you not know how to operate?'

'Do you?' Anahera asks him, kindly.

'Oh no,' he says.

'Maybe pull the string?' Cynthia asks.

Anahera breathes in three times, says, 'I know that,' and pulls the string once, twice more, and they're moving.

'Wholly!' Gordon says.

'But I don't know how to stop,' Anahera tells them. Cynthia shrugs, there's no need to worry yet. It's all exciting, like a party. Anahera stumbles in a forward rush to grab the steering wheel, and Gordon and Cynthia make sparkling eye contact.

He's like a boy, she thinks – adorable. 'To the rocks!' she shouts.

'I thought it was only one?' he asks her.

'We just start with one,' she says, 'and then there are more.'

Gordon nods. His cans clang and fall as they drive, and Cynthia watches Anahera for a reaction but she doesn't even seem to notice. The direction she's picked should be good, they're going away from town, and also from the island.

'Already,' Gordon says, looking at Anahera, 'I see that the view is very much something, and extraordinary.' Cynthia nods. It really is. Anahera's hair is in a plait, and at the end under the ponytail it fluffs out in a tuft. The water's a foamy mess where the motor spits it out behind them and they're going fast towards a mass of huge, jutting rocks. It's rapturous to be finally moving away from those other, bigger boats, and where they go will be entirely theirs. Anahera's hands are confident at the wheel, and she and Cynthia stand together, blinking in the mist of the mussed-up water. 'Inside we go to make sandwiches. Nutella.' Gordon nudges her. It's a good idea. Cynthia touches Anahera's arm and follows him in to do that.

When they're halfway through sandwiching, and Gordon's cheekily eaten one, Anahera calls them out, and she's pointing to some rocks. 'There? You see? We can't get much closer, but we're going to drive alongside them.'

'All of my dreams!' Gordon nods excitedly. They're wet and shining, sharp like jewels. 'It is a beautiful country,' he says, and they both agree. Cynthia's really proud. When the excitement of the rocks subsides, and Anahera turns them off in another direction, Cynthia and Gordon head back in to finish spreading. 'Do you think we'll see a dolphin?' he asks. 'They are one of my great loves.'

After she's spread Nutella on each slice, and Gordon's slapped them all joyously together, they take them out to Anahera. She pulls the string on the motor again, and nothing happens. Gordon and Cynthia watch in silence. She looks the motor over on the side, then the top, then on the other side she finds a red button and pushes it.

It stops. Then, 'No offence to your good time,' Gordon says, 'but I am very sleepy. I might give you $200 to sleep in the bed?'

'Sure, $250,' Anahera says. It seems neither of them feels the need to check with Cynthia that everyone's had sufficient fun for the day. So Anahera goes to the front of the boat, under the washing-line, to read a book, and Cynthia sits down to watch a bit of *The Real Housewives of Auckland* on her phone, at the back, by the motor and the steering wheel. Nothing much is happening on *Real Housewives*, but most weeks nothing happens, and Cynthia enjoys watching it out of patriotic love.

After twenty boring minutes, she pauses on a shot of Angela smiling. Angela's smile always looks the same, all she does is turn her face at different angles. Cynthia peers deep in. It's not plastic surgery, she doesn't think, it's a more profound sort of tautness. The way Angela's features are set makes her think hard. There's something not quite right, some emptiness in everything. She puts her phone down, and gets up to walk around the side of the boat, to where Anahera's reading.

Anahera's lying on her front, with one hand supporting her chin and the other holding her book. She shuffles over to make room for Cynthia, but doesn't look up. Cynthia stands, looking down at the neck of her shirt and some escaped hair touching it.

'You could have told me,' she says. 'I would have understood.'

'What?'

'He's your husband.'

Anahera's mouth drops and her eyes widen, so Cynthia regrets saying anything. 'Cynthia, you saw my husband. At my house.'

Cynthia stands dumb, and shakes her head. 'Oh,' she says.

Anahera winces and pats her shoulder, firmly at first, then more gently. This Gordon character has thrown their relationship back at least a month.

No one remembers or bothers to put the anchor down, and they drift. When Anahera and Cynthia decide to sleep they do so separately, and not till late. Gordon moves peaceably from the bed.

33

There's a jolt in the night. Cynthia wakes and hears Anahera awake beside her. 'I'm sorry,' she says. She feels wonky. 'Sorry,' she says again. Another jolt, so she knows Anahera's awake. 'I shouldn't have asked,' she says.

'Don't worry about it,' Anahera tells her.

'Sorry,' Cynthia says again. She doesn't sleep again till much later, and then she wakes twice more, feeling crooked and squashed, but each time she hardly slips out of sleep before she's back in it. Then, later, in the almost-morning, Anahera's rolled against her. Her face is low, breathing warm wet air on Cynthia's chest, and one of her knees is bent up, pressing Cynthia's thighs.

Cynthia's pushed hard against the wall, and she doesn't move. She tries to release air slowly through her nose, and to keep her ribs still under Anahera's head. Anahera is warm, and very lax now. The silk leg of her pyjamas is scrunched up over her bent knee, so it rests bare against Cynthia's thighs. She's heavy. Cynthia squeezes her hands in fists and keeps them to herself. She's not quite breathing properly, and her bones feel compressed. Still, this weight and warmth is beautiful. Anahera breathes gently, and her feet move.

The air lightens around them, and Cynthia can see the side of one of Anahera's closed eyelids. Her lashes look like they've been drawn by a child, they're so thick and curling. So black. Cynthia looks around, the feeling's odd. Things are not at the angle they were when they went to bed. Everything is above them.

Gordon appears, and clears his throat. He says, 'Yes, we are run aground.' Then he pauses, and peers curiously down at her, lying as she is nearly underneath Anahera's sleeping body. 'Gosh,' he says. 'Are you happy?'

Cynthia doesn't answer, but notices one of her hands has moved, and is moving up and down along Anahera's neck. She stops. 'What?' she says, quietly.

'Yes, we are run aground,' he says again, louder. Anahera shifts and makes a gentle waking noise, rubbing her ear against Cynthia's chest.

He says it again. Cynthia glares at him.

'Well?' He looks back at her, astonished.

'What?' Anahera says, awake now.

'We are run aground,' he says.

Anahera gets up quickly, and stands beside Gordon, looking around. She shifts her feet. She's standing beside a plastic cup, in a small pool of bubbled Sprite. Cynthia sits up too. The boat shifts, and there's a crunching noise from beneath them. It's tilted. It's leaning sideways, so everything's up higher than her and the bed. Anahera's already moving for a sweater.

'We just get out, and we push it back in,' she says.

'Are you sure?' Cynthia asks. But Anahera and Gordon are already moving outside to look around. Through the window above the kitchen she can't see anything, just half-dark sky. A few stars. Their voices are outside, moving around the edge of the boat, behind her head. The window frame shifts a little, and Cynthia thinks their moving is pushing them deeper into the sand. Then, their voices are further away. They must have jumped off, onto the beach. Gordon says, 'Okay.'

She recognises the odd, weird feeling then. Static. The boat is so still. But why don't they sleep, and then shift it? Clearly they're not listening to her. She stands and wipes her eyes, then walks around the edge of the boat to sit and look down at them. They're just standing there for now, gawking this way and that. It's lighter. Cynthia looks up at the vanishing stars and understands – Anahera's afraid that they'll meet people, and have to speak to them. She's frightened of the police, and of their own foreignness to this place. It's a small town, and they'll immediately be registered as strangers, and so suspect. They're caught at the beach where Gordon parked the dinghy before they went to the supermarket. She can see some public bathrooms and a road with no cars on it. 'So you'll just push it, then?' she asks, sitting on the deck.

Anahera's standing with her hands on her hips, and she doesn't answer. Cynthia wants to tell her not to worry. There's no one around, they have hours. What they should do is think.

'Okay,' Anahera says, and she and Gordon both push.

'Alright,' Cynthia tells them, although it still seems like a nonsense idea. They should be calling in a person, a professional.

'Push harder,' Anahera tells Gordon.

He stops, shrugs, and pushes again, but his face doesn't change.

Cynthia pulls her knees up, near her chin, and holds her ankles. She notices her guts, caught inside her arms and between her legs like a huge fruit, whole, in a small jar. It makes her feel sick, all of that new fat. Sick, and hungry.

She bites her knee. If Gordon wasn't there she could tell Anahera how she feels and how sorry she is and Anahera would make her feel better. But no, there he is.

'Push,' he says to Anahera. She doesn't. She's stopped, and she's looking past Cynthia, squinting at the sea. She waves. Cynthia turns, and there's a yellow boat anchored near them, with a guy standing on the deck. He waves back, then disappears around the side of his boat.

'Well,' Gordon says to Cynthia. 'Do you know what this is? It is reality! We are out of your little-cellphone-little-TV, we are really stuck!'

'Excuse me?' Cynthia says. He very clearly knows exactly nothing.

'Well, that stuff's all, what is it? Devised.'

She stares at him, and he shrugs as if he hasn't said a thing at all.

'So?' Cynthia says, and feels her lips puckering.

Anahera's not paying attention, she's still looking at the other boat. Cynthia turns and the guy's paddling over in an inflatable dinghy. Gordon just stands there, looking up at her. She wants to put her fingers in his mouth and wrench the skin off his face. 'Do you think people aren't told what to do in real life?' she asks him.

He shrugs again, and looks behind her. She can hear the guy's paddling. Cynthia officially doesn't like Gordon now; he's not a person she can speak to. She gets up and goes inside for some breakfast. When she's got Nutella on her bread she realises she can't go out and eat it in front of them, not politely without offering them some. So she eats fast, wipes her mouth, and re-emerges to see what's going on.

He's so stupid and dumb. When she arrives back on the deck, under the washing-line, it feels like they're deeper in the sand. 'What did you do?' Gordon asks her. She ignores him. The guy's parked his dinghy, and he's standing with his hands on his hips beside Anahera, who maintains the same position. He's got on an orange singlet, and some little black elasticated shorts. Gordon's leaning on the boat, stretching one of his arms out after all the pushing.

'Gordon, I know you plan everything you say,' Cynthia tells him.

'I mean,' Gordon says, scratching his nose, 'we could just do more pushing.'

'Cynthia, why don't you come down and help?' Anahera asks her.

Cynthia starts. 'I hardly think –'

'I'll tow you.' The guy interrupts her, then touches Anahera's shoulder.

'Well, thank you,' Anahera says, and turns to him.

Cynthia goes inside again, to pull up her shirt and look at her stomach. She grabs what of it fits in her two hands and squeezes tight. It hurts, insisting on being part of her, and she squeezes harder, more hatefully. Her legs are bent up and she shakes them, they wobble under her knees. She pokes her stomach hard, trying to make a specific organ feel it, but it's all of her that's the problem. All of her is flab now. Suddenly, it's like she doesn't have organs at all, she's nothing but this new hurting excess. Only her breasts have stayed the same size. She tries to comfort herself with them but can only think of udders and cows. They used to feel better in her hands, warmer, maybe, and now they're just two flesh-sacs. The boat moves, Anahera and Gordon are clambering back on it. She tucks herself away, and it stills again.

They talk outside, on the deck, then they're talking to the guy again. He's handed them a rope. He must be in a dinghy. He says alright then, and they say alright then back.

A long moment while he paddles, then Cynthia hears his boat, and Gordon shouting something at him. He shouts back, and the boat moves in a shudder. There's a horrible scraping noise, and Cynthia worries about the bottom of her boat. Then, a gentle feeling. The back of the boat is on the water, floating, and the dragging feels softer. Through the window, Cynthia sees that a lady's stopped on the footpath to look at them. She glares back and hunches down. The tide must go out then, because it feels like they're flat again, and even sinking into the wet sand. She goes to stand on the back deck, by the steering wheel. Gordon and Anahera are there, staring forward, along a long, thick blue rope, attaching them to the guy's yellow boat.

The tide's left them. It's on its way back in, but they need to be out and away, in reliable water as quickly as possible. 'Pull,' she shouts at the guy. Anahera looks at her briefly, and Cynthia wonders what face she turns back to him with.

He makes a gesture to say he's waiting for the tide.

'Pull!' she yells again.

He shakes his head, they're waiting. The water's around them again, but not under them, as it was. They've sunk in.

'Pull!' she yells a last time. He does. The rope makes a strained, gratified noise, and she nods. Again, the boat lifts. It's floating. 'Faster!' she yells, she doesn't want another tide to get them. He maintains the same speed, and gives her a nice, placating wave. Cynthia grimaces back, it's important to get along with at least some people. Gordon's got his hands on the steering wheel.

It's okay, they're in the water and they move smoothly.

'Come for a coffee!' Cynthia yells at the guy, and he makes a smile so big she can see it through the distance. With a nice, jolly look about him, he gets in his dinghy and paddles over. Cynthia stands in front of Anahera and Gordon, smiling and encouraging him. He arrives and he's sweet, looking up at her. He's got a round nose.

'Do you want coffee?' she asks him, and he nods.

He ties his dinghy up to the ladder, next to theirs, and she waits while he struggles onto the deck. She can feel Gordon waiting beside her, before he interrupts the quiet and says, 'Thank you for helping us.'

Cynthia was going to say that when she'd sat him down inside. Anyway, it turns out he's boring, so it hardly matters. Still, Anahera gets perky talking to him, and Cynthia nestles in beside her, with a head on her shoulder. Their hair mixes together, into a shared soft mess.

'Sorry,' she whispers.

'It's okay,' Anahera whispers back, then shrugs her off.

'Not for not helping with the boat,' Cynthia murmurs, 'for –'

Anahera interrupts her. 'I know.'

'Northland College boy, me,' the guy's saying.

Anahera laughs. 'I went to Okaihau,' she says. 'We were afraid of you.'

They both chuckle away together, and Gordon looks back and forwards between them, smiling. Cynthia sits and waits for something she can laugh at too.

34

The guy goes, and Anahera goes for a swim. Cynthia gets back in bed but can't sleep. She gets up again and Gordon's fishing. His arms are huge and veiny. He's using ham, which is excessive, considering it's his hobby and an unattractive, unproductive one at that. There's porridge on the stove, but he doesn't mention it. She eats it straight from the pot, cold, and sits watching him. He lumbers, he's ugly and German. Anahera's a woman of dignity – Cynthia can't think how she imagined him to be the husband.

'Holy fucking shit,' he yells. She looks over, and his line's bent. He grunts and bends down, letting it run, then he grunts again and pulls it back. He doesn't seem to think she's watching him. This is his natural state, she thinks, swallowing a spoonful. How revolting. He's leaning back and pressing his crotch forward, against the edge of the boat. He groans now, like he's gargling a throat full of liquid. All his muscles are tensed, right down to his calves, and his bare toes press so hard into the floor the blood runs out and they look yellow. She shifts her porridge around and looks at it. His groan becomes a moan of release, and the fish slaps wet against the side of the boat. It's not humane, she thinks. He holds the line in his hands and pulls it up; the fish, in a twirling panic, gasps and wets everything.

'That is so not okay,' Cynthia says loudly.

'They don't have minds!' he shouts, excited. The fish swings and hits him in the leg. 'Get a towel and wrap it up!'

'We are not using one of my towels for that,' Cynthia informs him.

'Ah,' he says, with the fish still swinging. 'Hold this,' and he tries to give it to her. 'I will use my shirt.'

Cynthia won't take it. The fishing line looks sharp, the way it's digging into his hand. 'I'd prefer not to be involved,' she says.

'Well how can I take off my shirt?' he asks.

'Why would you want to?'

The fish is hanging from its lip, with two more hooks banging against its face. Blood drips from its puncture onto the floor of the boat.

'I will wrap it in my shirt,' he says.

'I'm not helping,' Cynthia tells him. 'I think you should put it back. That is my political opinion.'

He blinks, as if that doesn't make sense. The fish hits his leg again, leaving a red, watery mark on the side of his knee. Its lip breaks, finally, and it lands with a splat on his foot. He kicks it aside, laughing, and removes his shirt. Cynthia gasps, sickened. His chest is fatty and muscular at once, nearly bald, but with a few long hairs. She should leave, her presence is encouraging him in this behaviour, but she can't. The fish's eyes bulge.

'It is only like a plant,' he tells her, bending down to pick it up with his shirt. 'Read the science.' It writhes in his hands, but Gordon holds the fish tight, stands, and pulls it to his chest.

'You can't gut that on here,' she tells him.

'Anahera will gut it,' he says, with his simple confidence. He hugs the fish, and reddish water shows through the shirt.

Cynthia goes to sit in the cabin.

After a while she comes back out. She doesn't say anything to him, just sits watching the nearly dead fish make its last, sudden flaps on the floor. They're all three of them waiting for Anahera.

Gordon sees her first, and he stands and holds the fish for her to see. It's only now that Cynthia notes the size. It's at least forty centimetres. Its eyes still bulge, and its stomach's palpitating. Gordon shifts it up, down and sideways, as if it's tugged by waves. Anahera giggles and swims faster.

Cynthia takes her phone to sit at the front of the boat; she won't be there while they gut it. The washing-line's hard and thin to sit against, and the window's at a weird angle – she can't get comfortable leaning on either of them. She wants to go home.

The smell's as repulsive as she knew it would be. She imagines bones, and more and more of its blood. All their knives are blunt, Anahera's always saying so. How thick is a fish's skin? Or, maybe it doesn't have skin, maybe beneath its scales there's only a thin, papery film, like under the shell of an egg. She remembers Anahera's calm hands, and her long fingers. Where will she put the blade first? It might still be moving now, and it might still be moving when she kills it. She might have already killed it, and still it might be moving. Maybe Cynthia will become a vegetarian. She thinks about Anahera's nails and the webs between her fingers, sticky and wet with blood. If Anahera were to hold Gordon – if she put her fingers at the nape of his neck, or the top of his pants – there's a sheen all over him, and if Anahera were to touch it? Cynthia mustn't think of it.

She peers down through the window. Gordon's on the bed, under the covers, laughing and making jokes. Cynthia can't hear them, but there's a hum of Anahera's laughter under his. Her face isn't visible, but she's cut down the belly-middle of the fish, and

Cynthia can see her fingers inside it. It's pink. Neither of them looks back at her. He's oiled with something, false somehow; evil, even. For a horrible moment Cynthia thinks: Gordon is what they deserve, after the boy. But they weren't anywhere near him, he was too high to hear anything Cynthia yelled.

She stays there all day, even though her phone goes flat at two and she never finds a comfortable way to sit. She doesn't want to lie down. Anahera doesn't join her till four, and when she does she says, 'He's sleeping,' as if Gordon were a baby.

'I hope you charged him,' Cynthia says. 'Two hundred dollars, that's the price.'

'We have to think in larger terms,' Anahera says. Cynthia's ready to march around the side of the boat and tell him what he has coming. But Anahera puts a hand on her leg and says, 'To fund the sort of life you and I want long-term, we need money. Now, I can tell you for a fact that he's got $12,000, minus what he's already paid us.'

'How do you know?' Cynthia asks. The boat rolls over a wave.

'What do you think I've been doing in there?' Anahera gestures through the window. 'I'm doing everything I can to get us what we need.'

'I'll help you seduce him, if that's what's necessary,' Cynthia says sportively.

'I should be able to do it,' Anahera tells her.

That night they eat the fish. It's crumbed and crumbling, buttered, and so, so very good. Cynthia makes sure not to look at Gordon while she chews.

35

She's in a dream of custard, and the bed's empty. She rolls sleepily through the sheets and blankets, then gets caught in one and stops, waking. She remembers lapping the custard up in the dream, and loving it like a dog, but now the thought of lactose has sickened in her. Her feet are too hot. Her stomach's uncomfortable to lie on. Her face is against the pillow, and she's breathing back in the same air she breathed out.

Gordon's saying, 'Wonky, yes. That is it. Certainly it is on a lean, so I am telling you. But don't worry. It is taking on water.'

Then, Anahera's voice. 'What do we do?'

A masculine sigh from Gordon. 'I will tell you. I will lift the floor.'

Cynthia listens to Anahera snort, but then it's a giggle. 'She's awake, I think. We can do it now.'

Cynthia can't remember when they anchored, but the liquid feeling of her dream is underneath them, and the caughtness of waking in her tight sheets too; they're moving, but not really.

'Let her lie in her bed, and I will massage your poor foot,' Gordon says.

Cynthia waits for Anahera to say no, or that she has to go for her swim. But she says, 'Mmm,' and her voice is only slightly doubtful.

'Just give me a try,' he says, 'and we'll see how it goes.'

Anahera doesn't refuse, and there's shuffling, then quiet.

Cynthia thinks about waking up now, but it's too late, they must have started. What could she say?

'You see?' Gordon says. 'It is not so much a big deal, this foot. It is like I said.'

Anahera harrumphs, but almost happily, as if there's been a joke and she's taken a while to get it. Cynthia considers his repeated allegation of tilting. Does he think he's something special, or deserves something special for noticing it? No boat's going to sit perfectly straight. The real loss of balance is his weight, and their retention of him. Why do they need money at all? Cynthia refuses to think for an answer. She glares at the wall and thinks, *Whore.*

Anahera comes in to take a shit, and Gordon follows her. Cynthia lies silently, watching his back hunch to turn the stove on. He's lumpish, and his head looks small, bent down under the mass of him.

She leans over, slowly, and grabs his leg. He jumps.

'I love her, you know,' she tells him. 'But she's disappointing me. Breaking my heart.'

He regains himself and his hunched posture quickly, and shrugs so his shoulders obscure his head completely. 'She is a beautiful, cruel woman. What are we to do?' He chuckles. Then he's got the pot, and he's putting oats in it. He doesn't understand that Cynthia's love for Anahera is serious and adult. She desperately wants to tell him they don't want him, neither of them does, they only want his money. Instead she says, 'Your muscles aren't the hot kind, you know?'

He turns and smiles. When Anahera comes out of the toilet, Cynthia pretends she still has her dark black Gucci glasses, and that she's wearing them. She looks from one wall to the other.

'Tea?' Gordon asks her. 'You seem very stressed?'

'I am, yes,' Cynthia says solemnly, cryptically. He's standing up straighter now, and he's turned to face her.

'It's because the boat's on a lean,' Anahera says. 'I know it's been affecting me subconsciously.' She speaks like she's in a hurry to go somewhere.

'No,' Cynthia says. 'I've just been learning a lot about human nature recently.'

Anahera chews her lip.

Gordon says, 'It's okay, you are only young.'

He gives her some porridge and she eats it slowly. They don't have milk, they're out of maple syrup, and it's dry.

'Can you feel it?' Anahera asks her. 'The lean?'

Cynthia shrugs, and puts another glum spoonful in her mouth. It's hard to swallow, nearly impossible.

He turns and tells her, 'I'm going to take up the floor!' He's finished his porridge. It's easy for him, Cynthia thinks, because his mouth's so huge and spitty. Anahera's scraping the last of hers now too. Neither of them have noticed how much Cynthia hates her breakfast.

Anahera takes Gordon's bowl and washes it, then her own. Cynthia puts hers between her legs on the bed and looks at them.

'Are you alright, Cynthia-girl?' he asks.

'Yes, of course I am,' she says. 'I'm just sad at what I've learned lately, about people.'

Anahera doesn't turn, or even shift her head. When she finishes washing the pot, she says, 'Should we get started with the floor?'

Cynthia stands off to the side so they can switch the bed over. Anahera's quick at it now. Then, she and Gordon get on their knees together, with Cynthia watching, and begin on the floor. There's a layer of water-resistant carpet first, and under that panels of wood. One's painted blue, and they shift it aside to reveal a pool of thick, murky oil-water. Immediately the air is overwhelmed with oil and rot.

'You see, it is gunk!' he shouts, as if he's found something good. Anahera goes to get the flush-bucket from the toilet.

Cynthia makes a long, low, disgusted noise, and Gordon looks at her like he understands. They didn't have to smell it before, and they do now. Why should they not have left it? Anahera fills her bucket up and takes it outside. While she's gone, Cynthia notices again the silence of the weights in the ceiling above them. Gordon gets up and digs through the recycling. She asks him, 'Did you shift her weights, after she told you not to?'

'Oh,' he says. 'Oh yeah, I did.' He finds an old milk bottle and saws the top off with a butter knife, retaining the handle. When Anahera comes back with the bucket he uses the bottle as a scoop to fill it with muck. Cynthia sits down at the table and re-examines her porridge. She's hungry, so hungry now that she'd eat it without noticing the dryness. Now though, there's the air. She'd vomit if she tried to swallow anything.

She stares at Anahera's mouth and she doesn't like it. It keeps almost twitching. Anahera stands slowly, and goes to dump the slosh in the sea. Cynthia considers it: the dark, potent murk running into the water. She wishes she'd planned more to say to Gordon about the weights, but she didn't. Instead she goes and stands outside, watching the colours run and merge. Anahera comes out to rinse off the bucket, and Cynthia leans on the steering wheel. 'He moved your weights.'

'Oh,' Anahera says, unbothered.

'You know,' Cynthia tries again, 'I feel very ill. This is the second day in a row that he's really stuffed up the air quality on our boat.'

Anahera looks confused, so Cynthia says, 'The fish? The fish guts? I literally want to spew right now.'

Anahera shrugs. 'The boat was on a lean. Do you know what that means?'

It doesn't seem to mean much. 'Quite polluting,' Cynthia says, and nods at the water. There are flecks of rainbow on the surface, still being pulled away. Anahera puts an arm around Cynthia's waist, and says, 'What do you want to do today? Gordon's paying us $800 for the next part of the Island Boat Tour.'

'Why don't you go without me, in the dinghy? He'll pay more,' Cynthia says, watching Anahera's face. 'Actually, I need some time alone.'

Anahera purses her lips, concerned, but shrugs. They go, like Cynthia said. Anahera winks as they leave – she was right then; they did get a bit extra.

She spends the rest of the day in bed, lulled by nausea. The air is tight against her and terrible with oil. Her whole body feels invaded by the slick black of it, but her suffering is too deep, and she's too caught in it to move. She rolls onto her face. Then her side, her back, her other side, and onto her face again. She's watched the whole of *Bachelor Pad* twice now, and *Bachelor in Paradise* doesn't look as good. There's no prize money on the sequel show. She's tempted by an article on stuff.co.nz about a new Australian programme, *The Briefcase* (a take-off of an American one with the same name). Poor, suffering people are given money, but – *twist!* – they're then shown footage of other poor suffering people, and asked if they'll share some. Cynthia watches a trailer on YouTube. One family lost everything in a bushfire, and another woman had all her limbs amputated after a serious illness.

It's been hours since they left and Cynthia feels dizzy.

Now, this isn't why she's upset, but why would Gordon choose Anahera? She can't need or shiver like a girl, like Cynthia could, surely? Both he and Anahera are tan and muscular. What could be the purpose of a partnership between two people who both know how to lift things?

She gets up to pee, and checks her face in the mirror. It's been a while since she has. She's spotty and burnt now, with a dull, wild look in her eyes. Her hair's scraggly from being washed in salt, and she's got regrowth nearly two inches long. There's new fat all over her, expanding under her skin.

She thinks about going to sit under the washing-line, but she's worried that if they come back and she's out there they'll think she had a nice day in the sun. They don't return till night. Cynthia can't operate the gas oven, so she eats three packets of chips.

When they do come back Anahera brushes her teeth, then Gordon does his, although he doesn't have a toothbrush. 'So then, what did that guy Jason say?' Anahera asks him, continuing some conversation from earlier.

'Don't know.' Gordon pauses brushing to answer her. 'I stopped listening a bit before then.'

Cynthia hoicks up some plegm. She hoicks and spits five times over the side of the boat, and she hopes they hear it. Then she stands outside the toilet, waiting for him to finish.

36

Fear is only the healthy shock of remembering what's important. Cynthia's going to stage an intervention and sort out Anahera's priorities. She doesn't want porridge, so she asks Gordon to turn on the stove. He beams and does so. Anahera must be swimming. She makes omelettes. They look good, considering what she's got to work with, and she's proud. 'Has Anahera eaten?' She checks with Gordon.

He smiles again. 'No.'

'Have you?' she asks nicely.

'No.' He smiles bigger.

She puts a tea towel over them to save warmth, and gets back in bed to spend a little time on Facebook. She's turned chat off since they left, but she sometimes likes to scroll through the messages people sent her immediately after she did. They all say typical, lovely things: *Where are you? Are you alright? Wherever you are we miss you so much? Why don't you reply. Please, just let me know you're alright*, et cetera. Reading them is dreamy. She's already deleted the one obnoxious one from an auntie, which mentioned her father.

When Anahera comes back Cynthia is in the perfect mood. They set up the table together, and sit down to the omelettes. 'Delicious!' Anahera says, and Cynthia knows she means it because they really are good, and they're running out of food. Gordon nods and sits.

'Anahera,' Cynthia says. 'It would be really nice if you and I could spend some time alone together today.'

'Aha! Girl time!' Gordon taps the table with his fork.

They both nod and laugh at him. 'That's exactly what I've been thinking,' Anahera says.

He yawns, and no one mentions making him pay for the bed.

So they paddle together into the glistening water, and Cynthia's tempted to say nothing at all. When they're away from the boat, and nowhere in particular, she puts a hand gently on Anahera's arm, signalling for her to pause. She does. Anahera is beautiful and kind. It's hard to remember what she ever did that wasn't reasonable.

But she's looking at Cynthia questioningly.

'How's it going with him?' Cynthia asks.

'Good, I think. Just give me a bit and I'll have it.' Anahera rubs her thumb over the handle of her paddle and smiles.

'Excellent, because the police are after us, and he's a liability.'

Anahera shuffles back in her seat. 'Really?'

'Yep. Ron's been texting me. I mean, we'll be alright. But the last thing we need is Gordon coming along if we're questioned.'

Anahera shuffles forward again. 'What's he been saying? Ron.'

'His dad knows the family. They're making investigations.' As she's speaking Cynthia realises that they are, of course they are – a boy's dead.

'What do they know?' Anahera asks.

'Nothing. He was last seen at the dairy, by the school. There's a half coloured-in dick on the bottom of the slide at the playground, which they suspect is his. And an abandoned, nearly empty spray can there.'

Anahera nods, relieved, but Cynthia's tummy wrenches. What if they were seen with Toby? What if the police talked to the boat salesman? They'd know the mooring number then, and the name and colour of *Baby*. She's glad she took the photo from his office. Her face is hot, and suddenly she's crying. Anahera moves forward to hold her.

'It's okay, we'll send Gordon to get the groceries. We'll make him get a dinghy-full. We'll be fine. When we get enough money, and he's gone, we'll leave this place.' But she adds, 'Stop texting Ron.'

Cynthia nods. Maybe she should text him, just to check. 'Okay,' she says. 'And you finish up with Gordon. I don't care if we only get half the money, or three-quarters. This is important.'

Anahera nods seriously. They stay there for a long time. Cynthia puts her head in Anahera's lap, and Anahera runs her fingers through her hair and says, 'I'm sorry we didn't get to talk like this earlier.' Cynthia doesn't mention the weights, or the toothbrush. Anahera's saying the right things, and very kindly, but in a halting way. She keeps looking from Cynthia to the town, and back to the boat.

They paddle back slowly, with Anahera pausing intermittently to touch Cynthia's face and say, 'It's okay. Don't worry at all about it. We can go anywhere in our boat. Anywhere at all.' Cynthia wants to grab her head and hold it still so they look straight at each other up close. She wants Anahera to confirm it wasn't her fault, what happened with the boy. But she can't ask, she's too afraid. Something very good has happened between them, there on the dinghy, and she can't afford to tip it even slightly.

When they get back they leave Gordon sleeping and watch an Adam Sandler movie on Cynthia's phone. During a funny part, when they're both laughing, she puts a hand on Anahera's thigh. Later, when they're laughing again she shifts it up and in, so it's clasped between her legs. Anahera is beautiful muscle and clench, and she continues her laughing a moment after Sandler is off-screen.

37

The next day she scrolls through her contacts several times, and can't trust herself to trust Ron. Anahera's not making visible progress with Gordon, but that doesn't mean it's not happening. She watches him a lot, and feels the need to interrogate him. Where did he come from? What does he know? She understands; with every question asked she tells him something. He sees her looking, but stays friendly. That afternoon he catches another fish and Anahera guts it.

At night in bed Cynthia burns to speak, but she can feel Gordon alive in the cabin.

38

It's morning and he's brushing his teeth again, loudly. Cynthia gets a glass of water, and through the crack of the bathroom door sees his mouth in the mirror. His teeth are clamped hard together, and he's emitting foam through the gaps between them. She can't see his eyes through the gap, just his jaw in the mirror and his big arm moving.

Anahera's swimming. When Cynthia's swallowed her water she opens a jar of olives. 'I see you watching me,' Gordon says, coming back out. 'I see you watching me a lot.'

Cynthia shrugs, he's on her boat.

'It doesn't matter if you like me,' he says. 'I am a social scientist.'

Whatever, Cynthia thinks, and goes to eat her olives under the washing-line. When she's had enough and goes back in for something else, he says, 'She left again, in the dinghy.' Cynthia ignores him. He's deconstructed the bed and made the table.

'Look at this,' he says, waving the boy's cellphone.

'What?' She's horrified. Didn't he take it with him?

'Asses,' Gordon says, '*and*, tits.'

'Why are you going through our things,' Cynthia asks as calmly as possible. 'In what world would that be appropriate?'

Gordon's grinning and flicking through them. 'An amateur, someone is,' he says. 'All on the desktop, I found them. In a folder titled "Homework".' He laughs, hard.

'Anahera will be back soon,' Cynthia says, 'and I know she won't consider it acceptable that you've been snooping through our stuff.'

'Snooping!' Gordon whoops. 'I didn't know it was *your* item. I thought it was a thing of the boat, you know – came with the boat.' He gives her a sly look, and swipes right. 'Oh,' he says. 'Oh gosh, yeah, there is one.' He doesn't show Cynthia what he's looking at. 'Right under my sleeping bed, it was, in the cabin. Only my second night, I found it. It is the same charge-hole as my own phone.'

'You've got to buy us groceries,' Cynthia says. 'Anahera and I have discussed it. You'll fill up the dinghy. So you nearly sink.'

Gordon laughs. 'You're pretty interesting,' he says. 'There are some hugely interesting things here, to be found.'

She shuts herself in the cabin and weeps a bit. She'd like to have her crying done by the time Anahera returns, and to be engaged in an activity. But Anahera comes back sooner than expected, and immediately Gordon starts asking her things, and Cynthia knows he'll be touching things and touching her, so she stays where she is. He's unashamed, like a huge infant. When Cynthia does come back out, they're playing cards. Anahera asks if she wants to join in, but it looks hard, boring and stupid, so she says no. After dinner they play some more. In the cabin, waiting for them to finish, Cynthia looks at Ron's number again. When she's done more than enough waiting, she sticks her head through the door. 'Are you nearly done? It's a shit-hole in here. It stinks.'

Gordon laughs knowingly. It does.

Anahera scrunches up her face, as if confused. It doesn't matter, Cynthia doesn't move. Anahera says, 'If you want we'll pack up after this round, in say, ten minutes?'

'No,' Cynthia says, 'that's too long.'

She sleeps in the cabin.

Later, she wakes and hears them. There's talking she can't make out, then a sound of Gordon flopping over. They're in bed.

'Well, no. But – ' from Anahera.

'They all do the Tinder thing. It's their *normal.*'

There's a noise of shifting bedding, like Anahera's grabbed his head and moved on top of him. He groans, and she says, 'Gordon, you don't know a thing about women.'

He laughs in deep splutters, and Cynthia thinks there are thuds of Anahera pummelling his chest. Then she must stop, because he says in a deep, smooth voice, 'We all need someone, that's all I'm saying.'

Quiet, then, 'Hey,' he says. 'Hey,' and there's shuffling again. They've settled against each other. 'Hey,' he says.

'Yeah,' she tells him.

39

Breakfast is couscous with canned tomatoes. It must be an apology, and it's delicious. They eat together. 'Gordon, you're going to get groceries today, as many as you can. On your own card,' Anahera tells him. He salutes, and keeps eating. He's wearing Cynthia's father's pyjamas. Anahera washes the dishes, and he changes on the deck. When he's ready to leave he folds them and puts them in Anahera hands.

After he goes she tells Cynthia, 'If they haven't come for us, I don't think they will. We just need to get his money and we'll go.'

Cynthia shrugs, happily, but there's a change in Anahera's eyes. 'You must be tired?' she asks. 'He's big, I imagine, to be in bed with. You must be exhausted.'

Anahera sighs, like a mother or a cleaning woman, and gets up to dry the dishes.

'Don't you see? You don't have to dry them at all!' Cynthia says. 'There's a rack, you can just leave them on the rack! They dry themselves, effectively.' But she stops. Discussions on this subject only ever become sad and philosophical.

'This isn't a big boat, Cynthia,' Anahera says.

Cynthia doesn't mention that as the extra person, Gordon should be doing them. She says instead, 'We used to be such dirty girls, Anahera! Before he arrived.' She's embarrassed at the way Anahera's name seems to glug in her mouth, like it did before they knew each other. There's a hard clunk of her tongue over the 'r', and a quick 'a' at the beginning, like in the small, dismal word 'ant'. She knows, Anahera always cleaned. It just didn't seem like much till Gordon arrived. Still, as she must, she continues audaciously, 'We were kidnappers, and we suntanned, and we had better biscuits. He's going to come back with shortbreads, and they're so dry.'

Anahera flinches at *kidnappers*, but only says, 'I don't like Tim Tams, Cynthia, you like Tim Tams.' Then she sighs again, deeper and drier this time, and re-wipes a plate.

'I don't even know what biscuits you like!' Cynthia says, but it comes out more like wailing.

Anahera turns and shrugs in a cooperative way, as if it's not important.

'Tell me something,' Cynthia says quickly. 'While he's gone – who would you rather kiss: Katy Perry or Beyoncé?'

'Beyoncé.' Anahera puts the plate away, finally.

'Me too!' Cynthia's toes are wriggling. 'Do you miss our old days sometimes?'

Anahera pauses. 'Yeah.'

Cynthia beams. 'He's just so boring, and he's got a honky nose.'

Anahera looks at her, as if the word might still be hanging there in the air, in front of her face. She laughs. Cynthia blinks. Anahera likes her and that's the truth. They only need to get back to the island where everything went so wrong, and let destiny set it right. There, Gordon was nothing and they were in each other's orbit.

'We need to go back,' Cynthia says. 'To our island. To stretch our legs, because we can't go into town, and we can't be like this a moment longer.'

Anahera waves at the window, and the distance behind it. 'It's a crime scene. It's disappeared.'

This isn't true. 'Pussy,' Cynthia says quietly.

'What?'

She didn't mean it seriously, but the way Anahera's looking at her makes Cynthia feel like a rude, breast-sucking little boy. She's ashamed. 'Pussy,' she whispers, glaring at Anahera's face.

'We'll never find it again,' Anahera says definitively.

'He used your toothbrush,' Cynthia tells her.

Gordon returns in the dinghy, moving very slowly but paddling hard. He's red-faced, and Anahera gets him a cup of water. The dinghy's absolutely full, with food piled high around his sitting hips. Anahera ties it up, and it floats oddly, dangerously, as if it's on the brink of sinking. She unloads it, bending down towards him while he sits there.

Cynthia stands back and watches Anahera's hands move things from around Gordon's hips, then his waist, and finally his feet. There are ten big water bottles, the same number of instant pasta sachets, a bottle of dishwashing liquid, one of vodka, and a bag of apples. There's a way Anahera grabs the food products that Cynthia doesn't like, and she stops noticing what they are. When Anahera leans down, over the edge of the boat and towards Gordon in the dinghy, her breasts are at his face level. Her hands and arms graze him, and he sits there as solid and dumb as a post, still puffing a little.

Cynthia waits for some instruction, but it doesn't come. Not until Anahera's shifted every last thing onto the boat does Gordon, still with blood in his face, get out to help put it away. Cynthia swivels to watch them, now they're in the kitchen. Gordon's shoulders touch Anahera's, and a couple of times they each reach for the same item and Gordon beams so big that even though Cynthia can only see Anahera's back, she knows he's being smiled at.

Anahera pours three cups of Fanta, and drinks hers while making some mac and cheese with fresh broccoli on the stove. She uses three packets, which seems excessive. Gordon probably got too many. He swallows his Fanta in a glug, and pours himself some milk. 'Smells good,' he tells Anahera. Then to Cynthia, 'I am thinking,' he says, 'during my long paddle. You are a young woman, Cynthia, and I find your ambitions inspiring. Very.' He nods at her. 'To become a news presenter, you said to me. It was your dream.'

She ignores him. Anahera doesn't turn from her pot.

'I am thinking, we should act out our fantasises. Self-love is so nice here!'

There was another thing she told him: that she and Anahera were in a real relationship. It makes her want to drown herself, to slam her head down into the table like it's water. She bites forwards, but it's like apple bobbing, words are too big for her and slip away from her mouth. She can't breathe. She'd like to throw herself away, into the water, and to die. Still, she lies more. 'Yeah, my father thought I should do it. He knew the people. But then I got into a specific postgrad thing, and I felt that was more important.'

Neither Gordon nor Anahera asks a single question. Anahera slops mac and cheese into three plastic bowls and they eat it.

Cynthia's in the bathroom, examining her regrowth in the mirror. Gordon leans on the doorway and says, 'I invented a philosophy, it is: if you are not making your own dream, you are making someone else's. I ask you now, do you believe in your own self-love?'

She lets her hair go and looks instead at his eyes.

'Don't worry,' he says. 'I know your island. You will go back to it.'

She turns on him suddenly. 'How do we know we can trust you?'

'Oh!' Gordon shifts quickly backwards. 'Oh, for what?'

Cynthia pushes past him, to get out.

'I will think about it for you,' he tells her. 'I will think of a reason.'

They have tomato soup for dinner that night, with more broccoli, carrots and leek. Then sausages. After dinner, Anahera and Gordon play cards again. At ten, Cynthia tells them it's time to switch the table for the bed, she wants to sleep. They do, but Anahera doesn't lie down with Cynthia, she goes out to sit under the washing-line with Gordon, talking.

Cynthia creeps out into the deep night. The air and water are one big nothing, and her hands disappear in front of her, into the black. It's very difficult, but she plants her feet firmly onto the narrow walking platform along the side of the boat, one after the other, and holds tight to the support bar like it's a hand reached out to save her. The screws are loose, they must be, because the bar shifts when she does, but Cynthia doesn't worry or even think about drowning. She moves closer, slowly, silently, and hears Anahera say, 'All my problems, he solved them all. But he'd get this look on his face, you know, this smug-generous look. And it would just stay there for hours and hours, after I'd thanked him, thanked him twice and made his dinner, and I'd know he was waiting for me to thank him again.'

Cynthia clings tight. Her hair itches at the edge of her fore-head, but she doesn't move her hands.

'Mmm,' Gordon says. 'I know what you mean.'

It's the boat that shifts. Cynthia's feet slip and she squeals. Neither of them says anything, and both stay silent while she makes her way back around the side of the boat, then to bed.

He's a mindless speaking thing; a tongue, and he's crawled out of the cabin and smeared his spit and noise all over Cynthia's boat, her home and Anahera. A tongue: a big flaccid muscle, out and wriggling too far from its mouth. He's not where he belongs, and because of him there's no place for Cynthia either.

40

The next morning Cynthia's desperate in a sexy way. She licks Anahera's neck, unabashed like a dog, from her collarbone to the lobe of her ear. 'You're nice, really,' she whispers. Anahera grins, still mostly sleeping. 'Yeah, I am.'

Cynthia snuggles her till they're both hungry.

'I am too!' Gordon shouts from outside, where he's fishing, and Cynthia's not at all surprised by his listening. Anahera gets up and makes porridge, then tells them to save her some while she swims. Gordon takes more than he should, and Cynthia has to take less than she wants so there's some left over.

'I've made up my answer,' he says, 'to your important question of yesterday. You can trust me because you can trust Anahera. She is pressed down on me like a thumb. She kissed me so good, hard, last night.'

Cynthia doesn't go cold hearing this, she settles into the cold she already is. She's calm. She knows – and Gordon must have his own inklings – that they're bad women, and dangerous. Some kissing is nothing. Cynthia shrugs.

He sits, still waiting for a response, but she's given one. She finishes her porridge and throws the bowl in the sink. It clangs but it's plastic. Anahera's a whore, but Cynthia's not worried. What she understands is this: their shame, and their pride too, are engines, whirring now. The game's started, and Cynthia will play it.

Anahera clambers back onto the boat and stands dripping in the same place she did when she first confessed her island to Cynthia, announcing their destiny. She looks around, and notices the lack of porridge in the pot, then Gordon's fingers at the elasticated collar of his shirt. She notices Cynthia too – Cynthia can feel her guts and posture under Anahera's eyes. The hard coolness in Anahera's glance makes Cynthia think of the moment just before Toby fell from the tree. There's something she didn't notice then, but she remembers it now all the same; Anahera's face just before he fell, enraptured. He wanted to impress her, and he did.

Anahera's neck stretched right back, her face lifted to him, and a twitch in her lip as if a hook were through it, pulling. Light falling onto her cheeks through the trees, and into her eyes. Her hands held slack in the shadows, forgotten, beside Cynthia. But her heart, and her blood! Anahera's blood must have moved so fast as they stood there together, quickened by seeing him, and Cynthia's sure she has more of it than a usual person. Murderess, Cynthia thinks, and who knows? Anahera might have been thinking the same of her for weeks.

Her love for Anahera is laced with something better than love: destiny, fate. Clearly, Anahera is some things. No matter. All Cynthia wants is to stand beside her again, amid the trees. Cynthia's regrowth is black, and long now. Her hair at the ends is dry from salt. Even her new fat is something; she only needs Anahera to bite it off. They're of the same wilderness; the same badness. She's proud, she won't be hurt. Gordon simply can't be with them.

She won't use her new knowing immediately. She's daring now, but also in new self-control. She smiles sweetly at Anahera, her partner and lover, and ignores Gordon, then holes herself up in the cabin under the light of her phone, with their three squeezy last apples. In that dark little space, with her phone's brightness right down to save power, her mind opens wider. Cynthia's at war – with a man – for a woman. She watches *The Bachelor* for three hours. It's all about how to fight your enemies by lying, kissing, fucking and dressing really well. All she needs to do is remember everything she knew in her old life.

Either Cynthia or Gordon will be humiliated. The water and sky don't care which, and Anahera doesn't necessarily either. It doesn't matter about the truth of anyone's love. You either have the gumption and talent to win a place for what you'll call your love, or you don't and it means nothing – if you can't swim, the water won't hold you.

The *Bachelor* girls fight and cry hard. Vienna wins even though she's got a bad face, particularly when she cries, but Cynthia knows she's tougher. She's a killer, with new tan lines and an oiliness that won't leave the nape of her neck. At midday, Anahera passes some canned soup through the gap in the door. Cynthia takes it, then takes Anahera's fingers and sucks two of them. She pulls them hard with her whole mouth, right into the back of her throat. When they sit down to dinner, she's going to tell Gordon, 'You're an ugly piece of shit and we all know it. Your ex-girlfriend knew it. Your time here is finite.' He'll act hurt and wipe his eyes, but she'll tell him not to bother.

She'll ruin him at dinner, and seduce Anahera at night. How it works is, you tell a person what they are, then you tell other people what they are, and if they become that thing by your telling, you win.

41

It's baked beans, dinner. Gordon comes in and wipes his brow as if fishing was a hard day, and sits opposite them both. He combs his fingers through his hair, then pats where he's growing a beard. 'So, ladies,' he says, leaning forward towards them, onto his elbows, 'I hear the police here are silly and willy-nilly. Arresting everybody all over the place.'

'Oh?' Anahera asks. 'Who've you been talking to?'

'Just at the supermarket, my friends there.'

Anahera laughs, so Cynthia does too.

He waits for them to stop. 'I am thinking now, we should make a practice. For if there is an emergency questioning!' He grins, ear to ear, like an infant who's just been changed and spitefully peed himself.

They say nothing. Anahera leans over and touches his elbow. He leans in and holds her shoulder, then pulls her forward. They kiss, gracelessly, over the table. Anahera shifts her bowl of beans aside so she can rest on her arm. Cynthia takes a bite of her bread, then puts in a spoonful of beans. She won't listen to their spitty tongues, instead she chews, loudly, so they can hear. Sadly, she knows, this will be her chief act of aggression this evening. She adds more bread, swallows half of what's in her mouth, and recommences chewing.

Gordon unlocks his lips from Anahera's. In a new, unaccented voice he says, 'Do you have any awareness of the incident?'

'No,' Anahera says, but there's a flinch in her neck, and Gordon's seen it.

'Where were you at the time of the incident?'

Cynthia begins swallowing to answer, but Anahera interrupts her. 'What incident?'

'Ah,' Gordon says. His accent and smile return. 'Good.' He looks at Cynthia. 'Will it be fine if I steal her away tonight, for a little ride in the dinghy?'

Cynthia looks at Anahera, and there's a slight nod. 'Whatever,' she tells him.

'Thank you,' he says. He stands up and makes a little bow. 'You are generous and mature.' Then he turns to do the dishes.

The paddle moves gently at the ends of Gordon's huge arms. There are no waves, and the boat slips through the water like a tongue into a mouth, silently. They stop. It's dark, they've not gone far. The moon falls on them like a spotlight. He's murmuring to her, Cynthia can't make out what, and Anahera murmurs back. It's his moment, he's alone with her. For all Cynthia knows he could be reciting a poem. She can't see Anahera's face, but she's wearing a singlet, her arms are uncovered. The moonlight, or some reflection from the water, has glazed the skin of her shoulders just slightly blue. One arm is bent back, its elbow pointing, to hold the edge of the dinghy, and the other is lifted to touch the skin behind her ear, where Cynthia knows it's soft.

Cynthia goes inside, into the cabin. There, she unzips his bag. First there's a pile of clothes, she shoves those aside quickly. Underneath them is a copy of *A Good Keen Man* by Barry Crump. Three cans of beans, and two of spaghetti. The gin trap, some keys, and a cellphone (charged). There's a fluffy teddy bear, wrapped up in plastic similar to cellophane. It's peachy brown, with a shiny red heart sewn on its belly. There are words stitched in silver on the heart, *Forever and ever*. Lower, there's a GPS (also charged) and a handful of pens bound together by at least three rubber-bands. An A4 exercise book, with the first third of its pages torn out. Under that is a box of chocolates. They're heart-shaped, in a red, transparent-topped box. Cynthia looks at them closely; some are dark and some white, and they've all got little smiley faces drawn on their tops in chocolate of their opposite shade. Some of the faces wink. Under those are chargers for the phone and GPS. She checks the phone, but it's locked. She puts everything back in the right order. When they first met he told her his bag was full of shoes.

42

The next morning they're drinking beer outside. Anahera swallows the last of hers and stands up. They watch her. Gordon tips the rim of his bottle against his lips, slowly. Anahera's already wearing her swimming shorts, but she turns to face the wall and removes her shirt and bra. Her breasts swing out briefly, but she puts on her bra-integrated swimming singlet easily and turns back around. This is how she changed before he came, as if her body were nothing, no secret at all.

The air around her is plump with every feeling Cynthia has. But inside that air, Anahera's the same woman she's always been: fit and moving, unblemished. She doesn't look any different for the salt air, or their separation from the supermarket. There's nothing to take from her. She's her own system of temperature and weather; abandoning Cynthia all the time, without any change of movement or breathing.

Gordon doesn't look away. He sits, dumb as a dog, while she looks back down at them. But why should he? How can he feel so safe? His brain's as slack as his mouth. If Anahera bent down and touched his thigh, Cynthia knows, if she grabbed it, he'd maintain precisely the same expression. His brain is a drainage system, moving fluid continually through the same place. He doesn't know where he is. Cynthia watches him watch Anahera straighten the underwire of her singlet, which is still wet from her swim yesterday.

He'd want her if she were anything. But Anahera is something;

Cynthia can't sit there like he does. She looks at the kettle, then the ceiling, and down again at their little wobbly table. The whole room of their home is small. He sits in it with them as if everything is nothing and they're only animals.

Anahera sits back down. She isn't smiling, but Cynthia thinks she would if she let herself. She's holding it, like she holds her muscles while she exercises. She stands again and grins in a way that isn't a smile, acknowledging there was no reason to sit, then walks to the back of the boat and dives off.

Anahera swims powerfully away. Cynthia gets up from the table and stands in the kitchen area. She's thinking what she might eat. She can't think what to eat. She notices with horror the way Gordon's muscles pull his shirt taut around his shoulders. His jaw is hard. It's because of his body, and the way of his body. Anahera's body is perceiving the threat of his, and it's lubricating itself *down there*. She's mistaking that for real attraction. Even his nose has menace about it.

He sees her watching him. 'I am not what you think I am,' he says. 'I am not a tourist.' Cynthia says nothing and stands to look out the little window above the sink. His lips make a wet, vibrating, in-suck noise. 'I am everywhere I go on business,' he says. 'I am a sociologist.' Cynthia fills a glass of water, drinks some, and tips the rest down the drain. 'What does that mean?' he sighs, then answers, 'It means my job is to watch people. To find a place and sit down with my eyes –' He thinks for the word. 'Skinned? No, peeled. With my eyes peeled and fresh like a potato. Just my sitting here will change you. Is changing you. That is the power of me and how good I am with my eyes. I am like a potato, peeled by you. Bits of me are removed by your moving, as I come to new understandings. But you, too, you will lose your skins just as I look at you. Do not appear alarmed! This is not flirtatious. But sociology will leak in here, through me, through my eyes opened into an opening. We will all be washed clean, understand? And see the water in our filth. Won't that be healthy, Cynthia? When we, all three, are bare to each other.'

Cynthia hardly waits for him to finish. She says, 'You're not what you think you are. You're a moron, actually.' Then, without changing, or even letting him see her remove her socks, she goes outside to wash in the sea.

When she clambers back up the ladder, he's standing above her. 'I will give you the forecast,' he says. 'I am going to ask her the right question soon. It is not much I wait for.'

Cynthia pushes past him for a towel. It's her responsibility now, she understands, to save Anahera from unimaginable shame. She goes on Facebook, and Gordon fiddles with his fishing equipment. Together, they're waiting for Anahera. 'She doesn't owe anyone a thing,' he whispers loudly, out of nowhere.

A gull shits on the window. Cynthia understands, as suddenly as a slap, that *waiting* isn't enough. She crawls into the cabin and dresses herself, starting with a push-up bra and an invigorating thong. Then she pinkens and wets her lips, and puts on a short, frilly dress. Her dulled cellphone screen acts as a mirror, and she gets everything exactly right. After considering pigtails she settles on a high ponytail. Her eyes are lined.

Sexy isn't when you want sex, but when you offer it; sexy is what oozes from you when there's none of you left. She lies back in the dark, and she knows. She's going to stuff his rude, under-educated tongue back in his mouth and watch him choke on it. She'll seal the cranny in Anahera's mind before it cracks, before he can press anything through.

She looks at herself more – she knows what she can trust. Yes,

Cynthia has gained weight and got hairy, but she and Anahera are the same sort of woman, and those aren't the things they care about. By her own standards, and certainly by Anahera's, Cynthia's still a definite nine. When she's lounged and loved herself adequately, she emerges, tripping a bit on the second anchor, but righting herself.

She's surprised – she was paying deep attention in there – to find Gordon at the table, eating a four-layer club sandwich, oozing jam. 'Ah!' he says, with his mouth very full. 'You have made, what is it? An effort?'

She ignores him and sits down. 'Knowing what I do, I advise you to leave.'

Gordon laughs. 'What do you know.'

She says nothing, only stares back.

'Oh, never mind!' he says. 'Wow, you are so little. How could you become bigger? Make a huge deep breath of your lungs, I tell you! Breathe in power! You must! Are you breathing at all?'

'Turn this on,' she tells him, standing and gesturing to the stove, which she still can't operate herself.

'Sorry, you are a weakling,' he says as he passes her, like he's hurt her feelings. Still, he lights the thing and turns the knob. Cynthia's not afraid, she looks right up at the back of his head.

Anahera's going to be hungry when she comes back, so Cynthia makes porridge and slops it into two bowls. He clearly wants some, but says nothing. She makes custard in another pot with milk powder from the cupboard. She also finds a can of lychees, and puts them aside with a can opener. She'll open them for Anahera later, if that's the way they feel. She slops the custard on the porridge, and goes to wait with it on the deck.

43

Anahera's minutes away, swimming slowly. Cynthia's been waiting a while, and her hip hurts from leaning over the edge. Anahera flicks her head to keep some loose hair from her eyes, and a moment later, flicks again. She flicks twice more before Cynthia decides she's close enough, and tells her, 'I need to be alone with you.'

Gordon's doing something inside. It doesn't matter what – he'll be listening. Anahera tilts her head to show she hasn't heard, and Cynthia leans over further to repeat it, not louder, but with more obvious movements of her mouth. After a moment, Anahera nods. It's perfect; it's all going perfectly.

When Anahera arrives, finally, she's flushed and panting. 'I didn't know how far I went,' she says.

Cynthia laughs knowingly. 'I made you breakfast, I thought we could eat alone together in the dinghy. I'll paddle.'

'Sure, sweetie.' She looks into the bowls and raises her eyebrows. 'Looks good.'

Transferring everything from the boat to the dinghy was difficult, but it's done now. Cynthia beams, sitting close. She hasn't bothered to paddle them anywhere. He can hear them; she doesn't care. 'I got these things too,' she says, nodding to the lychees and forgetting what they are.

'You sure did,' Anahera says.

It's hard, opening them in the dinghy – there's a balance problem for one thing – but Anahera doesn't watch and Cynthia gets it.

Then, she realises – she didn't think of spoons! She says nothing of it, and hands Anahera her bowl. Anahera has an odd, curious look on her face, but she holds it out, waiting. Delicately and stickily with her fingers, Cynthia slops some lychees into Anahera's bowl, then her own. She ends up with more than she wanted – she's not really sure what lychees are – but doesn't worry.

Anahera's waiting for a spoon.

'Um,' Cynthia says. 'Yeah.' She nods at Anahera's bowl, and her fingers holding it.

'We could ask Gordon. We're not far – ' Anahera starts. They haven't drifted much, they're only a few metres away. Cynthia shakes her head, No. Then she picks up a lychee with her fingers, squeezing it confidently. The bowl's resting between her legs, nearly at her crotch. Anahera laughs and shakes her head a little, flicking some water from her hair. She lifts a smear of custard to her mouth and says, 'Good, with only milk powder.'

Cynthia nods, relieved. She's got a whole lychee in her mouth, and it's a lot, but she's deciding she likes the taste. She bites and it's hollow in the middle. When she's swallowed she lifts the bowl to her mouth and slurps some custard-porridge. Anahera laughs so she does it again, louder and slurpier.

Anahera doesn't laugh the second time, but her smile stays. 'What is it you want to say then, Cynthia?'

Cynthia pauses a moment, then leans her head on Anahera's shoulder, not heavily, but enough to be felt. Anahera slurps some porridge herself, and it's a loud noise in her mouth, right near Cynthia's ears. 'I've been thinking about me and you. I mean: men, what did they ever do for us, huh?' Cynthia murmurs.

'Hey? I didn't get a word of that,' Anahera says.

'What did men ever do for us?' Cynthia says.

Anahera laughs, slurping again. 'Your dad's – '

'No,' Cynthia says. 'I mean really *do*. We find this whole place' – she gestures around them, not at the other boats, but at the sea, sky and hills – 'then he comes. They're just lumps, I think. Men.' Anahera's hand pats her head, so she says, 'That's just my opinion.'

'I'll speak to him,' Anahera says.

'It's important to me.' Cynthia puts her bowl aside and nestles in closer. 'All the male race ever does is walk into beautiful scenery and ruin it.'

'Did you have a boyfriend, when I took you?' Anahera asks.

'No, because I knew I was waiting for something.' Cynthia takes Anahera's hand, which is now resting on the seat beside her, and moves it to her waist. Something momentous.'

'Something momentous,' Anahera repeats. Her face is still, and her hand motionless above Cynthia's hip.

'It's just, I always felt I knew you. From the very beginning at the gym.'

'You're alright, Cynthia.'

'But you noticed me, you saw me in a special way.' Cynthia's voice breaks and she shifts. The hand at her waist feels dead like a fish.

'We had several extremely good moments, and you're definitely attractive, but Cynthia, that's not enough – not, you know, when there are all these other things.' Anahera's voice is steady, low, and she shifts her hand up and down along Cynthia's side in time with her speaking.

'What other things! What other things can matter?' Cynthia's sobbing now, in quick little heaves.

Anahera doesn't answer. Clearly, she thinks the things are too obvious: Gordon, Toby, the dishes, their respective levels of maturity, and money – of course, money. Instead she says, 'I'll never in my life forget the way you looked in my classes when you were proud. When you'd achieved something, even something small, and you beamed. You were an extremely satisfying student' – she pauses – 'I'd say my most satisfying, Cynthia, even though you never lost any weight, or gained even a bit of muscle.'

Cynthia giggles, looking up at her. Her cheeks are wet, but the sun's hot, warming them. Their faces are close, she only needs to move forward a little. They touch lips gently. Forget Gordon.

Anahera maintains her hold on Cynthia's head when they pull their faces apart. 'There are things,' she says. 'You know there are.'

'They're nothing,' Cynthia tells her.

'It's been something for a while,' Anahera says.

'He's nothing.' Cynthia leans in again, and puts her lips around Anahera's bottom one, holding it. She shifts Anahera's hand inside her shirt, and bites her tongue.

'Will you take care of me?' she asks.

'I am,' Anahera says, indignant. 'I'm trying to.'

Cynthia puts her hand at the nape of Anahera's neck, and pulls it forward. This may not be going so badly after all. This time she bites a little harder, still only inquisitively, and Anahera's hand tightens on her waist.

Now's the time – Cynthia grabs Anahera's hair and pulls it back, hard and suddenly. Anahera begins to say something, but Cynthia says, 'No.' Anahera starts again, but Cynthia tells her, 'Listen up. I know he's a fake – he's got no feelings.'

Wind comes past them in a rush, then they're sitting in simple, hot sun again. Anahera says, 'He knows.' The boy falling. The dinghy lifts and lowers on a wave. Anahera won't look at her eyes.

'I'm not saying you can't have your pet,' Cynthia says. 'I'm saying, train him.'

Anahera maintains the same face; Gordon knows.

'What do you think I'm afraid of?' Cynthia asks. 'Him? The police? I'd rather be arrested ten thousand times than let him own you.' Anahera starts to speak again, about what he knows, but Cynthia stops her. 'He's a dog, and I respect you.'

'Cynthia, you're not being reasonable.'

The boy falling, and all the trees. The wind's gone. The water holds still for a moment. 'He watched us, do you know that? He watched you grieving, and he watched us sleep together in that tent.' Cynthia understands now. 'He waited.'

Anahera holds her breath patiently.

'He set the trap.' For days Cynthia's been having visions of Gordon tied up like a dog, eating all different colours of boiled gruel. They make sense now.

Anahera doesn't look so astonished, she already knew.

Cynthia makes sure to proceed calmly. 'Okay,' she says. 'He needs to give us all his money. Then we give him an allowance for shopping and if we can't afford the good corned beef, he steals it.' He'll be their criminal slave, that's the only way they can survive him.

Anahera nods to show she's heard.

'He's an evil degenerate,' Cynthia says.

'I don't know abou –' Anahera starts to say, but Cynthia stares at her hard and won't stop.

'Okay,' Anahera says, looking down into the water. 'I'll talk to him.'

Cynthia nods. It's not enough, but it's a start. She wants to kiss again now. Anahera feels Cynthia leaning and turns back from the water to reciprocate. Her tongue is almost utterly still, but Cynthia bites and sucks. Then, she slides down in Anahera's arms, and lands softly in the cushion of her lap. There she watches the water move, and feels it under them. She looks up sometimes, at Anahera squinting, as if to interpret some code in the waves. 'I mean it, what I said about prison,' Cynthia says. 'I mean it even more now.'

Anahera doesn't reply directly, but she does say, 'Tell me about your dad.'

'Eh.' Cynthia makes a deliberate noise. 'He bought me a lot of Barbie things.'

'Mmm,' Anahera says. Right in front of Cynthia's eyes are two bare knees, brown, one with a freckle-thing. She feels just as she imagines Snot-head must have, and closes her eyes, rubbing her head gently against the bottom edge of Anahera's shorts. Neither of them say anything else, but it doesn't matter. It could be an hour, two, or only fifteen minutes before Anahera says, 'Well, we'd better get back, I suppose.'

44

Cynthia did gymnastics for a while as an adolescent and it's definitely her best sport. While Anahera makes lunch, she invents an entirely new series of positions using the washing-line for support. The gymnastic feeling comes right back to her, and a blue pair of Anahera's underpants brushes against her shoulder. She hopes Anahera's watching. After ten lunges and ten squats, she lies down. It's a hot day. She rests and watches the shifting patch of water where, less than an hour ago, everything changed.

Canned tuna and tomatoes on rice. Cynthia muses quietly while she eats, and Anahera doesn't say a thing to Gordon. When they're nearly finished, Cynthia asks them, 'How are we all?'

'Exhausted,' Anahera says.

Cynthia nods, and looks at Gordon.

'Whatever, white girl.'

After lunch the dishes sit by the sink. Eventually Anahera and Gordon go do stuff, and Cynthia makes the bed from the table and lies down on it. She relaxes her eyelids, and her eyes under them, then her toes. The two of them come back in, occasionally, and move around her. She twitches her knees, and her glutes too. Anahera's going to speak to Gordon; she's probably speaking to him right now, telling him what Cynthia says is what.

Anahera taps Cynthia's forehead with two slim fingers, and Cynthia opens her eyes happily.

'What is it you think you do, Cynthia?' Anahera asks, peering down.

She looks up, dazed.

'You can actually be a very difficult person to get along with.'

'What did I do?' she asks, astonished.

'Firstly, I've washed the dishes once today. Gordon's been fishing since this morning, and the least you could do – '

'Is wash the dishes?'

'And flush the toilet,' Anahera says.

'What? I always flush the toilet. When have I ever not flushed the toilet?'

'But properly, Cynthia. So the bowl's full of entirely new water. You have to fill the bucket up, then tip the whole lot down. I don't think you've ever done the pump more than twice.'

She hardly opens her mouth, and Anahera says, 'Don't try to blame Gordon.'

Cynthia's shocked. This has never been a problem before. She turns over and pushes her face into the pillow. The boat shakes gently as Anahera walks away.

What's wrong with this picture – the answer is oafish and obvious – Cynthia, Anahera and Gordon? The weight distribution is terrible. Someone sits alone and two people share a seat. It won't float.

Cynthia doesn't open her eyes for practically the whole afternoon. There's nothing she wants to see. You can't move the seats around, they're fixed on the boat.

She shifts onto her back and presses her palms against her eyeballs till the blackness hurts. After a while of this, Anahera's fingers tap her again, this time on the shoulder. Cynthia doesn't move. More tapping. 'What?' she groans.

'Look, I am sorry.'

'Doesn't matter, what's said is said.' But Cynthia removes one hand from over her eyes. Anahera laughs a bit, and Cynthia covers it again. She's ashamed of the voice she uses, it's moany, but still she speaks. 'You think I'm just silly and white and too much mess.' Anahera will say, *No, of course not*, but Cynthia's prepared to listen through to the truth.

'Well,' Anahera says, as if the whole thing is a joke.

'But – you know – you don't know anything about me.'

'What don't I know?' Anahera says, like she's being really patient. It's confirmed; the worst. Cynthia removes her hand, briefly, and sees Anahera's kind face looking down. She slaps her eye covered again. Anahera sees her only as what she is, as if that's all she is.

'I'm really complicated,' Cynthia mumbles, almost gurgling.

'What?'

'I said,' she says clearly, and louder, 'that I'm really complicated.'

'Yeah, well. Of course you are,' Anahera tells her.

Cynthia's not going to speak for the rest of the day. Enough's been said, more than. She clamps her lips together and closes her eyes. Anahera rubs her shoulders a bit, then goes away.

Gordon's captivated her. There must be something in the way his muscles tense when he hauls fish in from the sea; he must have a proud, boyish smile when he turns to her, with them still flapping on the end of his line. His lips peel back in Cynthia's mind now, and the teeth behind them are big and white.

That night she and Anahera share the bed, but it means nothing. Cynthia's body is weighty with new fat, and it pushes her down.

45

She wakes at her usual time; something like eight. She's in bed alone, which is typical, and the sun shines on the boat, coming strong through the windows like always. But, there's no noise at all. Gordon's gone too. She fills a cup with Coco Pops and eats them un-milked. They make a good noise between her teeth. She fills it twice more. When she's done she doesn't wash it, but bangs it on the floor twice so the leftovers fall out, and puts it back in the cupboard. She feels weird and jumpy, and gets up to pee. The boat doesn't move, even when she does.

She watches a video on her phone. It's of a woman in front of a blackboard in a pencil skirt. She writes 'Penny Lee, substitute teacher' on the board, and giggles. Beside the blackboard there's a poster with an apple on it. After Penny Lee flicks her hair – which is a very good part – Cynthia skips forward.

'It's your what?' Penny Lee's mouth drops. 'Your big cock?' She puts a lot of emphasis on some words and looks offended, but also aroused. In the moment before this, Cynthia remembers, Penny's just asked why all the girls want to sleep with the student, who's in detention for sleeping with all the girls.

Penny Lee touches her top, then flicks her hair again. There's no one else in detention. They're away. She's on the boat alone. She doesn't know where they are or what they're doing, but she knows exactly what Penny's about to say. She never leaves the guy time to reply, or even for Cynthia to think what he'd say if he did.

It's big, anyway.

Penny strips unhurriedly, while keeping Cynthia abreast with the situation. The guy's wanking his big cock, and Penny admits it's only fair that she should get completely naked. She's got a British accent, she says com*plete*ly naked. Then there's a good bit where she shows her bum, and Cynthia pauses it there.

She looks at it for a long time, and slowly it begins not to look like a bum at all. It becomes two lumps of flesh, and then a mass of beige like an old pudding. Cynthia looks out the window at the water – still barely moving – then back at Penny's bottom, and she cries a bit. She gets up for more Coco Pops, but sits again. She's crying a lot. Penny's bum's blurry through her tears, and liquidy. The water outside stays silent and static, ignoring the small heaves of Cynthia's body.

She gets the whole bag, even though they're stale and dry. Then, back in bed, she pours them in her hand carefully. It's full of them, but – they'll never fill her up; they're hollow, milkless. She shoves the fist of them against her mouth, but it can't open wide enough to receive them all. About a third are crushed against her face, and fall down her shirt, onto her legs and the bed. She fills another hand with them, then swallows what she's got in her mouth. After putting the second load against her face and in her mouth, she shakes her top out, so the crumbs fall onto her belly and stick there.

What are they doing? Talking about? Cynthia doesn't know anything at all. When Anahera goes to the toilet, or swimming, or even just looks at Cynthia, Cynthia forgets that their love isn't a mutual love. When Anahera does anything at all Cynthia forgets. It's only Gordon that reminds her, and with each remembering she finds herself newly abandoned, floating alone on the vast loneliness of the sea. It swells and settles, and once it's settled she forgets again that it's right there beneath her.

Cynthia hears the splashing and laughter of their return, brushes most of the Coco Pops from her face, and settles in sombrely to wait for them. Anahera takes a hand off his arm before coming through the door, but Cynthia saw it. They stand together above her, dewy, salty and fresh with the calm morning.

'Have you eaten?' Anahera asks.

'No.'

Anahera begins making porridge.

'Do you think you might get up? I will make this table,' Gordon says, scratching his head. He sits at the foot of the bed, and Cynthia pulls her legs quickly up and away from him. 'Okay,' he says, and shuffles away too.

'What does she see in you, do you think?' she asks him, quite loudly.

He recommences scratching, now at his ear, and looks at the wall. Anahera turns and says, 'I thought we might all have breakfast, Cynthia. At the table. Gordon has something he'd like to tell you.'

'Oh?' Cynthia says, wriggling her feet so they take up more space, and glaring at him. 'Yes?'

'Cynthia, get out of the bed. Gordon's going to make the table. We're having a meal,' Anahera says, scooping porridge into three bowls.

Cynthia giggles and says in a husky, kinky voice, 'Yes Ma'am,' but really she's annoyed. She stands back and watches Coco Pops fall everywhere while Gordon pulls the bedding off.

They all sit down, with a bowl of porridge each. Behind the

window the yellow boat that pulled them off the beach only three days ago sits gently on lilting water. Cynthia moves her finger towards the glass. Anahera and Gordon eat, and watch her. When she hits it, he says, 'Oh, sorry.'

'What?' she doesn't turn, but pushes harder. The finger bends at the first joint, and goes white at the tip. Further down it's red. *Interesting*, she thinks, but it isn't.

'Oh, nothing anyway,' he says.

She shrugs, removes her finger, and slams it forward again as suddenly and hard as she can.

'Yes,' Anahera says, putting her spoon down. 'Something.'

Cynthia's listening now, but she doesn't shift or lessen the pressure of her finger on the glass.

'Ah,' Gordon says. 'Yes, it is that. I am to tell you. My game I have been playing is irresponsible. Ah, cruel. I am to stop immediately.'

Cynthia sucks her finger, it hurts now. She doesn't look at him, but at Anahera, who looks back and fills her mouth with more porridge. Gordon makes a noise as if to say more, but Anahera turns – suddenly – and says, 'Nothing else. That's it.'

'Should he apologise?' Cynthia asks.

Anahera nods, and says, 'He will apologise.'

Gordon is red. Little veins are visible in his cheeks. 'I will apologise,' he says.

They both look at him, with eyebrows raised, waiting.

'I will say –' he begins.

'No,' Cynthia says. 'Say it.'

'I am sorry.' He looks down into his porridge, and scrunches his face up as if very confused.

'Good,' Anahera tells them both, looking from one to the other.

46

Right after dinner, Gordon tugs Anahera outside by the arm, to watch the sunset. Cynthia makes the bed and gets in. She stretches her four limbs out tight so they hurt. There'll be no space for him. They stay out there for minutes, and Cynthia's thigh cramps. When Anahera does finally come back in she appears shocked at seeing Cynthia so aggressively star-fished.

'Oh!' Cynthia says. 'There's room for you.'

She shuffles over quickly, but Anahera says, 'It's only eight?'

'That's fine,' Cynthia says, shifting her arm and leg back, lest he attempt to slip in.

He strolls back in and stands beside Anahera, looking down and yawning, 'Gosh,' he says. 'Do you want to play cards?' he asks Anahera.

She looks again at the bed, there's no table.

'Oh,' he says. 'Want to go for a paddle about?'

Anahera nods, goes out, and he follows her. Cynthia lies, waiting. If she goes to pee, even with him in the dinghy, even as quickly as she can, he'll attempt to claim it. He knows how much it means now. She lies there for at least an hour, then sleeps.

Her hand touches a leg, rough and hairy: his. It moves.

'Gordon!' she hisses.

'Yes. Oh, yes – she said, she will take a turn in the cabin.'

'Excuse me?'

He repeats himself.

She logs in to Facebook. There's no chance of sleep now.

'Are you scrolling through a wall?' he asks, immediately.

She's turned away from him, blocking the screen with her body. He'll only see the light. She moves down the page silently, and thinks she can feel his eyes blinking behind her back in their slow, dumb way. 'You all just post pictures of things,' he says. His lips are as wet as a baby's, she can hear it in his voice when they separate. 'Things you think are pretty.' His mouth is a pond of spit.

Cynthia raises her eyebrows in the dark, and likes someone's link to an article about sugar taxes. If she leaned over with a knife right now, and stabbed his throat, would he gurgle? She scrolls. He would.

'Are you afraid of drowning?' he asks. 'Or have you already drowned in your social media device?' The blankets shift down low, near his muscled toes. He's wriggling them.

She could conk him on the head with something. 'How would I drown in my phone, Gordon?'

Anahera shouts at them from the cabin. 'Little bit quieter, guys.'

'Righto!' he yells back. Then he whispers to Cynthia, 'Ah, I mean, metaphorically. In the *feed*. Are you hungry, Cynthia, or are you *fed?*'

She hears his age. When they first met and he seemed wild, he seemed young too. As young as Anahera. That was a long time ago now. He's acquired a decade from nowhere, and he's weak.

He very diligently ignores her lack of response. 'You don't believe in reality,' he whispers. 'You believe in *reality TV*.'

He's naïve. Cynthia remembers when he dressed in a suit for

their Boat Island tour; he combed his hair. She likes a picture of a three-legged dog.

'If I threw you over' – his whisper is even quieter now – 'would you be afraid you might drown? No? Because you can swim?'

'I can swim,' Cynthia turns and hisses back at him. 'It's just fucking boring.' Her face is much too near to his. She can feel him breathing.

He clears his throat; a deep, reverberating noise, like a rock falling in a cave. 'Because you think Anahera, that nice strong girl, would save you? You think you know she'd save you?' She can feel him grinning now. His lips are stretched. 'Think of Anahera – she is a lion. She would murder a goat with her mouth and eat it. And she knows how to speak nicely to people.'

'Guys,' Anahera says from the cabin. 'Quit muttering.'

Cynthia closes her eyes. Not to sleep – she won't surrender – but to rest. He's probably a farmer in Germany, she thinks. He's got the waiting intelligence of a dog, and the muscled tongue of a bull. Here, he has found himself so at home in New Zealand, our dirty country of animals. Cynthia doesn't know any farmers, but you only have to watch the news to know what sort of place this country is.

47

In the morning she wakes in bed alone.

Gordon is clean – his clothing and his smell, his articulation and the way he moves through the boat. His body's sectioned into tidily cleared parts like those of a Ken doll.

He's clean, but Cynthia finds a bottle of piss in the cabin where he sleeps. It's tucked away, where the walls narrow and the ceiling meets the floor, behind some cushions they don't use. She opens it and peers in. It's a big old Fanta bottle, nearly full. At its neck the liquid's surfaced with five or so little bubbles. She takes a whiff – *putrid* – then screws the lid back on tight, and replaces it behind the cushions. What a revolting man he is, she thinks again and again, kneading the cushions with her feet.

For the rest of that blessed afternoon she ponders what to do about it. During dinner she decides that at their next meal time she'll pour it very gently under the table onto the crotch of his pants. She only needs something good to say afterwards. Something he can't reply to.

The piss bottle is from when he first arrived with them. When he stayed in the cabin at night, unsleeping. He behaved properly in their home then.

48

The next day Anahera's swimming and Gordon's having breakfast; it'll have to wait till lunch. When Anahera comes back Cynthia's having seconds.

'You look cute,' she says. 'Happy.'

Cynthia nods, it's true – she does and she is. 'What will you do today?' she asks.

Anahera shrugs and leans forward, towards her. 'You?'

'Just some stuff,' Cynthia says.

Gordon's standing at the back, shouting at the guy on the yellow boat. It's closer now, not twenty metres away. He's so noisy, Anahera rolls her eyes.

'Hey!' Cynthia giggles. 'Hey, hey – wait a sec.' She touches Anahera's nose, and clambers into the cabin. It's the perfect time for the chocolates. He's distracted, and she and Anahera are both beautiful today, and near love, or just near each other.

He's folded the clothes in his bag, and she doesn't want to mess them up and disturb him prematurely. The chocolates are right at the bottom. She's got the bag on the floor, and she's lying on a lower bunk with one of her legs sticking through the cabin door. Anahera taps her foot with something cold, like a spoon. Wet, maybe – with Anahera's spit, maybe. Cynthia stops worrying about the foldedness of the shirts. She pulls out the chocolates, then fists everything back in. The spoon taps her again, and she turns to see Anahera's face smiling through the gap in the door.

'Yeah?' Anahera says.

'Yeah!' Cynthia throws the box at her.

They sit opposite each other. Gordon's yelling at his buddy. 'Women!' He laughs uproariously. 'They're always screaming! Ha!'

Anahera hasn't opened the box. Cynthia wants to take them back and do it. She wants at least ten chocolates in Anahera before Gordon says they're his. But, Anahera's examining the little smiley faces. 'These look expensive,' she says, beaming.

'Yup,' Cynthia nods. She can feel herself squinting, and she's pulling at her thumb with her fist, so it aches at the socket.

'What?' Anahera asks. 'What is it?'

'I just want to see you eat five at once,' Cynthia says, still squeezing and pulling. She looks behind Anahera, through the door at the deck, but she can't see Gordon. He's quiet now, he must be listening, either to them or his friend.

Anahera's only silent for a moment. Then she laughs and rips the box open. 'Five?' she asks.

Cynthia nods, waiting.

'Do you want one?' Anahera pauses.

'I just want to see you,' Cynthia tells her.

Anahera laughs again, in a lovely flattered way, and puts one in her mouth. Then, counting them, four more. Her cheeks push out huge, and her eyes seem pressed from the insides into a new, splendid brightness. She laughs more, and chokes a bit. Cynthia's very satisfied. 'Are you going to swallow?' she asks, taking one herself and looking at it. They're quite big, the size of your average marshmallow. She looks down at the little iced wink on the one she's holding.

Anahera's trying to swallow, but laughs too hard. Her shoulders lift up and down, and the chocolate shows in flashes in her mouth.

Some falls on the table. She moves for it, but Cynthia gets there first. She wipes most of it up with her fingers, it's wet and spitty, and puts it in her mouth. Anahera smiles. She's stopped laughing now, but she's still breathing loudly through her nose.

They might be a bit off. There's a slightly metallic taste, but Cynthia thinks that's Anahera's spit. She doesn't swallow, she just sits there and meanders her tongue around, tasting. *I love you*, she tells Anahera with her eyes, and she sucks each syllable.

'Alright, friend!' Gordon shouts, and Cynthia remembers him. Anahera gives her a meaningful look back.

He re-enters, stomping loudly. Neither Anahera nor Cynthia turns to see him, but he arrives, standing right over the table. 'Oh,' he says. 'You have stolen my love gift.' He turns immediately to Cynthia, who looks back at him, empty-mouthed now, and defiant.

'This boat is private property,' she tells him, smartly. 'It got mixed up with our stuff.'

She hears Anahera's effortful swallowing of the chocolate, but doesn't look to her for support. She won't shift her eyes from Gordon.

'You bitch,' he says, laughing. But then he yells. 'You fucking little bitch!' His accent is gone.

'Gordon!' Anahera says, loudly. 'Stop that immediately!'

He says, calmly, accent returned, 'Hello there, Cynthia, you fucking little bitch. I am going fishing.' Then he walks back out to the deck, presumably to set his line.

Cynthia snorts, noisily, so he can hear. But she looks at Anahera, and says, 'Did you know his accent was fake?'

Anahera holds her face deliberately, and says, 'I had some idea.'

49

Cynthia finishes the chocolates and makes plans. At lunch she'll tip the piss on him. Then, when he jumps and shouts, she'll say in a calm, almost maternal tone, 'Are you okay, Gordon?' When he says no, he's covered in two litres of his own piss, she'll explain back to him concepts he's spoken of earlier, of self-love, and breathing deeply. Cynthia won't laugh at all when he jumps up screaming, but Anahera certainly will, because it'll be very funny.

He'll be driven wild and reveal his true nature. She imagines his big hands squeezing their frail table-bed so hard it crunches, then smacking her across the face. If he hits her she'll cry and Anahera will comfort her, ignoring him. He'll shout for hours without stopping, dripping piss, then eventually collapse on the floor in a drenched puddle. He'll cry louder and longer than Cynthia, because he's a man and when they get started that's how they are.

When her eyes are dry, and they've let him go on for a while, she and Anahera will share a look. A look communicating Cynthia's plan: Anahera forcibly ejects him. She biffs his wet, angry body into the bigger, wetter rage of the sea. He'll be weakened by his own stench and shame, and the sight of seeing Cynthia hit will propel Anahera, she'll be at her strongest. Cynthia will then zoom the boat off. That bit's a concern, actually – Cynthia's never operated the motor, she might have to step aside and let Anahera do it.

Gordon's shouting again, at his friend, but she doesn't pay attention. His whole life is meaningless.

She's just eaten the last chocolate when he comes in, with his buddy. 'Sit, please,' he says, ignoring the empty box. 'What can I get you?'

The guy's wearing the same little black shorts and orange singlet as he did when he pulled them off the beach. He sits at the table opposite Cynthia, and shrugs. 'Coffee?'

Gordon does the thing with the gas then the lighter, and the kettle hums.

'He doesn't own this boat,' Cynthia tells the guy, gesturing at Gordon's back. 'Or a single thing on it. He's a guest who will be uninvited soon, probably tomorrow.'

Gordon turns and says, 'You've already met Cynthia, and you know what? She's only fourteen.' His fake accent's vanished again.

The guy looks from Gordon to Cynthia, and back. If it were a room he'd leave. She gives him a smile, she understands. Then she gets up and stands behind Gordon. He's hunched down and bent over, into the small gap between the raised kitchen cupboards and the bench. She turns briefly back to the guy, and pulls her fist back, ready to punch, then gives him a nod. She makes sure he's watching properly, and with all the force she can muster she slugs Gordon in the back of the neck.

'Ow!' He stumbles, and bangs his head on the wall. The boat rocks at his movement, and Cynthia waits patiently for him to regain his balance. When he does, he doesn't turn back to look at her. She punches his lower back twice, but it does nothing, he's holding the bench to steady himself.

'I know you're not German,' she snarls.

Gordon turns to look at her then. 'I'm not German,' he repeats, as if mildly surprised. His eyes are white, and he looks dully down with them for a long moment, and blinks twice. Then, he looks over Cynthia, to the guy sitting at the table. 'Good day fishing?'

Cynthia returns to her seat, across from the guy. He's scratching his chin, and looking at the door.

'What are your interests?' she asks, to make him feel better.

'Aw, fishing, I guess.' He shifts his singlet, so the areas around each of his armpits are equally uncovered. They're very hairy, like he's hiding mice.

'Cool,' Cynthia says. 'Do you want coffee?'

She can see Anahera's ankles through the window behind Gordon's head, coming around the side of the boat.

'Yeah,' the guy tells her.

'Cool, Gordon's making you one. Do you want sugar in it?'

'Yeah,' he says. 'Or, either or.'

'Gordon, put sugar in it.' Anahera's off the edge, and must be on the deck.

He turns and stares at her, then spits in the sink.

Anahera sits down beside the guy. 'Hey there.' She gives him two friendly, hard pats on the shoulder.

Cynthia notices Gordon not adding sugar, but says nothing. His friend can suffer the wrong sort of drink, she doesn't care. 'This guy enjoys fishing,' she tells Anahera.

Anahera laughs. 'I know.'

He makes a crackly chuckle too, and finally settles into his seat a bit.

Gordon puts down three coffees: his own, one for Anahera and another for the guy. 'I didn't know if you'd want tea,' he tells Cynthia. Then, 'Caught much?' he asks the guy.

'Nah, but I took a nap.' He shrugs.

Cynthia looks straight forward at his pecs, still flabbily

exhibited at the big arm holes of his singlet. Is now the time for the pee? It doesn't feel right. She waits patiently. Anahera and orange-singlet both know a family in common: the Henares. How boring.

Orange-singlet asks Gordon, 'How long have you been around here?'

'Only months.' Gordon shrugs.

'He got dumped,' Cynthia says.

'Should I make lunch?' Anahera asks, smiling broadly.

'Aw, nah. Don't trouble yourself,' the guy says, but he's leaning forward a little. He likes her, he's been running a hand through his hair and smiling since Cynthia mentioned Gordon's having been dumped.

'Lunch'd be pretty good right now.' Gordon rubs his belly.

Anahera opens a can of corned beef, then their last loaf of bread. She boils the kettle again, and they have sandwiches and tea. 'Victoria Beckham kissed her daughter on the lips,' Cynthia tells them. 'Then posted it on Instagram.'

Anahera says, 'That's nice.'

Cynthia thinks it's gross, but she lets them do the talking, chews her sandwich, and checks Facebook instead. When he finally leaves, she looks up at the guy and says, 'Pleasure.' He nods and smiles, and Gordon shows him out.

'Interesting man, that,' he says when he comes back in.

Anahera agrees, and says she'd like to have him over again. That doesn't seem consistent with their plans of not getting arrested, but Cynthia doesn't worry. She only needs to wait a few hours till dinner.

50

Dinner is canned peas, canned corn and more corned beef. It looks nice and tidy, all scooped out in sections on their plates. Cynthia and Gordon are waiting for Anahera to finish washing her hands in the bathroom. The bottle's behind the cabin door. She knows she can reach it from where she's sitting, and doesn't think they'll see. She sections her foods off from one another with careful scraping movements of her knife. Gordon tells her to stop, and she finishes the corn, then she does. The peas roll a bit, but the water's okay tonight, so not too much. She puts one between her lips, a pea, and holds it there a moment. She sucks it back in and says, 'Will you wash your hands, Gordon?'

'No. Will you?'

'No, I never do. Before dinner.'

Anahera joins them, and Cynthia wonders how she's even going to manage this. The excitement and nerves are making her hungry. She eats a large mouthful of peas. They're actually not good, very watery. She's got the bottle behind the cabin door, and Gordon's beside her, between her and the wall. How to unscrew the lid without them seeing? She just has to do it, she decides. She won't put it off.

She puts some corn in her mouth and it's sweet. She smiles at Anahera, then turns the same face to Gordon.

'Definitely an interesting guy, your friend,' she says. 'What with how he liked fishing and all.'

'I wasn't so sure about his politics,' Anahera says.

Gordon laughs, as if he understands her or New Zealand politics at all. Anahera and Cynthia let him. He's eating quickly, he'll be done soon. She didn't account for his way of swallowing without chewing. She shuffles sideways and down, towards the cabin door and the bottle behind it. He's still laughing.

Anahera's looking at her corn. 'We won't get these peas again,' she says.

'Nope,' Cynthia agrees, and she's got the bottle by her fingers. She lifts it a bit so it's not dragging loudly along the floor, and gets it through the door. She can't go back now. She's not sure if it's visible from where Anahera's sitting or not. 'Not *these* peas,' she agrees a second time. It's under the table, touching her left foot. She shifts the foot, so the bottle's between her two feet. It's much bigger than her feet, and she's worried it could topple, but she uses her ankles and calves to hold and shift it. It makes a dragging noise, but she's watching their faces, and they don't hear it.

Gordon extends his plate towards Anahera, and she lifts her own and shoves the peas over. Cynthia rests her head on the table, so she can get her arms low to the bottle. 'I'm bored,' she says. 'I get bored with politics.'

Anahera nods at her oddly. That's not what they're talking about anymore.

'Also, these peas,' Cynthia says, smiling. 'Gordon, you can have my peas too, they're so tiring.' She slides the plate towards him, still concentrating on shifting the bottle.

'I don't want your peas,' he says.

She's got her fingers on the lid now, and she's turning it carefully, and holding the bottle still with her calves and feet. She shrugs her shoulders as if to say it's fine about the peas, and she's nearly got the lid off. Neither Anahera nor Gordon reacts to her shrugging, so she does it again. The lid's off. A bit of pee spills. Her fingers are wet. She thinks she can smell it, but she's careful not to sniff. The bottle cap falls to the carpet then, and makes a soft sound.

Anahera looks at her.

'*Peas,*' Cynthia says. '*Peas, peas, peas.*' She nearly sings it.

She's got to move quickly, they're watching her now. Or, Anahera is. She can't see Gordon's face, and she's worried if she turns she'll tip the bottle. Anahera puts a fork of corn in her mouth. Then, quickly, Cynthia lifts the bottle and it shakes in her hands. It's going to fall, so she half throws, half shoves it at his crotch.

'What the fuck?' He wrenches Cynthia around to face him. She pulls away. The smell is deep, musky and acidic. Anahera's head tilts and her eyes stare hard. Cynthia's legs are wet. She can't remember what to do now. 'Breathe deeply?' she says, and she's shocked by the height and panic in her voice. Her legs are warm and dripping.

'Pardon?' he asks her.

Cynthia looks at Anahera. Her eyes widen, and her eyebrows lift right up. It smells citric and rotten, like an off lemon.

'Cynthia,' Gordon says, in a measured voice. 'Did you just tip piss on me? Old piss?'

Anahera waits, with her eyebrows.

'Yep,' Cynthia says. 'I did.'

Silence.

'Why?' Anahera asks.

Cynthia says nothing.

'Cynthia, do you know how disgusting it is?' Gordon says. Cynthia doesn't turn to look at him, but he's swivelled right around to stare at the side of her face. All she can think is that he phrased the sentence wrong, he should have said 'this' and not 'it'. He leans forward, closer. 'I am dripping urine,' he says.

Anahera drops her head into her hands.

'It's your own piss,' Cynthia tells him. 'It's you.' She looks down at her corn, and wishes they were still eating.

'Cynthia,' Anahera asks through her fingers, 'have you done this to make a point?' Cynthia can't look at her either. She stretches her neck right back, so quickly it hurts, and stares at the ceiling. The piss is sinking in, she can feel it tingling around the hairs on her legs. 'You already know what my point is,' she mumbles.

'Excuse me,' Gordon says, standing up. He shifts past her. 'I am going to wash.'

Cynthia puts some corn in her mouth, but Anahera looks up, and looks like she's waiting for something, so Cynthia shrugs and gets up to wash too.

Gordon's already in the water. He says nothing, and turns away towards the sun. It's setting and the water's not warm. She gets in and out quickly, and goes back in to change. Anahera watches her dripping on the carpet, but says nothing. Cynthia finds a shirt and shorts, and changes in the bathroom, dripping more water by the toilet.

She doesn't say another thing to either of them, and goes to sleep alone in the cabin. If Anahera isn't prepared to stand up for her ever, why sleep together? She can get squashed to death under Gordon for all Cynthia cares.

Anahera knocks on the door three times, but none of them to apologise. Twice to ask if she's alright – Cynthia doesn't answer, and Anahera doesn't open the door – and once to leave water outside the cabin, which Cynthia ignores.

She lies like a corpse, caught in an understanding as simple and putrid as death: some truths are not to be accepted as facts. A fact brings with it a horde of contingent truths, more potential facts. If you don't stop accepting them, you might never. Then you're in an ocean. Anahera never loved Cynthia, and Cynthia stops thinking at that.

On silent, she watches a girl shove a huge dildo in her mouth, then her vagina, then her bum. She turns it off and they're talking about her. He says, 'Where did you find her?' His voice is muffled, like he's talking right into Anahera's chest.

There's shuffling, then, 'Gordon, probably just don't touch me. I can smell it on you.'

He mumbles, still against her, 'I can wash again. If you want me to, I'll go out into the cold water and wash?'

'I just want to sleep.'

Cynthia doesn't breathe or move in the husk of the cabin. She waits.

Gordon's voice is clearer, and sudden. 'What the fuck is your plan now, tell me?'

'Gordon,' Anahera says, 'no one invited you here. You got urine tipped on you, whatever. Don't think it's my problem.' The boat shakes, and Cynthia hears Anahera stomp out and around to sit on the deck. Then she stomps back and says, 'Gordon, you ruined everything for me, do you know that?'

51

Cynthia lies awake, thinking of Snot-head, and her father. Randy. Ron. All of them, boys; such innocence, so loving and lovely and Cynthia's thrown them all away, for what. She mustn't think of Toby, and his elbows. She remembers Snot-head's legs instead, and the bones in them. So short and knobbly; little grandad bones. His big tongue, big eyes, and the heat of his nose and panting mouth. The thought of him in someone else's bed is all she has left to make her happy, but she keeps crying and imagining him dead, then getting sadder when she realises he probably isn't; he most likely really did find somebody.

Gordon's mouth asks her through the door, 'What will you do with your life?'

'Fuck off.'

'I had a job when I was fourteen.'

Cynthia very deliberately says nothing. Anahera must be asleep.

When she left university, she applied for jobs at McDonald's, Burger King, Pizza Hut and Kmart. She didn't get work anywhere, but McDonald's had her fill out a questionnaire online that, in response to her answers, gave her advice on becoming her best self: she needed to develop a can-do attitude, and care more about other people.

'Let me guess? There was a boy and he didn't love you, so now you *mope* – so now you have taken it upon yourself to destroy my relationship.'

'Oh, with who?' She looks deep into the dark.

'There are a lot of boys who don't love you, Cynthia,' he tells her. 'And a lot of women who aren't your mother.'

The survey said to Cynthia, 'Consider how you would feel working in an environment where open and honest feedback is a regular part of your day.' They asked how she'd respond to someone stopping her on her way out for her lunchbreak with some constructive criticism. She answered honestly: she'd rather eat. They replied in kind: they found her unreceptive to love. Food is love, and they questioned her right to handle theirs.

Gordon says, 'You think because you have a little body, a child-ishly taut body, that people will continue everlastingly to spoon food into your mouth, and carry you about on their shoulders?'

'No,' Cynthia says, alone in the dark. She feels stupid, but continues, 'I expect to die.'

He goes on as if he hasn't heard her: 'She will not want you now, or even me, after what you've done. But after your murder of the teenager, you see – oh yes, I know you know that I know – we're all together now, probably forever. Breathe, Cynthia. It's important that you breathe.'

She clamps her lips shut, to spite him.

'I saw her face when she smelled it. Every love opportunity is over.'

The smell, the rank, deep, sharp smell, and Cynthia remembers how it felt lukewarm on her leg. She wasn't looking at Anahera, not when it first poured out. She can't remember where she was looking. At the wall, probably.

'You must be going limp,' he says.

But she's hard, strained; the air in her is stalled. She scrunches up tight against the cabin wall. His is the language of debtors and employers – love yourself, it says. Make yourself contented. She listens to him settle back into the bed. Anyway, Cynthia never got a job.

When he's silent she stands on the deck, watching the water. In the dark it's only more darkness, and that's all water is. Transparency and transparency on top of itself until you can see nothing through it. Her father was moustached and rich and distant. She never saw him in shorts, and she can't imagine him with tanned legs or pale ones. He hasn't texted her in over a month, no one has. She remembers her old bed, and how soft it was. The laxity of Snothead's sleeping limbs, and his gentle breathing.

There's sound from inside. Cynthia peers through the doorcrack and can see only the lines of someone's limbs moving through shadows, but they're Anahera's. Things are being picked up, and there are shuffling sounds. The noise of a zip, and the thump of a full bag being put down on the ground. Anahera's packing. Cynthia squeaks, her knees are weak. She holds the doorknob for support.

Anahera lifts her head up into the light from the window, big-eyed, and says, 'I thought we might have a day out tomorrow, hey?'

Cynthia bites her cheeks and stares back.

'I've just got some Weet-Bix, Nutella and a sweater,' Anahera says.

Cynthia says nothing, and continues to stare while Anahera puts the bag down, gives her a nod, and gets back under the blankets with Gordon.

She needs to regain the bed immediately, by force if necessary. She stands in the doorway to examine the situation. They're each lying at far edges of the mattress. All she needs to do is place herself between them, and sleep. She pees first, even though she doesn't need to, so that after claiming her position there'll be no need to relinquish it. Then she steps, carefully, over Anahera's body so she's standing on the bed. Gordon rolls and moans by her feet. Silently, she lowers herself down, onto her knees, then her elbows, and finally her stomach. There she is, then – that easily! – lying between them.

She doesn't really sleep, her tendons feel tight and weird. She just lies there, tensed and breathing. He smells salty. Then, when the morning light is still only arriving, Gordon rolls onto her, opens his eyes and yells. He doesn't make words, only a deep, long roar. When he's exhausted and regained himself, he looks at her and says, 'Creep.' He shoves her hard against Anahera, and Anahera pushes back silently. Cynthia struggles for breath between them.

'I'm sorry, excuse me,' he says. 'I do not feel comfortable with your body so close to me in bed.'

Cynthia pulls in as much air as she can – they're still both pushing – and says, 'Then you know what to do, Gordon.'

He stops pressing. 'Oh, I'm not sure?'

It's still dark, but Anahera fake yawns and gets up. 'Well,' she says. 'Today we're going for a trip. All of us together. Confined space clearly isn't aiding our psychological health.'

Gordon gives Cynthia a hard shove, and she falls onto the floor. Immediately, she clambers back up and over him onto the good side of the bed – the safe side, by the wall, where he was, and where she won't be expelled nearly so easily again. He doesn't fight her, and she doesn't know why till she sees Anahera's backpack, visible from where he is now, leaned against the kitchen cupboards.

'Is your plan – extensive?' he asks Anahera.

She nudges the bag with her foot and smiles, very nicely. 'I've packed some food and things. I couldn't sleep last night.'

She's lying. Cynthia moans and bangs her head against the wall.

'You see,' he says, speaking over her, at Anahera, 'you are giving us agony.'

Cynthia hears herself moaning and moans louder. He's turned to face Anahera, and his back obscures her from Cynthia's view. All she can see is wall and ceiling; all that flaking paint. There's more light now, it's nearly daytime.

'What do you mean?' Anahera says.

Cynthia watches his mountainous back shrug.

'Well,' Anahera says, 'I'm awake now. Thanks to both of you. So I'll go for a swim, then when I come back we'll go?'

The lump lifts and fall again, another shrug. His muscles ripple. Anahera goes, and Cynthia and Gordon lie still for twenty minutes. Then, she reaches up and digs her fingers into his back. His muscles are hard, her fingernails can't find purchase. Then, one of them catches on a mole. 'I'm not giving you my bed back, ever,' she says. 'You came here, and you ruined my life.'

He slumps onto his back, and covers his face with his hands. 'No,' he says. 'Nothing that happens to you means a thing, you are too young. Your life is not possibly ruined. Do you have a father? It is my life that is a great heap of ball-sack. It is you who have ruined my great dreams.'

He's pathetic. She looks at his body. His thighs are thick, and his chest's very solid. She leans over, and touches his stomach with a fist. She presses it down hard, but nothing happens. He doesn't have any squishy part at all. He opens his eyes, and tells her, 'You know she thinks she's going to run from us?' He laughs and laughs. 'She will not run from us,' he says, and he twists and resettles himself under her fist, still pressing. She lifts it up and punches him once in the stomach, so he makes an 'Urrgh' sound.

Satisfied, she lies back to watch the ceiling for twenty minutes more.

'A lot of boys would like you, Cynthia,' he says casually, 'but not me. There are specific qualities I look for in a woman.'

How annoying, and after that he pulls one of his knees up, and squeezes it against his chest. He releases it, blows out three short, sharp breaths, and looks at her sideways. 'Well,' he says. Cynthia wishes she knew a stretch she could do lying down. She can't copy his, but she feels very tense. He does his other knee, still looking at her.

'Anahera practically said I was allowed to make you my criminal slave,' she tells him.

He raises his eyebrows and releases the second knee.

'But you're just too shit. I was going to make you steal corned beef, and steal that guy's yellow boat, but you're just too shit.'

'Where would you contain me?' he asks.

She doesn't hesitate. 'I'd tie you to the table.'

'But then where would Anahera sleep?' He lies there, ogling her.

She's about to say that, actually, she'd lock him in the cabin, when he puts a finger to his lips and nods towards the door. Anahera's on the ladder. 'See how mature I am,' he says. 'I will give you the whole bed.'

He gets up and pours the last of the Coco Pops onto his face, and into his mouth.

Anahera arrives in the doorway and looks down at the carpet

where a good deal of them have fallen. He stamps them in with his bare feet, and says preemptively, 'There were a lot already spilled there.' The big toe on his right foot twitches, and he grabs it by the ankle to lift it and remove a half-crushed Coco Pop from the crevice between that toe and the ball of his foot. Having flicked it away, he tells Anahera quietly, 'You won't leave us.'

'What? Why?' she asks, panicked.

'What, or why?' There's a fleck of Coco Pop caught in the slight hair above his lip.

Anahera gives him a reducing look, then goes back onto the deck. 'Cynthia,' she says, loudly. Her voice is bright with deceit, but Cynthia comes, like a called animal. 'There's the busy town we've been going to,' she explains, pointing to Paihia. Cynthia nods, she knows. 'But then,' Anahera shifts her arm, so she's pointing in the opposite direction, 'on the other side of the estuary is a much quieter place, Russell, with secluded beaches. I thought we could all go there for the day.'

It doesn't make sense, what Gordon's been saying. Anahera could have left on her own in the night, in the dinghy. She could already be gone. She moves behind Cynthia now, and touches her hair. 'I'll plait it,' she says. There's no wind, it's quiet, and her voice sounds almost girlish, sweet in the cool, still air. 'Fish-tail or French, you pick?' Cynthia's thinking of Snot-head. He had very watery eyes, some days. The hair's pulled softly at her scalp. The tips of Anahera's fingers slide under Cynthia's ponytail and wriggle, loosening it. 'Fish, then,' Anahera says, and Cynthia can't help her posture rising up towards her touch.

52

They're silent and squashed in the dinghy like sardines. 'So,' Anahera says, and neither Cynthia nor Gordon says anything. 'Well,' she says. Then, finally, 'Alright then.' Gordon paddles. The sky's thick and weighted with waiting rain. Cynthia and Anahera sit side by side, and Anahera's arm twitches.

When they arrive, Anahera tugs Cynthia up, and they walk to sit on some grass at the edge of the sand. The only visible buildings are high above them, on the hills. Gordon joins them after shifting the dinghy from the sea, yawns loudly, and lies back. His shirt lifts right up and shows his hairy belly-button. Around them, the grass is rough, and in patches it's beige like skin. The water's grey, and tides heave up onto the beach, one after the other, near to where he's left the dinghy. He didn't drag it far.

Anahera's looking around, worried they'll be seen, but Cynthia doesn't bother. Let them take us, she thinks, and lies back as peaceful and loose as Gordon, to imagine herself being caught, photographed, shamed and locked away forever.

Rain falls on them in plops. 'The town's over there,' Gordon says, shuffling up on an elbow to point where the beach curves around, away from them. Then he lies down again, and brings his lips to Cynthia's ear. 'This place connects to the mainland, you know,' he whispers.

Anahera's sitting up, and she turns back to them with a lazy, forced smile, then unpacks the picnic. They're nearly out of food.

There's a Weet-Bix for each of them, and Nutella to spread on top. 'We can put it on thick,' Anahera says hopefully. 'And to wash those down . . .' She presents a huge bottle of water, one of their last ones, almost grimacing. Gordon takes a Weet-Bix gingerly in his big fingers, and slathers it like he's been told to.

'I always loved these,' he says.

Cynthia ignores him. No one loves Weet-Bix.

He laughs hysterically. 'Just kidding, I am German.'

'Fuck off already, Gordon,' Anahera says. She's been sitting, looking dumbly at her own wheat biscuit, and now she throws it into the sand and stands up. She walks to the water.

'Boof!' Gordon puffs out after her, but quickly all his attention is on the Weet-Bix, and he's brushing the sand off with the careful soft of his fingers. He places it down at his side, away from Cynthia, on his cardigan. Only then does he screech after Anahera, 'What do you know about the incident, woman?'

She doesn't turn.

He yells again, 'Suspect!'

Cynthia couldn't care less about any of that nonsense; the boy, the police or anything. He makes a little wheezing laugh under his breath, and together they watch Anahera ignore him.

Water laps at her feet.

'Killer,' he says.

'You're a child if you think we'll be hurt that way,' Cynthia tells him, and begins to crunch through her Weet-Bix, dry.

He laughs, and nods at Anahera. 'She will be hurt, she is that way.'

Cynthia wants to tell him what sort of person he really is, but there's not enough saliva in her mouth to swallow what she's chewed. Anahera's kicking the water, and she stops to squat down and look at it. Cynthia takes glugs from the water bottle, and swallows her mouthful in three portions. When she's done the moment's passed, and she and Gordon watch Anahera together. The air between them feels peaceful to Cynthia, as if there's no truth left to be spoken or changed.

'We were going to take all your money,' she tells him. 'Before we knew you knew about the kid.'

He shrugs. 'You thought that.'

She narrows her eyes so Anahera becomes a dark blotch before the reflected light of the sea. But, what else would she expect him to say? She closes her eyes and lies back. 'You see?' he says. 'She is a sweet woman. She could have paddled off, but then you and I would have no dinghy. So she took us here, so she could run, and we could use it to get back to the boat. A real darling, she is.' He yells at her, 'You're a real fucking sweetheart, are you not?'

When Anahera does come back to them, she says, 'I thought I might just go for a little walk.'

'Where?' Gordon asks.

Anahera waves her hand off to where the land curves away, behind a corner.

Cynthia wriggles her feet, thinking to get up and go with her, but Gordon speaks. 'You can go,' he says, coldly. 'You can go wherever you like. I will not follow. I will not tell the police any bad thing of a good woman like you. You can trust me.'

Anahera squats down, grasping her thighs and looking hard at him. Cynthia sits quietly alongside.

'It is Cynthia,' he says, 'that you cannot be sure about.'

Anahera swivels, and she's looking at Cynthia. Her lip twitches. Cynthia tries to look up sweetly, to push all her generosity and love into her face, but it doesn't seem to be working. Anahera blinks, and wipes some hair from her eyes, then continues her deep looking. A laugh-choke comes out of Cynthia.

Gordon adjusts himself in the grass. 'Cynthia,' he says, 'I put it in her bum, in my tent.'

There's not a thought, just dull, vicious noise. Anahera's eyes, nose and mouth are all Cynthia sees. They turn away from her, all at once, to face Gordon.

'Fuck off,' Anahera says.

She turns back to Cynthia, but Cynthia's eyes have opened so wide they hurt. Her guts are rising in her throat, and all she can think of is vomiting on Anahera's so-close face. 'What?' she asks Anahera. What he said is true.

'Please, ignore him,' Anahera whispers.

Cynthia shouts back, spitting, 'What?!'

Anahera says nothing.

'What? So you can run off and leave me with him? So when you leave me I won't call the police on you?' Cynthia spits more.

Anahera doesn't move or wipe her face till Cynthia's done. She waits, and says, 'Right, I think we should all head back to the boat.'

Cynthia's fingers are in her mouth, and she's pushing them back. For a moment she finds them there, pauses, then continues pushing deliberately. Anahera grabs one of her elbows, trying to pull them out, but Cynthia slams her head against them, harder. She doesn't think why; doesn't think. Bile comes up and touches her fingers. Her fingertips are wet and her throat burns. Anahera pulls Cynthia's arms harder, so the joints hurt, and their faces are near each other again. 'I'm sorry,' Anahera says. 'I'm sorry, I'm sorry.' She's crying. She's going to say more, so Cynthia throws herself up, out of Anahera's arms, and runs.

Gordon's ahead of her, putting the dinghy back in the water.

She runs past him, screaming, into the sea. She trips and falls when it's at her knees, cries out, stands, and continues running, but falls again.

Anahera's yelling, 'Don't, don't,' then she *catches up and grabs* Cynthia. 'Don't,' she keeps saying.

'Don't tell me don't!' Cynthia kicks at her legs, but Anahera's holding her by the stomach, and her grip tightens. Cynthia swings her arms, still kicking, not touching the ground anymore, and screams louder.

Gordon looks over, from where he's waiting now at the dinghy. 'Just let her go,' he says. 'She'll come back.'

Cynthia bites, but she's only biting salty air. Anahera lets her go, and she runs, struggling against the tides, till she's in water too deep to stand in. She can't see a thing through her tears, the water and her hair which has slapped wet in one mess over her face. There's water in her throat, her mouth and her eyes. She's heavy, but she tries to swim back to the boat. She remembers waiting for Anahera outside Countdown with Snot-head, and a man coming out and looking at her, and she thinks, Of course, of course, over and over again.

Anahera's voice isn't far away, calling her name. She looks sideways and the dinghy's right there, floating gently in the water beside her. Anahera's hand's out, waiting. Cynthia doesn't want to touch it. She swims over, and struggles to pull herself up, out of the water, but slips four times. Before the fifth, Gordon offers his hand, and she takes it.

He paddles. The water all around them is unbearable green. He's sitting opposite them, and his whole body rolls forward and back with each stroke. Anahera's hands are on her thighs, and her knees press tightly together. Cynthia looks at her, then at the water again, and her throat burns with salt. She swallows to soothe it, but it won't feel better. Anahera leans forward, with her hands and her fingers spread, murmuring to comfort her.

'Anahera,' Cynthia says, 'who did your husband catch you having sex with?'

Gordon coughs and stops paddling. Anahera's hands are up, suddenly at her hair, pulling it back so violently her eyebrows wrench up. One side of the paddle catches in the water, and they move in a slow, wonky circle.

53

In the cabin, Cynthia just sits. She's got the last of their food: one more Weet-Bix, and a can of peas. What she feels is almost boredom. She knows everything now; it can only go on as it is forever. The bedding's still moist from the night before, and she can feel it getting wetter. She's sinking in.

She coughs like a dog coughing up a dog. He's listening – she listens back. They don't knock and ask for food, but still. She knows him, the way he lounges all over things and people with his big, ugly body, and she knows Anahera now too. They fucked. He slid his cock into her, and now Cynthia can't let them live unwatched.

She opens the door and finds Anahera at the table with her head in her hands. 'Cynthia,' she says in a pinched voice, 'will you please join us for dinner tonight?' Cynthia thinks they just want her peas, and she's about to say Anahera can get stuffed, she already ate them, but Anahera says, 'Gordon found some beans.'

'Oh, Gordon found some beans. Wow.'

Anahera nods dumbly, she's got nothing else to say.

A dead bird floats up against them. 'A bird corpse,' Gordon says. 'Come look!' Cynthia and Anahera stand at his sides while he pokes it with a broom handle. 'What do you think?' He turns between them. 'Dead?'

54

Rain falls in a continuous thud on the roof. They're inside, at the table. Gordon's philosophising and Anahera's acting interested because, as Cynthia now knows, that's what she does. He says, 'I'm not the police, as you know. But I could have been.' Anahera turns to Cynthia, probably expecting solidarity. Gordon registers the loss of her attention, and changes tack. 'Alright,' he says, 'I have a scary story. It starts with a boy – '

'You're being lame,' Cynthia interrupts him. 'Honestly, neither of us feels bad about that anymore.'

Anahera gives her a look.

'What?' Cynthia asks. 'It wasn't even our fault.'

Anahera wipes her face, and when she removes her hand her expression is neutral again.

'No,' Cynthia says. 'What?'

'Well, it was a bad idea,' Anahera says. 'To take him.'

Gordon's head swivels, from Anahera to Cynthia and back again. Cynthia feels herself make a noise, and goes to stand outside on the deck. The sky and water are separate blues, then a ways away you can't see the line between them. She cleans her ears with a pinky and wipes it off on her pants.

She's going to do it soon, and she won't feel guilty. The sky's heavy, deep and dark above her. She's going to wipe her boat clean of fluff and spillage, and see clearly what she and Anahera are; really are to each other. She doesn't need to talk to them anymore.

She reads one *of her* romance books on the deck.

55

Anahera calls the two of them to dinner. Cynthia sits, looks at it and says, 'Gee, thanks a lot. This looks like shit.' Anahera smiles anyway, and shrugs. Gordon says nothing. They're the beans from his bag.

'Cynthia,' Anahera says. 'We're both really, really sorry.'

'Oh, for what?' Cynthia looks up, and pauses briefly from spooning them around. 'I'm not into beans,' she says.

'It isn't that I didn't want to tell you. I wanted him gone, you remember, but then' – she looks at Gordon, and he nods – 'he knew about the boy, and my feelings changed independent of my control.'

'Independent of your control?' Cynthia slaps her spoon against her beans. A nice splat comes up, and some lands on her collarbone. Anahera's mouth is open, she's about to explain herself more, so Cynthia asks, 'Have you been fucking often then, since he, uh, joined us?'

'No,' Anahera says. 'No, only once.'

Gordon shuffles quietly in his seat. Cynthia looks, and his face is a deep mauve.

'Hmm,' she says, turning to face him. 'Not much luck then?'

He looks down at his beans. His eyes are scrunched up, and his bottom lip's pushed over the top one, like he's sad and only ten years old. Cynthia chuckles at that, and leans over to slap-pat the side of his face. Her hand makes a good, sharp noise against his cheekbone. He looks up at her then, and says, 'It's your fault.'

Cynthia laughs, harder, spitting some beans on her shirt. 'Where are you from?' she asks him.

'Palmerston North.'

They sit, waiting, as if sense is going to arrive to them on their boat in the post.

Cynthia sleeps in the cabin that night, because it doesn't matter. She's ready to destroy herself to sink him. She only needs to wait for the decision to move from her mind to her body.

56

She lies all day in the cabin listening to splat after splat of bird shit fall on the roof. At five o'clock he shoves his monstrous head through the door. 'Peas and corn,' he says. 'I found some cans.'

They all sit at the table in front of their portions. 'We'll be hungry after this,' Cynthia says, although they all know. Tonight the water's rough, an aggressive mass moving beneath them, so they eat their peas first. There's rain on the roof. One pea rolls from Gordon's plate and off the table, and he doesn't move to pick it up. He finishes first, then Cynthia. 'Well,' she says. 'Do you have more up there?' He looks right back at her, with his mouth closed. His eyelids blink, slowly, three times.

Cynthia checks in the cabin, and her peas were the ones they just ate – he must have taken them last night, while she used the toilet. She has a look through the cupboards. There's nothing, and they swing closed loudly.

'Cynthia, go easy on those,' Anahera says.

'Why?' Cynthia asks, not turning. 'They're my cupboards.'

'We all have to live here.'

'Oh? Do we?'

Anahera and Gordon get up and look too. Cynthia sits back down to watch them. The answer is simple: his death. He squats to look in the lower cupboards, and she notices him being as rough with the hinges as she was. He finds a chip packet she missed, pinches some crumbs in his fingers, and lifts them to Anahera's mouth. Anahera ducks her head away and steps back, then puts out a hand for him to place them on.

'You need to shop, Gordon,' she tells him, after swallowing.

'Yeah,' he says, not looking away from the empty hole of the cupboard. 'We have porridge.'

Cynthia was thinking that.

'That's morning food,' Anahera says. 'We need it in the morning.'

He looks at her hands, near the handle of the cupboard with the porridge. Cynthia knows what he sees. Anahera's fingers are purposeful and quick. Coloured like copper, strong and elegant. 'Tomorrow,' Anahera says. 'Tomorrow, before you get groceries.'

Gordon nods without looking up at her face.

'This is shit planning,' Cynthia tells them.

'What should I get?' he asks Anahera in a dreamy voice, ignoring her.

Anahera turns suddenly, and smiles. 'Get whatever Cynthia wants.' Cynthia stares at the wall and nods, pleased.

She goes to bed early with a dry, hungry mouth. There she waits, for an hour, or hours, holding her hands up in the dark above her face and letting them touch each other. Anahera never snores, so there's no way to tell if she's sleeping. Cynthia's hands tire, and she lowers them to her face. She'd like to know what expression she's making. She touches her lips, but they only feel mouthy.

Anahera stays silent, but Gordon wheezes. The door opens gently. Their cabin's lighter than hers. The curtains are thin, and shifting gently. She waits in the doorway for the right feeling. She should know what to do before she moves, she thinks. But then she doesn't know, and she moves anyway.

Anahera's beautiful with her body so still; the blankets rise at her breasts, and dip in at the gap between her legs. Her eyelashes fan out towards her cheeks, and her nose has a smoothness Cynthia never noticed before. Beside her, Gordon's face twitches in the forehead, but otherwise he's still too, like calm water. She wants to touch both of them.

All their knives are blunt, she's heard both Anahera and Gordon say it. She looks around, and considers the kettle. She can't see anything else. When she lifts it from the stove it makes a metal noise against the element. Anahera moves, but doesn't wake. Gordon's still. It's filled with water. If she tips it in the sink, they'll hear it, and if she tips it outside, they'll hear that too?

They will, she decides. It's heavy, but how much of that is liquid? Should she just whack him with it full? Would the extra weight help her? No, she bends down and pours the water into the carpet. She's careful with the angle, so it runs out slowly, and she doesn't hear a thing. When she stands back up there's a noise from one of her knees. They both shift in bed, just a little, and she stands back and waits for them to settle. The kettle's too light now, and she wonders briefly – should she go outside and fill it again with sea water?

The skin of his eyelids looks incredibly soft, and his eyes form perfect mounds beneath them. The edges of his nostrils, too, appear extremely delicate. Perhaps she could lift him, so quickly he'd not have time to wake, and slam his head against the wall? She'd have to knock him unconscious with the first hit, then slam him five or so times more to kill him. It seems improbable. The moon moves and the light in the cabin lessens. She's standing in the water from the kettle, and her toes are wet. She struggles to think harder. There's nothing of the necessary weight on their boat, she thinks, but – there must be?

The anchor. She opens the cabin door carefully. It's dark in there, completely. She knows the spare anchor's on the floor, tangled in a lot of rope. She's careful picking it up, but still, it scrapes a little on the wooden floor. She doesn't think it's loud enough to rouse him, but Anahera? She turns, slowly, with her feet gentle on the ground. There's rope coiled around the anchor, and it tangles with her hands and hangs on her feet. She moves back through the door so she's positioned above him, then looks down. His eyes are open, and they open wider.

She slams the metal down on his face. He moans, and pushes her back with a big, meaty hand. The anchor drops, and hits her hip as it falls. There's still rope caught around her arms, but she limps as quickly as she can to the back deck, dragging it. It scrapes along the ground, banging at the step before the doorway. He's in the cabin behind her, moaning and moving. Cynthia pauses, and thinks she hears Anahera cooing to comfort him. The dinghy's adrift, tied to the boat with a long, white rope. She pulls it as fast as she can, and gets in.

She's struggling with the knot in the dark, and in panic, when she hears him clear his throat. He's on the deck, smiling, just behind where she was a moment ago, with his hands on his hips. She can't see his face well, but she thinks his lips are hanging oddly, and that one of his eyes is shut. His nose looks weirdly flat. He'll raise a hand soon, she feels, to wave her off. *He knew all of this would happen.* But he doesn't, and something moves in the shadows beside him. Anahera's hand reaches up. Her face is there too, only slightly behind his, with its mouth hung open slack, and her hand continues to reach up, so slowly, to touch her cheek. Unable to settle, it drops back down, to swing limp and graze his hip.

The knot comes undone, no one says anything, and Cynthia uses the paddle to push herself away from the boat. The moon's strong, and the water pulls her out of *Baby*'s shadow. Water ripples between Cynthia and her home, and she feels herself leaving faster and faster.

57

Because of the rain, the dark and her own drifting, Cynthia can't see *Baby* anymore. She doesn't want to. She curls up, and hours pass. The rain stops and the sky lightens. She looks around and sees nothing but water. She's got dandruff. She scratches her head and watches pieces of scalp twirl in the new light before her eyes. It's because she hasn't been shampooing often. She digs her nails in hard, as if peeling an egg. He's better than her. He fucked Anahera, and she couldn't kill him. Now she's alone.

Anahera could never have loved Cynthia, or made any serious love to her at all. She'd never have seriously touched Cynthia's so, so white body, with its pale stomach and pink elbows and knees. Cynthia remembers her own smugness at first imagining herself small under the older woman, squashed. Now she's left only with her shame; her desire's run forward and away from her, as helpless and dumb as a bug.

There are hours and hours, marching past like ants. The sun arrives, and quickly there's too much of it. Cynthia leans, slowly at first, one way then the other. The dinghy shifts, gently then violently, and water slaps both its sides. The sun's up now, on her back, watching her curiously, and Cynthia feels she's watching herself as she tips the dinghy. It flips easily, it'd been waiting to all along.

She's only under it a moment. The water moves. All of it shifts aside in a tide past her, and she's in the sun again and breathing. She holds its side and it settles. The water sparkles, wet and blue like an eye, wanting her. If she softens, it says, it will be soft against her. She only needs to breathe in three times, relax, and accept that Anahera doesn't love her, and never did. It'll be kind. She sees every curve of Anahera at once, but not her eyes, not their colour or anything at all behind them.

Her tears disappear into the sea. It shifts at her hips, appreciative. She closes her eyes and tips her head back, giving the nape of her neck to the water. It licks, cooling her. Cynthia doesn't mind, she doesn't mind anything. She stops kicking and lets her arms go still. She holds her eyes open while she sinks, to see the blue and the blue getting darker. Her toes are cold, numb, then her knees, her hips, and her whole body.

The water doesn't end. She stays loose, with her fingers hanging from her hands, and her hands from her arms like string. There's no bottom, only quiet. She can't remember how long she's been sinking, or feel her toes. Water presses her ears and nostrils. Her lips will quiver open soon, she feels, suddenly, and it will all come in.

His laughing, a deep noise in the murk like he's about to choke, but he won't – she will. She's going to die – that's the cold certainty at her toes, what she's sinking to. She panics, her mouth opens. Water floods down her throat and she can't close her lips against it, her body's sucking the liquid down. He laughs on and on, all around her in the water, burning her inside. He's alive, still so alive. She coughs and she's sucking in more.

She kicks, but can't feel herself moving. There's too much weight above her. The water's still, down low. She slaps at it with a hand and fingers herself in the eye. Cynthia kicks, and kicks harder. Then her hands, she remembers them and cups them to pull water down beneath her.

The water thins, the blue becomes lighter. Her toes return to her feet, and her feet are attached to her legs. She struggles higher and higher, towards the sun. There's warmth at her head and she moves through it.

She arrives – slows her limbs and breathes. The water's shifting gently, and Cynthia can look around and see the surface of all of it. Light and warmth are incredible all over again, and she throws her hands up in the air so the water falls off them and rolls down her arms in droplets. She'll survive.

The dinghy hasn't floated far, and it's hardly rocking in the water. She swims slowly, and slowly her survival becomes humiliation. They fucked. She's only moving, like food in bowels. She gets near the dinghy and it's upside down and still nowhere. There's going to be a long time waiting, she knows, and after that she doesn't care what happens. She rests against the dinghy, then tackles it the right way up.

The paddle's floated a few metres away, and she settles in to watch it move further. It doesn't, hardly. She waits hours and it only moves three metres. After a while she's sunburnt. She's only got a shirt and a bra on, and there's no way to lie properly, so she's red all over.

Of course, Cynthia knows that elsewhere there are bellied and pimpled girls who love themselves and are right to; girls who are perfect and enough just as they are. She tries not to think of them. Her stomach's cooked, searing hot, and she squeezes it tight between her fingers.

They'd have eaten together. She imagines him with one of his cans in one hand, spooning spaghetti into her open mouth with the other. In Cynthia's mind Anahera lies supine and he puts more and more in her mouth so it spills all over her, and heaves up and down on her chest as she wriggles – loving it – with her breasts shifting, and her lips spreading wider as if her mouth could hold more.

Cynthia remembers a noise from when she used to have sex: the wet unsticking of two sweaty bodies coming apart, and the feeling to that sound; the disappointed satisfaction of it being done.

Anahera and Gordon would have overexerted themselves every time, both being so into sports, and what was Cynthia doing? She was in the boat, waiting, watching nonsense on her phone and dreaming of Snot-head, who was almost certainly dead, even by then.

After resting they'd have walked back to the beach together, and looked at *Baby* moving on the waves. He'd have touched Anahera's arm to send her home, and, sated, she'd have swum through the water Cynthia floats on so glumly now.

58

The yellow boat settles not far away, under the sun, and rocks patiently for several moments, thinking. Gordon's friend peers through his window at Cynthia in her dinghy, then vanishes and reappears on the deck. The guy shouts something, and waves his arms, then revs his motor and putts closer. 'What are you doing?' he yells again, a hand alongside his wide-open mouth.

Cynthia shrugs, what does it look like.

'Do you want some sunscreen?'

She doesn't answer, but he gets some, and throws it at her. It hits hard against her burnt thigh. He's waiting to see her squeeze and apply some, so she turns away, scraping her raw torso on the bottom of the dinghy.

'I'm going that way,' he yells, stupidly – she can't see where he's pointing. 'Towards your friends, I could give you a tow.' His nose balls at the end, she remembers. He yells again, 'I could give you a tow.' Tow; his nose is round at the end like a toe. It's hard to think. Does he want his sunscreen back?

'What happened?' he shouts.

Anahera fucked Gordon. The boy fell out of the tree. Cynthia waits minutes for him to leave, and he coughs. It's agony, the way her sunburn's lying against the wood, but she doesn't want him to see her move. 'Ah, alright then,' he yells. But still, she doesn't hear him go. Then, with rasping anger, 'What do you expect to happen to you, like that?'

His boat splutters off, finally. The sun loosens its grip, and tightens again. That's all, the time for one cloud to pass and there's more shouting – Anahera. 'Cynthia, are you alright?'

No sound of Gordon. Cynthia's eyes must have been shut, because they open. The boat's coming towards her. It stops and starts in gentle fits, till it's positioned alongside the dinghy. Anahera cuts the motor, and Gordon stays unmoving where he's stood against the door. 'Boil the jug,' she tells him, but she's looking at Cynthia.

Cynthia's curled on the dinghy's small floor, and Anahera doesn't look away from her as she moves around the edge of the boat, then lowers herself down. A silky leg arrives at each side of her shoulders, and Cynthia squirms up to see Anahera's face, hallowed by sun. 'It's very hot,' Anahera says, and squelches something. The sunscreen from the floor, and she rubs it on Cynthia's cheeks, chin and forehead. She's looking down intently, but not at Cynthia's eyes. Cynthia chokes a bit and swallows it.

Anahera stops rubbing. 'Are you hungry?'

Cynthia swallows again. Chocolate snaps between Anahera's fingers, and it's in Cynthia's mouth. Cynthia darts her tongue out of the way of it, and the fingers, and tries not to suck. Anahera makes a soft sound, and squirts more cream on her hands. 'Sorry I let you go,' she says. 'I was frightened. I didn't know what to do.'

His eyes are peeled. Cynthia looks up, and there he is, staring down through the window. Gordon doesn't blink.

'I really did like you,' Anahera continues, 'when you came to my classes. I always noticed you.' She rubs Cynthia's shoulders, smoothing the cream in and stopping just before it hurts. She does her arms and even her fingers, although they're not burnt at all.

'You know sunscreen's to prevent sunburn, not to – ' Cynthia starts, but Anahera shushes her, and rubs her tummy and waist. The sunscreen's sticky and warm, dried out a little. She can feel lumps of it, congealed and rolling, between Anahera's hands and the fat of her belly. 'Look,' she says, 'why don't you stop?' She's still wearing only a bra and shorts, Anahera didn't think to bring her clothes.

Anahera does, and wipes her hands off on her pants. 'Sorry, I really just don't know what to do anymore.'

'Yeah, well,' Cynthia says, and stands up. The dinghy rocks, and she grabs Anahera's head for balance. The side of the boat's too steep and smooth for her to climb, so she sits again.

After waiting for her to settle, Anahera dives off after the paddle. She doesn't come back to the dinghy; she goes to Gordon, on the boat. He looks sideways at Cynthia, only briefly, before asking Anahera, 'Well?'

Anahera touches his wrist and Cynthia hears her say, 'Listen, Gordon,' before following him through the door. Once they're inside, there's her voice making statements, and his moaning. Cynthia rubs a wet patch of sunscreen with her thumb, where it's caught between her clavicles. The boat rocks beside her, he's stood up from where he must have been sitting at the table, and he's looking down again through the window. He marks a point where they make eye contact with a finger, and slaps it covered with his palm. He holds it there for several minutes, shifts it briefly, and winces to see Cynthia still looking back.

When Anahera's told her to, and Cynthia's climbed up the ladder, she stands waiting, touching her own elbows. Anahera and Gordon are side by side with their hands hanging down, quiet and looking a bit confused.

'Hello,' Gordon says, after a moment. 'Anahera doesn't take a single concern of mine seriously, and so here you are!'

'Leave, if you'd like to,' Anahera says, and she hands Cynthia the hot chocolate he boiled the kettle for earlier.

'Oh boy, I would like to,' he says, shaking his head. His bottom lip wobbles at the right side, and his eye on that side is swollen shut. The hot chocolate is delicious. 'But,' he tells Anahera, 'I am worried for you.'

Cynthia shakes her head. 'That's not why,' she says.

'Gordon, I'm trying to do the right thing.' Anahera rubs her own wrist, nervously or impatiently, Cynthia can't tell.

He's standing with his elbows tight at his sides, staring at Cynthia's forehead. 'Anahera wore my backpack, swam and got us food,' he says.

'Cool.' Cynthia's not listening. She's proud to see his baggy lip shake as he speaks, and the swelled mound of his eye lift into a bulge when he pretends to smile.

'How's your brain?' she asks him, swallowing the last of her drink.

He laughs, sudden and loud. 'How would I know!'

She can't help it, she laughs too. He listens and watches her eagerly. Anahera goes in to sit at the table, and they follow her, him standing back to allow Cynthia through the door first.

He stands, and picks up a soggy box of Baked Oaty Slices from the table, but he's like an animal – too frightened to look down and eat. 'She's clever, you see,' he says, nodding at Anahera. 'The box is cardboard, but they're each inside plastic packets.'

Cynthia nods, waiting for him to open them.

He changes tack, trying to be funny again, and says, 'Hmm. How does it feel to have nearly killed a man?'

'I can't remember,' Cynthia says, and it's the truth.

'Hmm,' he says again. He's scratching the damp corner of the box, afraid to look down and tear it.

'Gordon,' Anahera says, 'give it to me.'

He doesn't look at her, throws it, and misses. Anahera gives one bar to Cynthia, and one to him. He struggles with the wrapper, and most of his crumbles to the floor, but he puts what's left in his mouth and chews, gaining confidence.

'Anahera thinks it would be good for us all to do an activity. Yoga, she thinks. Her friend who found you is coming back for yoga.'

'Probably not into it,' Cynthia says.

He shrugs, and then, while chewing, looks at Anahera. Cynthia turns too, and Anahera's looking back at him. His face is wiped blank – they've communicated something and she missed it. He steps back towards the cabin, where it's darker.

'Do you want to sleep?' Anahera asks her.

'No.'

Anahera's face is disappointed; wincing. Cynthia can feel his new, loose lip twitching behind her, where he's standing in shadow. Anahera summons a smile. 'I could make the bed up,' she says, even though Cynthia's already said she doesn't want to sleep.

A noise from his mouth. A cracking noise, maybe from his nose. Cynthia turns to look at him, and he pulls his face together again, waiting for her to speak. She takes another slice from the box.

'You got burnt,' he says. The lump of his eye pulsates.

She chews. Eventually he goes to sit on the deck. She chews that mouthful for a long time, and Anahera goes out to join him, and murmur things. Cynthia can't quite make out what she's saying, but he interrupts her quick and loud: 'You don't take what I'm telling you seriously.'

She keeps talking, at her same calm volume – Cynthia imagines her with a hand, placating and cool, on his thigh or shoulder – and he keeps interrupting, saying, 'She won't, you know that she won't.'

Cynthia eats two more slices.

59

'It really isn't difficult,' Anahera says, and Cynthia can hear the instructive smile in her voice. Yoga. She's watched their three sets of feet troop around the side of the boat, through the windows. Now she turns to see them through a different one, at the front, where they've all stopped to stand in a collection at the washing-line. There can't be much space. They remove their shoes and wiggle their toes. Cynthia watches Anahera's, then Gordon's, then the other guy's. The guy's are pasty, with dark hairs, and she'd know Gordon's anywhere; he's the first to stop wiggling.

She grabs an Oaty Slice and goes to sit on the top roof and look down at them, squashed on the deck. 'I could make space?' the guy asks her, gesturing beside him as if he could move further that way without being in the water. She shakes her head and settles in. Anahera says, 'Downward facing, we'll take turns.'

'Dog,' Cynthia murmurs. She knows this one. The men step back, against the bar edging the deck, while Anahera demonstrates. The downward dog is one of the most nauseating yoga positions. Cynthia eats her slice.

'Good circulation,' Anahera says, pausing before she begins. The deck is sloped, high in the middle and falling off at each side. She gets on her hands and knees with her fingers spread wide. Then, quickly – Cynthia's never sure how this bit works – she lifts her bum right up in the air. She looks up through her legs at the men, and they're both standing back, mindfully quiet.

Gordon scratches his nose, and Cynthia remembers why he should be killed. Anahera looks up, specifically at him, and says, 'If your hamstrings are tight, bend at your knees.'

He nods. Then she says, 'My hands are engaged,' and he nods again.

'Righto.'

She stands back up, and waves her hand for the guy to take her place. He does, and she sits down beside Cynthia. She touches Cynthia's ankle.

'Thank you,' Cynthia says. 'Just watching this is making me feel better.' It takes a while for the guy to get it right, and Cynthia can't think what time of day it is. Gordon's being patient, with his hands clasped behind his back. When he's finally in position, the guy deep-breathes, goes red, and stretches his neck. Anahera lets him finish after only twelve seconds.

'What?' Gordon says. It's his turn. He does it quickly, and wrong.

Anahera says, 'Your knees. I said that with hamstrings like yours, Gordon, you should bend your knees.'

He turns his head sideways, and makes a pouty face.

'What you're doing right now is actually bad for your back,' she tells him.

He makes a big exhale, and adjusts his feet.

'Don't bother,' she says.

He bends his knees, then. 'Feels weird.'

'Looks stupid,' Cynthia says, and gets up to go back inside. There, she takes two Oaty Slices and a packet of chips, wobble-squeezes her belly, and goes to eat in the cabin.

Usually at the doorway she bangs her feet on the spare anchor, but it's not there. They leave her alone, and she concentrates on chewing. The sunscreen's dried up and turned oily, and it's flaking off with bits of her skin into the bedding. She rolls a large conglomerate between her fingers, and it disappears. They're talking again, behind the door, but she doesn't bother listening.

She's got a notification on her phone from Panty Deal. Someone wants to buy the G-string Anahera wore. Cynthia's remembering how pink it was when the door opens. 'Dinner time,' Anahera says. 'We're having potatoes, gravy, sausages and cauliflower.'

'Cute,' Cynthia says, and rolls onto her guts.

Anahera doesn't quite shut the door before saying to Gordon, 'It doesn't matter if that's true, that's what I've said. That's what I'm saying.'

Cynthia gets up, bangs her head on the ceiling, opens the door, and there they are; both of them at the table, waiting, not even touching their cutlery. She sits by Gordon, and he grasps his fork. Anahera's watching, so they eat.

'Oh, Cynthia,' he says, pausing, 'don't worry about all the chocolate oat bars from the box.'

After dinner, Cynthia goes back to the cabin and sleeps. She doesn't know what time it is when she wakes, but they're quiet. She's pretty sure he won't attack physically, not in cold blood. Perhaps it'd be easier to think outside, under the stars, but she presses her feet against the wall and stays where she is.

There's some noise outside, in the bed. Moving. Then the cabin door creaks and opens. Cynthia's blood quickens. She watches the gap, waiting for a face, but sees the eyes first. Anahera's. For a moment this is more alarming than if they'd been Gordon's; what could Anahera want? Then the door opens wider, there's more light, and Cynthia sees her face. The eyes twitch, and Cynthia understands – Gordon's afraid, and Anahera's been sent to watch her and protect him. Anahera asks, 'Is there room?'

Cynthia squishes tight against the wall and there almost is. Anahera says nothing of how half her body must be hanging off the side of the bed. She wriggles, trying to find balance. Eventually Cynthia hears her put a foot down on the floor, and they can both relax.

Anahera's fingers aren't in Cynthia's mouth, or on her body; they're not in or on her at all, but somewhere in the little bunk Cynthia knows they're there, resting. Everything's waiting, Cynthia feels it all over again. Her mouth is full of teeth and she roves her tongue through it.

'He's going to apologise to you tomorrow,' Anahera says.

'Cool.'

When Cynthia first thought of killing him it was a dream of gushing blood and screaming. It was like a movie with her arm, and her whole body, going *stab-stab-stab* like a boy's hips fucking something. Now, she only feels quiet. He'll wheeze soon, sleeping, and when Anahera hears him she'll leave. They both wait. Then, there it is, guttural puffs of air blowing out his nose. Anahera says nothing, but Cynthia hears her foot adjust on the floor. 'Maybe go back to your own bed, Anahera, so we can both sleep,' she says, but Anahera lies silently for several minutes. It's too hot. 'I'll sleep, don't worry,' Cynthia says. She's tired.

Without saying a thing, Anahera goes.

Cynthia lies, waiting, then moves quietly outside to look at the sea. Anahera's silent, and the sun's just now beginning to press the horizon and the surface of the water. Cynthia's eyes are hard, she can feel them, boiled. Anything, that water would take anything.

She thinks she's dangerous now, standing where he did while she floated away a night ago, but is she? She steps back, through the door, towards him, and he doesn't wake. He stays with his blood soft and slow and his muscles relaxed in his fat. He's got a knife there, sticking out from under his pillow. She touches the blade and it's sharp. The blanket's pulled up around his neck and under it, unconscious and breathing, he looks like something natural. He must be warm, beside Anahera. His eyebrows are soft, and full, and his top lip waits for the bottom one to stop sagging, and join it in smiling. He looks young again, boyish.

She leaves him to wheeze and goes back to the cabin, but she can't sleep. She's thinking of Anahera's eyelids flickering, the lashes twitching – her sleep was fake.

60

She wakes late, with her leg bent weird against the wall. She opens the cabin door with her other foot, and he's sitting at the table eating Nutri-Grain. There's the knife again, black-handled by his plate. He nods down at it. 'I sharpened that.' Then he puts his spoon in his mouth and stares at her.

'Okay,' Cynthia says, and sits opposite him. 'That's the first helpful thing you've done since you arrived.'

'Who ever loved you?' he says, spooning up more.

'Excuse me?'

He refines his gaze and holds the spoon steady in front of his lips. It's piled high, and she thinks he must be concentrating on keeping it steady and watching her simultaneously. His mouth opens much wider than necessary, and he puts it in.

'I've been assured of an apology from you,' she says.

One of his bloated fingers lifts and taps the table gently beside the knife. After a long, slow swallow, he says, 'Look at Anahera,' and gestures at the empty seat beside him. He looks from Cynthia, sideways, at the empty space, but only for a moment. She looks too, at the seat. Anahera's face, her body, her hands. A light falls on her, a gorgeous beam of it; their attention. Gordon, seeing that Cynthia's looking where he's pointed, chances a second look that way too. He gestures with his hands, adoringly, at the air where he says Anahera is, indistinguishable from the space in which he plans to make his point. It's Cynthia's hate that she sits in. But she sits comfortably in all that empty air. It seems she's revealed now – that this is what she always wanted; to be wanted this way, so hotly. To have everything waiting for her, because of course, Anahera's gone swimming.

'You see, Cynthia? Her parents had to go to WINZ, you know.'

'Her dad was a logger,' Cynthia says.

'Doesn't matter. I gave her her first fitness job.'

Cynthia gasps, appalled.

'That's right,' Gordon says. 'I instruct too. Women have sex with me because they respect my skill set.'

She gapes at him.

He laughs. 'They're cutest when they beg. Anahera, in particular, is inclined to say a lot of special things.'

Cynthia begins taking twenty big breaths.

'Do you not eat, Cynthia?' He's excited. He's using his stupid fake accent again.

She stops at seven. 'Gordon, I know you're from fucking Palmerston North.'

He ignores her. 'It is because you were beautiful, now you don't have an idea. Where's Louise gone, Thelma?'

Cynthia walks past him to stand on the deck and consider the sea. She watches the water shift and remembers how the blue nylon of his tent caught light, and how fecund and green it was with moss lower down. There wasn't much space in there, but in all that dark moisture, under that blue, Anahera moved so Gordon could insert himself into her. He stands near Cynthia now with a hand at his chin, pretending to think. What he's said doesn't hurt her, not particularly. What hurts is the size of him, his slow-moving strength, and knowing that however strong she is Anahera let herself be less in comparison, under him, or maybe as a game on top.

He coughs, he thinks he's thought of something. 'You could never be on television,' he says, excited again and gesturing with his knife. 'You are not flirtatious.'

'You're right,' Cynthia says, 'and I lack practical skills.'

'It's more than that,' he says.

'Yeah, I lack other things as well.' Having observed the repetitive swell of the water, Cynthia turns back inside, to the table. 'I'm not always good at following through on stuff, and sometimes people think I'm boring.' She sits down again, where she was.

He follows her, and sits too. 'It's not boring, exactly,' he says. He looks at her thoroughly, trying to think of a word more precise. Then, thinking harder, his head shifts slightly so he's looking out the window behind her head. His fingers flex around the knife. 'Hmm,' he says, then he gets up, and takes it with him to the toilet.

She hears him in there, loud like a horse and humming. Then he stops. 'Cynthia?' he says.

'Yes?' she answers, sweetly. She gets up and moves the slat back in the ceiling. Standing on the table, she struggles to lift herself up, and inside. The first time she doesn't make it, and twists her ankle when she lands back down on the table.

'Oh, nothing,' he says. He recommences peeing, and after that, humming. He's lost the tune and he stops and starts. 'Cynthia,' he says again.

The second time she struggles harder with her fists and wrists, and gets herself rested midway through the hole on her elbows and belly. She wriggles her hips and struggles forward. 'Yes, Gordon,' she says when she can breathe again. Her voice is muffled and echoing. There's not much room in there, or light. She can only lie on her belly, and see nothing, but she throws her hands out and forwards.

He stops peeing.

'Yes?' she answers again, puffing, in case he didn't hear her.

He hums, deliberately ignoring her. She wriggles her hips forward, and throws her hands around, then hits them. The weights. She clutches them, but they're tied together and the rope is nailed down.

The toilet door opens. He says nothing, but she can hear him breathing, standing in the doorway. She pulls her feet up, out of reach.

'What are you doing, then, Cynthia?'

'Sorry,' she says.

'What?'

The nail won't budge. She can't see the knot to untie it.

'Cynthia, how safe do you think it is up there? That is frail wood.'

She doesn't answer. She's chewing on the string, but she can't get through it. She should have taken a knife from the drawer.

He knocks on the wood under her. 'Excuse me, what are you doing?'

She feels where the string's tied around the weights, it's tight. 'Gordon,' she says down at him. 'How do you feel?'

'Oh, good, for sure.'

Then his hands are pushed up, through the hole in the ceiling. One of his blind fingers hits her thigh. She's careful not to move it, as if she hasn't noticed. She grabs a weight and pulls as hard as she can. It feels like something's about to snap, but that might be her arm. She stops, and touches the nail and the string around it. It's hammered in at the centre of the knot, not all the way in – the nail doesn't hang through the bottom of the ceiling, but enough that she can't pull it out. She takes one of the weights and bangs it against the nail, from one side then from the other.

'Cynthia!' he yells, and whacks the ceiling under her so it shudders.

'Yes?' she says, still banging at the nail. It's loosening. She hits it from each side, trying to enlarge the hole. Soon, she can take it between her fingers and tilt it in different directions. The wood's old. She spins it in circles, each time pushing it further outwards so the circles grow. Then, she can squirm it up and down.

It comes out smooth. She lifts the weights up, the big tied-together mass of them, as carefully and quietly as she can, and shuffles to reorient herself, so her head's at the ceiling-hole.

'Gordon,' she says.

He looks up. His teeth are bared, and his good eye squints meanly. 'Oh,' he says, 'you are unhinged.'

She lifts them, and plonks them onto his face. He falls with a thud to the floor. He's won't be dead, not that easily. She half falls, half clambers onto the table, and lands on her knees and chest. On the floor, his neck's bent and his head's propped up against the table-pole. One side of his face has collapsed completely, and only his bulged eyeball looks as it did earlier in the morning. Cynthia doesn't waste any time, she gets on her feet, squatting above him. Then takes his knife and stabs him three times in the chest.

The blood doesn't gush, it seeps. Twice the knife doesn't seem to go in properly, it just hits bone, but the third time she feels it move past that, into something soft.

She drags him by the feet through the door and onto the deck. His head lifts and falls, banging against the floor the whole way. He's heavy, but she doesn't rest. Anahera will be back any moment. She pulls him up to the side of the boat, then lifts him over the edge so he's face-down and his head's hanging towards the water. His knees are crimped up, and his feet are set on the floor. She pulls his shoulders over, and from there the work is easy. She gets a knee between his legs, and hoists the rest of him off the edge and into the water. One of his bare feet kicks out when he falls, and he floats. His head, hands and legs sink lower than the rest of him, so his back seems to balloon up and curve down into the water. It settles around him, and gains colour. His centre discharges a hazy red cloud, brownish and disappearing.

She can't have Anahera swimming through his blood, so she gets in after him, and grabs him by the arm. It's twitching. He's half sunk and hard dragging, the water's against her, but after minutes and minutes she gets him around the side of the boat.

61

There's blood on her shirt, so she takes it off and uses a clean patch to smear around the red on her arm. She throws it out the window, and sits down for a breather in her bra. Anahera will be back soon, and Cynthia would like to be doing something relatable. Gordon's gone, so she skips putting on a new shirt and gets breakfast. Nutri-Grain. Before pouring it, she remembers the knife on the floor. She stops, and takes it outside to drop into the sea.

Anahera's only metres away, treading water and staring. All that's visible of her is her head, and where her hands push the water away in ripples. Cynthia shouts, 'Hello!' as brightly as she can, and bends casually to slip the knife into the water, where it can stay.

Anahera doesn't reply, or come closer, but Cynthia can feel her eyes. She wishes she still had the knife in her hands, so she could stay bent, and drop it again. 'Hello!' she yells a second time.

'Hi,' Anahera says back, and when Cynthia looks up she's swimming forwards, but slowly, not even kicking her feet.

Cynthia's plan was to be sitting down, with a spoon on its way to her mouth when Anahera arrived. Then she wanted to look up, as if surprised. Now that's all ruined – before even touching the boat, Anahera says, 'Where is he?

Cynthia stands, still waiting, with the tendons stretched in her legs, before realising that the question's already been asked. 'What?' she says.

'He said not to worry, he was going to make it okay with you.' Anahera grips the ladder, and begins climbing up.

'I think he ran away,' Cynthia says. 'Before I woke up.'

'He had a knife.' Anahera's standing beside Cynthia now, damp and smooth in her togs. 'I thought it would be alright.'

'Did he?' Cynthia remembers his blood, and the wet noise of his mouth when she dragged him and his head banged on the floor. 'Maybe he'll go back to his girlfriend in Germany.'

Anahera doesn't shift or blink. After a long moment she shoves Cynthia aside and dives back into the water. It's still brown with his blood, and the murk reforms quickly after her body's cut through it. Cynthia waits, but there's nothing. The air's windless and the water stills. There's no sound but her own breathing.

Then in the distance, screaming. Anahera's head's bobbing up and down twenty metres away. She stops and sobs, then she's silent. Cynthia can't make out her eyes or nose, just her hair hanging wet over her face like a curtain. Her head's small and isolated, lifting and falling like a toy in the water.

She shifts to face away from *Baby*, and after twenty minutes Cynthia goes into the cabin and finds the bear in his bag, to comfort herself. She tears the plastic away gently and touches her nose to its soft face. She'll give it to Anahera later, maybe tomorrow. The heart on its belly is made of silk, which Cynthia thinks is real. She reads the words sewn there, *Forever and ever*, trying to forget Anahera's head, silent and caught in the water's moving.

After a while she sits the bear down and goes back out to stand on the deck. Anahera's spreadeagled on her back now. Her arms lift while her legs fall, each wave moving under her body in parts. Cynthia stands there, looking sometimes at her, and sometimes at the ocean or sky. The blood vanishes, and the water's clean again.

Then, Anahera swims back.

After climbing the ladder, she wipes the hair off her face. Her eyes are red, and her teeth bared tight. She says, 'We got Nutri-Grain. He wanted Nutri-Grain.' Her hair drips.

'Cool,' Cynthia says.

'He was good to me when I was your age.' Anahera pushes past and lays out two bowls on the kitchen bench. She takes up the whole kitchen and doesn't even let Cynthia pour her own milk. Cynthia holds her bowl and looks into it. All the pieces are floating. Some aren't wet, because they're sitting on top of other floating pieces. She lays her spoon on them, and applies the tiniest amount of pressure so they absorb fluid. Then she spoons a single piece into her mouth. She sucks the sweetened milk out of it, and lets it soften into mush. 'I saw him looking at you a lot of times,' she tells Anahera, 'in a way I didn't think was appropriate. A sexist way, actually.'

Anahera hasn't touched her own breakfast. She says nothing.

'He always turned to face you. He's like a dick you only saw when it was hard. But I saw him all droopy and evil, from behind.'

Anahera swallows in a way similar to choking. Then, 'What do you want to do?' she says.

'Go back to the island.'

Anahera can't have any spit left to swallow, but her throat's still moving.

When Cynthia was younger, only months ago, she wanted to become an animal, eating, fucking and wild. Now, though, it seems she is one, and wild isn't it. Animals move as slowly as humans when they're comfortable. She stands and goes to find a sweater.

The pink one. She sits wearing it with the last few Nutri-Grains in her mouth, sucking milk. Her dream again – barer now

– Anahera licking her forever in a way that will give her something better than cumming, and Cynthia licking back, again and again till it isn't even tiring. On the island.

62

Cynthia watches the distance between them and the land. She feels Anahera propelling them, against the water and through it, and she says, 'You know he's just a silly old thing that escaped from the meat factory.' Anahera looks sideways, away from her, and keeps paddling. Cynthia looks that way too, but there's nothing there.

If Gordon climbed out of the water, and appeared again, she'd leap on him with her mouth wide open and chew right down his body, starting at his head. She touches Anahera's arm. 'Someone wants to buy your thong. The pink one.'

Anahera looks back at her, like she can't remember.

'The pink one.'

Anyway, might they not make love? Cynthia looks up and watches the clouds moving. It's not hard to see two merging into one. Anahera might lie down on the beach, and Cynthia will crawl along the sand to her. If the wind blows and she gets grit in her mouth, Cynthia will swallow it. She'll arrive to Anahera with a clean, smooth tongue. The clouds continue to merge. Cynthia looks away from them, to Anahera, and when she looks back they don't seem to have shifted.

Anahera's hair is mostly settled in the calm air, and her shoulders are soft like the hills behind them. Her eyes are dewy and glinting, deep. Water surrounds and lifts them, shifting through blues into greens, and now Cynthia knows how far down it goes. Anahera looks past her, over her shoulders, and paddles in regular, strong strokes. The bones and muscles in her face are unmoving, set. There's only a short slice of sand at the edge of the island, and at either side of it are sharp rocks and trees balanced precariously on cliff edges. Closer, and the water lightens. The tide pulls them in.

63

Anahera forgets to shift the dinghy from the water, and Cynthia follows her into the bush. The air glows green with leaf-filtered light, and fades into moss and darkness lower down. Sun pierces through the canopy, falling on Anahera as if God's just opened his eyes and noticed her walking through Cynthia's love. She moves in deeper, quickly. Cynthia watches her step easily over roots and trees, away and into the centre of the island, to where Toby must still be.

How must it feel to be in her body? The trees are high and noisy with birds, but in her new way Cynthia doesn't feel below them. 'Forget him!' she shouts. 'We both know he's nothing.' Anahera doesn't hear, and walks faster.

There's a damp earthy smell, and Cynthia stops to breathe and touch the bark of a tree. Her throat had been feeling taut, but it's okay now. Soon she'll push forward. If the bush hurts her it doesn't matter, she only needs to reach Anahera's body with her own.

For now, she sits on a log to rest.

Encircled by gently leaning trees Cynthia is in her own small room of dappled light. The log is covered in dewy, airy mounds of moss. Cynthia thinks of Snot-head with his wet little nose. Wherever he is he'll be loved. Cynthia is giving Anahera space, which is what she needs, and while waiting she feels beautiful. Blond. She'll give Anahera time to tire herself out, then catch up with her. They'll go back to the dinghy together.

For now, she shifts her head from one side to the other, resting it. Time passes and the trees are silent. A small winged bug lands on her wrist then flies away. She doesn't notice.

ACKNOWLEDGEMENTS

Thank you Nick, for every draft you read and every tangent you waited to hear the end of. Thank you so excruciatingly much to my class (2016!), for talking about Cynthia as if she were a real person before she was even a proper character, and for being such a team. Thank you very much to my teachers: Emily, Pip, Anne, Robert and Ellie. Thank you very much also to my earlier teachers: Beth, Ms Evans and Jill. Thanks enormously to the people at VUP, Holly in particular. Thanks Fergus and Tracey. Thank you Verna and Denis Adam. Thanks James Daly! Thanks Jona and Danielle. Thank you Kirsti, for helping me grow up, and thank you everyone I studied with at MIT. Thanks Huntleigh. Thank you to my family. Thanks Mum, and thanks Dad.